"Kamir—" I begin.

"Yes?"

"Kamir, in my race there are two types of people, because of our way of reproduction—" I begin a clumsy exposition of gender and sex. What's the matter with me? I never have trouble with this part of alien contact, never thought about it before.

I am halfway through when Kamir bursts out laughing. "Yes . . . yes . . . we also have two. And—?" Another of those killing smiles.

"And which are you?"

"Do you ask?"

"Yes."

"I thought it was very plain. Perhaps because I am so ugly it is not."

"Ugly? But you are very beautiful, Kamir."

The lovely face turns on me, the incredible deep-blue eyes wide. "Do you *mean* that, 'Om Jhared?" A hand comes timidly to clasp my forearm.

"I mean it. *Yes.*"

Very softly Kamir says, "I thought never to hear those words." Then, whispering, "I am an egg-bearer. What you call a female."

It is incredible, whether a chance meeting of pheromones across the light years, whatever, I am trembling. I look down at her graceful back, with its lacy frill proclaiming her alienness, and it does not seem alien at all. My mermaiden.

But I am in mortal danger. I must straighten up and fly right.

The Tor SF Doubles

A Meeting with Medusa/Green Mars, Arthur C. Clarke/Kim Stanley Robinson • Hardfought/Cascade Point, Greg Bear/Timothy Zahn • Born with the Dead/The Saliva Tree, Robert Silverberg/Brian W. Aldiss • Tango Charlie and Foxtrot Romeo/The Star Pit, John Varley/Samuel R. Delany • No Truce with Kings/Ship of Shadows, Poul Anderson/Fritz Leiber • Enemy Mine/Another Orphan, Barry B. Longyear/John Kessel • Screwtop/The Girl Who Was Plugged In, Vonda N. McIntyre/James Tiptree, Jr. • The Nemesis from Terra/Battle for the Stars, Leigh Brackett/Edmond Hamilton • The Ugly Little Boy/The [Widget], the [Wadget], and Boff, Isaac Asimov/Theodore Sturgeon • Sailing to Byzantium/Seven American Nights, Robert Silverberg/Gene Wolfe • Houston, Houston, Do You Read?/Souls, James Tiptree, Jr./Joanna Russ • He Who Shapes/The Infinity Box, Roger Zelazny/Kate Wilhelm • The Blind Geometer/The New Atlantis, Kim Stanley Robinson/Ursula K. Le Guin • The Saturn Game/Iceborn, Poul Anderson/Gregory Benford & Paul A. Carter • The Last Castle/Nightwings, Jack Vance/Robert Silverberg • The Color of Neanderthal Eyes/And Strange at Ecbatan the Trees, James Tiptree, Jr./Michael Bishop • Divide and Rule/The Sword of Rhiannon, L. Sprague de Camp/Leigh Brackett • In Another Country/Vintage Season, Robert Silverberg/C. L. Moore* • Ill Met in Lankhmar/The Fair at Emain Macha, Fritz Leiber/Charles de Lint* • The Pugnacious Peacemaker/The Wheels of If, Harry Turtledove/L. Sprague de Camp*

*forthcoming

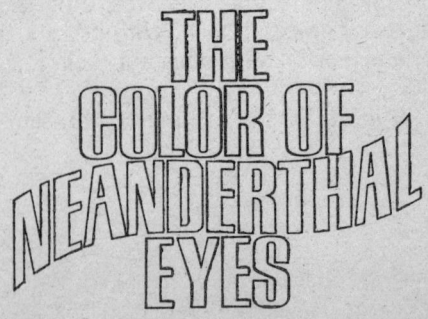

JAMES TIPTREE, JR.
THE COLOR OF NEANDERTHAL EYES

A TOM DOHERTY ASSOCIATES BOOK
NEW YORK

This is a work of fiction. All the characters and events portrayed in this book are fictitious, and any resemblance to real people or events is purely coincidental.

THE COLOR OF NEANDERTHAL EYES

Copyright © 1990 by the Estate of Alice B. Sheldon

All rights reserved, including the right to reproduce this book or portions thereof in any form.

A TOR Book
Published by Tom Doherty Associates, Inc.
49 West 24 Street
New York, NY 10010

Cover art by Dave Archer

ISBN: 0-812-55964-9   Can. ISBN: 0-812-50204-4

First edition: January 1990

Printed in the United States of America

0 9 8 7 6 5 4 3 2 1

It's my fault, all of it, and Kamir is dead.
But something must be done.
Now it is afterwards and I am recording this on shipboard so that you will understand. Much of this belongs in a Second Contact Report. Much more does not. But I am too torn-up and tired to make a formal report. I am simply talking out what happened so you will see that something must be done.

• • •

It started while I was lazily cruising along just outside an island coral reef, on the beautiful sea-world unimaginatively christened "Wet." I see it now: turquoise sea and creamy small breakers, and across the green bay the snowy expanse of sand, backed by the feathery plumes of that papyrus-like plant I learned to call *cenya*. The sun has started down, so I start my motor and go along the reef, looking for a pass. I find one, and cautiously zigzag through; my little new-rubber dinghy is too precious to risk hitting that sharp coral. Once through, I stop and turn, watching. Something has been following me all afternoon. I don't want to spend the night alone on a strange beach without checking out the creature.

Will it follow me in here?

I am, so far as I know, alone on Wet. And I'm tired. I'd been on a very strenuous year-long tour as Sensitive on an Extended Contact party six lights away. It's hard work, building up an FVV—First Verbal Vocabulary—and the aliens I was dealing with had complicated, irritable, niggling minds. The niggling made for an accurate vocabulary, but it was tiring for the lone telepath on the team. And it was a high-gee planet, which made for more fatigue. I had earned my post-tour leave. When we passed near Wet, I opted to be put down in a lander for weeks of restful solitude.

Wet has been visited only once before, by a loner named Pforzheimer, who stayed only long enough to claim a First Contact. His notes in the Ephemeris say that there are humanoid natives, confined to the one small continent, or large island, on the other side of the planet from me. Besides that, what land there is consists of zillions of small islands and islets, mostly atolls, long looping chains of them everywhere, archipelagos forming necklaces around friendly seas.

Wet seems to be in an interglacial period with the ocean at maximal height, and only a tiny ice cap on the south pole. And its sun is yellow, like Sol but smaller, so that even here near the equator the noon heat is merely pleasant. A tropical paradise in this season. There is even a magnetic field; my compass works. I left the lander at my base camp due south, and have come exploring this pretty chain of islets.

Ah!

In the pass I am watching there bobs up a round head, rather like a seal's, but glinting a fiery pink in the sunlight. The creature is following me into the bay.

What to do? Is it a predator? If so, it has had plenty of chances to make for me while I was diving, but did nothing. More important, is it a marine animal or an amphibian? Much of Wet's wildlife seems to be amphibious, their lives and bodies undecided between sea and land—a natural development here. If my follower stays in the sea, well and good; but if it comes ashore, I won't have a reposeful night.

As I look, the head swivels, apparently spots me, and submerges again. A ripple in the water shows it coming on in. I float quietly, undecided. Perhaps it is merely curious. That might imply high intelligence. But what persistence! It has been around me, now near, now farther off, since noon. What should I do?

Then something happens! A swirl in the water behind the creature, and a glimpse of something white. I have a notion what it is—one of the giant white crabs I have seen (and avoided) on the reefs. Our passage must have attracted it.

At this moment the creature accelerates to a very respectable speed and heads straight toward me. The swirl of the crab accelerates, too. I receive a mental flash of excitement, mixed with a trace of fear. Clearly the creature is racing to get away from the crab; but why toward me? Does it feel I am somehow a refuge?

I check my impulse to start my motor and take myself out of the path; I feel responsible for my follower's plight.

I shilly-shally until there is a commotion in the water alongside. The alien creature has arrived right by me. Then two pale green arms shoot out of the water and grasp the dinghy, and, so suddenly I have no time to react, the creature boosts itself up and tumbles into the bow of the boat—with a startlingly Human laugh!

Can it be Human? No—a humanoid, I see as I get a better look at its waving feet. Long membranous flippers are folding themselves around its toes, and the fingers are webbed. But the form is Human—quite beautifully so, I notice. And the creature is sending out a wave of excited pleasure.

I have evidently encountered the hominid inhabitants of Wet.

My first reaction is—damn it all. I'm in no condition to exercise my special talents, to do a Contact routine. But somehow the laugh beguiles me. I don't need to do more than a minimal scan to grasp that my visitor is in no way hostile.

But there's no time for more—a big white pincer-crab claw has lashed across the boat and is coming at the alien. I fumble for my harpoon.

Before I can find it, the situation is solved. Still laughing, the alien expertly grasps the claw and whips out a shell knife from its belt—yes, it is wearing a belt and loincloth—and runs the knife down the claw, severing its "thumb," or lower pincer. The thumb drops to the bottom of the boat, the now-harmless claw batters about a bit, and a second, smaller claw comes aboard. The process of de-thumbing is repeated. For a moment both ex-pincers are battering and waving, and then the great crab, seeming to grasp its trouble, gives up and slides back into the sea.

The alien, grinning, bends and retrieves the thumbs, shaking its flaming red hair back from its face. With its knife, it scoops the meat out of their shells and leans aft. It is offering one claw-meat to me! I take it, puzzled. It is like a big white banana.

The alien pops the other piece into its mouth and bites, nodding and smiling at me. Good! Cautiously, I taste it without swallowing. It is delicious—but alien food like this can contain an infinity of hazards. The crab's flesh could be laced with something lethal to me—as simple as arsenic—to which the locals are immune.

Regretfully, I lay the luscious white meat down on a thwart and gear my mind up to communicate the thought, "Thank you. It is very good. But we are very different. I come from another world."

To my inexpressible surprise and relief the alien, its deep blue eyes fixed on mine, sends back, "I know, I know." So they are natural telepaths! How rare, how wonderful!

And more is coming: "Other one came from sky a long time past." A foggy picture of what must have been Pforzheimer forms in my head, evidently a passed-on image. "Are you like that?"

Mind-questions are hard to ask. The alien does it by superimposing a figure I see is me, and flashing back and forth fast to the Pforzheimer image with an eager feel. "Yes," I send. "We come from the same world."

The alien eats more crabmeat, considering this.

Then comes another, more complex question I don't get. Foggy flashing images of Pforzheimer opening and shutting his mouth, blurry pictures of what might be planets of different sizes and colors ... "many worlds ..." I am roused to make the effort to probe for the alien's verbal speech, and try a guess.

"You say, the other-one-like-me said there are many worlds, many peoples?"

Enthusiastic assent. I've hit it.

And from then on, we converse in an irreproducible mix of verbal and transmitted speech, unmatched for fluency and ease. I report it here as close as purely spoken speech can come.

"Yes, that's true," I tell the alien. "There are many races. Some stay on their worlds, others travel much—like me."

The alien smiles broadly, the blue eyes in what I realize is a very beautiful face bright with pleasure. He snuggles down into a comfortable position in the bow, reaching for my rejected crab claw.

"Show me! Show me all!"

He is evidently prepared for a long session of entertainment. But the sunset is casting great golden rays across the sky, tinting the flocks of little island-born cumuli and generating lavender shadows on the blue-green sea. I must prepare for the night.

"Too many to show all. Too many to know all. I will show you one, others later. The night comes."

"Yes, I know how you do in the night. You take this"—he slaps the boat with the knife—"onto land, and sleep. I have watched you two days." There is a smile of mischief in his blue eyes.

What? But I only spotted him this noon. However, I recall some vague impressions of sentience nearby that had caused me momentary disquiet. So that's what they were—emanations of my new acquaintance, watching!

"Good. Here is one other world." I send a nice detailed view of the fiery planet of the Comenor, with a few of its highly intelligent natives hopping about or resting alertly, tripedal, on their large, kangaroo-like tails. The Comenor had been one of the races I trained on.

"Ah! And they think, they speak? Do they make music?" The alien raises its voice in a provocative little chant.

"Yes . . . yes . . . let me remember—" I try to render one of the Comenor's pastoral airs.

"Hmm . . ."

As he sits there reflecting, with the golden light playing on his flaming hair, I realize I may be mistaken. I have been calling him "he" because of his breastless body, flat belly, and slim hips, and perhaps also because he is apparently alone in the open sea. But that face could belong to a beautiful woman. And he is *not* Human; there is a strange fold running down the throat, and the pupils of his eyes are hourglass-shaped. Nor is he even mammalian; no nipples mar the pale green curves of his pectoral muscles, although he has a small navel. Perhaps "he" is female, or epicene, perhaps it is the custom of his race for females to wander far alone. Whatever, my new friend is enchanting to look at; even his accoutrements of knife, belt and loincloth are charmingly carved and decorated.

"Wonderful," he says at length. "And you have seen this and more?"

"Yes."

"I would like to do so."

"It might be possible, someday. Maybe. But now I must go ashore." I send him an image of himself getting out of the boat so I can drive the bow up the beach.

"Yes, I know." Again the hint of mischief in the smile. He pops the remains of the crab claw in his belt, and in one graceful flash is overboard. As he sails past I glimpse that strange fold on his neck opening to show a feathery purple lining. Gills! So he is truly aquatic. No wonder I didn't see him until he decided to show.

I start the motor and examine the beach. As often here, a small stream meanders to the bay in its center, marked by clumps of the tall, plumy papyrus-like plants. I'll have fresh water to top off my canteens.

I choose the larger expanse of beach and head for its center, where I'll have maximum warning if anything approaches. I've searched inland on several atolls, and so far found no sign of any predators—indeed, of anything larger than a kind of hopping mouse and a wealth of attractive semi-birds. But I'd prefer not to have even hop-mice investigate me in the night.

I rush the dinghy up a smooth place, jump out, and drag it beyond the tideline. There are low, frequent tides in this part of Wet, generated by a trio of little moons that sail across the sky three times a night, revolving around each other. Like everything else here, they are attractive—one is sulfur-yellow, another rusty pink, the third a blue-white.

The alien offers to help me with the boat. I warn him about punctures and letting the air out. He steps back, warily.

"Thank you."

When I detach the motor and batteries, he comes to examine them.

"More wonders. How does this work?"

"Later, later." I am puffing with exertion as I take out all my gear and turn the boat over to make a bed, hopefully out of reach of the little nocturnal crabs and lizards on these beaches. The alien watches everything closely, nodding to himself. When I have dried the dinghy's bottom and laid out my sleep shelter, he sits down on the sand alongside.

"Now you will—" Quick images of me relieving myself among the papyrus and returning to sit on the boat and eat.

I laugh; the pictures are deft cartoons, emphasizing our mutual differences and also the—I fear—growing plumpness around my belt.

"Yes. And I fill my canteens. The beach last night had no fresh water."

"Good. I, too, will eat." He opens his belt pouch and extracts the crabmeat, together with two neatly cleaned little reef fish. Raw fish must be a staple here.

When I return, he is still delicately eating. I offer him water but it is refused. "You don't need fresh water after such a long time in the salt sea?"

"Oh, no." I reflect that their bodies must have solved the problem of osmosis, which dehydrates seagoing Humans. Perhaps that beautiful pale greenish, velvety-looking skin is in fact some sort of osmotic organ.

I settle down with my food-bars, enjoying the unmistakable sense of companionship that emanates from the alien. We are both examining each other between bites, and I find that his smile is contagious; I am grinning, too. Extraordinary! Especially after my last aliens.

Now I can see more signs of his—or her—aquatic origins. A rudimentary, charmingly tinted dorsal fin shows at the back of his neck, running down his spine to surface again just above its end. There is a frilly little fin on the outside of each wrist. All these fishlike trappings fold away neatly when not in use. The flipper-fins on his feet fold over the toes so as to appear merely decoration. And his hair isn't true hair, I see, but more like the very thin tendrils of a rosy anemone; a sensory organ, perhaps. Am I seeing a member of a race that has evolved directly from fishes? I think so; these appendages look more like evolutionary remnants than new developments to my untrained eye. He is on his way out of, rather than back to, the sea. But could he be cold-blooded? No; when our bodies had brushed together, I had felt solid warmth under the thick, cool integument.

But perhaps he is not "on his way" at all; on this world, his adaptations seem perfect. There is every reason to retain his aquatic features, and none at all to lose them. I think I am seeing a culminant form, which will not change much, at least from natural pressures.

He for his part is looking me over with care.

"You do not swim well," he concludes, extending one foot and flicking the flippers open.

"No, but we have these." I reach under the dinghy and pull out my swim-fins to show him. He laughs appreciatively, and I reflect that my race, like seals, *is* returning to the sea—by prosthesis.

"My world has much dry land," I explain. "My race grew up from land animals who never went to sea." What am I doing, assuming a grasp of evolution theory on the part of one whose mind may not be much more than a fish's? Yet he seems to understand.

"Wonders." He smiles.

Next he is fascinated by my teeth. I show him all I can, and he in turn displays the ridges of hard white cartilage I had taken for teeth.

And so we pass the evening, chatting like amiable strangers, while the golden sun turns red and sinks, silhouetting the fronds of the papyrus. We exchange names late, as is customary with telepaths. His is Kamir. He has a little trouble with mine, Tom Jared. His people, he tells me, are three days' travel away, to the east. Why is he alone? That one is difficult; I can only guess that he means he is exploring for pleasure. "It is the custom."

Somehow I cannot bring myself to take up the question of sex, even though I know he is curious, too; once or twice I catch a tendril of his thought lingering around my swim trunks.

But through all our talk, I am amazed by what can only be called its courtesy. Its civility. Never do I strike a hostile or "primitive" reaction. It is a little like being questioned by a bright, well-brought-up child. Innocence, curiosity, those are neotenic—childlike—traits. Neotenia has been a feature of Human development. Kamir's race is neotenic, too. But beyond that, he is indefinably but unmistakably *civilized*. Whatever may turn out to be his technological level, I am communing with a civilized mind.

It grows darker, and a myriad unknown stars come out. I grow sleepy, despite the interest of the occasion. Kamir notices it.

"Now you desire sleep."

"Yes."

"Good. We sleep." And he pulls up the back flap of his loincloth to make a pad for his head and simply lies back peacefully. I wriggle round in my sleep shelter and do the same.

"Good night, sleep well, Kamir."

"Sleep well, 'Om Jhared." Then suddenly he adds a question I sense as deadly serious: "Will more like you come?"

I am glad to be able to reassure him. "No, unless you ask. Oh, maybe once a small party to record your world, if you do not object."

"Why should we?"

And so we both relax, the alien on his warm white sand, me on my galactic dinghy, and the little crabs and lizards and other creatures of the night come out and sing or fiddle or chirrup their immemorial chorus. I remember thinking as I drift off that they are a good warning system; only when all is still do they sing.

• • •

When I waken in full sunlight, all is calm and still. Too still; the sea is like glass. I check my barometer. Yes, it has started downward.

Kamir is nowhere in sight. I feel a sense of loss. What, has he abandoned interest in me to return to his watery world? I hope not.

And—good!—in a moment or two there's a splash out on the reef. Kamir surfaces. He comes quickly back to shore, towing something. When I go to meet him, I see that it is a silky purse-net, full of flapping fish.

Too preoccupied to greet me, he hurries up the beach and kneels over his catch, his beautiful face tense. He begins quickly decapitating them, finishing the last one before cleaning any. Then he sits back, sighing relievedly.

"Their pain and confusion are hard to bear," he tells me. Then, smiling, "Morning greetings, 'Om Jhared!"

"Greetings." I know what he means. I once made the error of going too near a meat-killing place; it had taken me a fortnight to recover.

"I wish we could eat some other way. We all do," Kamir tells me, working on the fish. "But plants are not enough."

I agree, looking over his net. An elegant little artifact, clearly handmade. His is not a machine culture. "I think there is a storm coming."

"Oh yes." He touches his shining hair. "My head is full of it."

"When?"

"This evening for sure." He looks me over again, curiously. "What will you do in the storm, 'Om Jared?"

"Take my stuff farther up on land and wait it out. What will you do?"

"Well, of course, we go down into the deep water where all is calm and wait it out, as you say. Very boring ... But today I think I will stay with you. I haven't seen a storm on top since I was a child. Would you like me to be with you? I can help carry your things." His head cocks to the side as he looks up, shy, coy, absolutely charming. I can no longer stand this convention of "he."

"Kamir—"

"Yes?"

"Kamir, in my race there are two types of people, because of our way of reproduction—" I begin a clumsy exposition of gender and sex. What's the matter with me? I never have trouble with this part of Contact, never thought about it before.

I am halfway through when Kamir bursts out laughing. "Yes ... yes ... We also have two. And ... ?" Another of those killing smiles.

"And which are you?"

"Do you ask?"

"Yes."

"I thought it was plain. Perhaps because I am so ugly it is not."

"Ugly? But you are very beautiful, Kamir."

The lovely face turns on me, the incredible deep blue eyes wide. "Do you *mean* that, 'Om Jared?" A hand comes timidly to clasp my forearm.

"I mean it. *Yes.*"

Very softly Kamir says, "I thought never to hear those words." Then, whispering, "I am an egg-bearer. What you call a female."

And her—her!—red head goes down on my forearm, hiding her face.

I can only stammer, "Ah, Kamir, I wish we were not of different races!—"

"I too," she breathes.

It is incredible, whether a chance match of pheromones across the light-years, whatever, I am trembling. I look down her graceful back, with its lacy frill proclaiming her alienness, and it does not seem alien at all. My mermaiden.

But I am in mortal danger, I must straighten up and fly right.

"Kamir, I do not think you should stay with me through the storm."

"Why not?"

"It—there might be dangers—" It is impossible to lie to a telepath.

"If you can endure them, so can I! Ah, why do we speak nonsense? For some reason you are afraid of my nearness."

"Yes," I say miserably. What can I tell her convincingly? Of the iron Rule Number One in ET contacts? Of the follies that Humans, men and women alike, succumb to? Of the fact which I have just realized, that I have been a very lonely man? Why else, I ask myself, should I be so smitten by a purely chance resemblance to Human beauty?

"Look," she says, lifting her head to the sky. "The storm is coming much faster . . . I don't think I will have time to swim to a really safe place. If my presence disturbs you, I will stay far, very far away. When we have moved your things."

Little mischief, is she lying? My senses tell me so. But when I, too, look up, I see that the sky has taken on a curious yellowish tint, though no clouds show yet. The sea is so flat it looks oily, and the air is ominously still and hot. She is right, whatever is coming is moving fast. And these seas *are* shallow, it may be a long way to a deep place. In any event, it is time to secure my possessions.

"Very well," I say with profound unwisdom. "Then if you want to help me, we will move my boat and the rest up into the dunes behind the beach."

She smiles radiantly, and we go to it.

But it is a slow process; she exclaims with interest and curiosity over all my things, wet suit, waterproof recorder, pump, repair kit, camera, lights, charging device, scuba gear, first-aid kit, my lighter—I find she knows fire, which her people accomplish by twirling hardwood sticks—and all, down to the binoculars, which charm her, and the harpoons, which turn her very sober.

"You kill much."

"Only for food, like you. Or to save my life."

"But this is so big."

"Well, I might be attacked by something big, like the crab. You killed it, you know. Without claws it will die of starvation."

"Oh, no! It will eat algae. And the claws will grow again. We use them like that to pull building supplies." Image of a big crab with a harness hooked on its carapace, hauling a laden travois. "When they get dangerous, we chase them back to sea."

"Ah."

Some perverse honesty compels me to show her my waterproof laser, which I carry in my swim trunks.

"This is for use if I am attacked on land." I demonstrate on a nearby shell. She runs to examine the burn.

"It would do this to flesh?"

"Yes."

"Why, when I came in your boat, you might have done this to me?"

Blue, blue eyes gaze at me, horrified.

"Not unless you attacked me so viciously that my life was in danger."

"Oh, but could you not *feel* the warmth?" She flutters her hand from herself to me and back. I think. Yes—from the first moment, I could. Damn it.

"Well! You are strange." Shaking her head, she resumes lugging a battery up the dune. She is very strong, I notice.

We have found a splendid hollow in the high dunes in which to ride out the storm. Somehow nothing more is said about her staying far, far away.

Finally, we stake my big tarpaulin over the heap of belongings and bring up the boat. I rope it upside down to three stout plant roots. The scrub "trees" growing here resemble giant beach gorse and have great hold-fast roots.

By now, the air is so humid and strange that our voices seem to reverberate on the still beach. And we can see a level line of white cloud rising up at us from the horizon, growing against the upper wind. Under it is a tinge of darkness, the first sight of the squall-line. And in the far distance beyond towers pale cumulus. It looks like a whole frontal system coming on us. Will the weather change?

"You may grow cold here, Kamir."

"Oh, I am used to that."

"You could put on my wetsuit." (What, and leave me naked? I am mad.)

"No, when we cover our skins, we grow too thirsty."

Aha, I was right about the osmotic protection in the skin. Perfect adaptation.

"Well, if it turns cold, we can always make a fire. Let's gather some of these heavy stalks and stems."

When all is ready, we sit on the dune-top, swinging our legs and eating our respective provisions, watching the squall line rise until it divides the visible world. On our side all is still and sunny and hot; we are caught in an eerie stasis. A kind of water animal I haven't seen before paddles about in the bay, followed by a line of small ones.

"Jurros," Kamir observes. "They are very tame. Only the big fish bother them."

I wonder about those "big fish." Are they shark-like? But in response to my query Kamir only laughs.

"Oh, you pop them on the nose. They run away."

Well, I have heard people say that about white sharks. I resolve to watch out for any "big fish."

The storm is closer and closer, but still nothing stirs around us. Half the sky is shuttered with black roiling cloud, yet here it is impossibly bright and calm. The barometer must be falling through the deck, it is suddenly a little hard to breathe. I check it; yes, it's at the lowest point I've seen it. This is going to be ferocious.

We watch quietly, gripped by the drama of the scene. The water-animal has now disappeared.

Just as it seems that nothing will ever happen, a shudder runs through the world. Still in total calm, the sea wrinkles itself like the skin of a great beast. A tiny puff of cool wind lifts our hair. And a few big drops of rain, or perhaps hailstones, plop into the surface of the water and onto the beach.

And then, with a rush and a bellow, the storm hits.

In a moment the flat water has reared itself into a thousand billows two meters high, running unbroken from shore to shore. The breeze becomes a blast of wind against us. In the last rays of sunlight, a million specks of diamond flash from the waves into darkness. And then the sun is eclipsed by cloud, the world is twilight-dark.

Eerily, the papyrus plants all bend over with a whipping sound before we feel the wind that bent them. And then it hits, and the boat bangs up and down as if it will tear from the earth.

We scramble back from the dune-top and get under cover of the boat, holding it down over our heads. Then the sky opens, and tons of water dump on us, drumming intolerably on the boat. I am sure it is hail that will tear the boat, but when I stick out a hand, it is not. The world is in uproar around us.

Kamir is going excitedly "Whoo! Whee!"—I can barely hear her over the storm, but I can see her eyes flashing blue fire and her little back fin standing straight up.

"This is not boring?" I yell.

"No!" Laughing, grinning with excitement.

"But—" I begin and am drowned out by a *crack!* of lightning, and thunder like a gigantic bolt of tearing silk. Then the cracks and flashes and roars and rumbles are all about us. The strikes seem to be hitting the beach and the dunes. I see Kamir's fin suddenly clamp itself into her back, and her laughter changes to a squeal. I realize she hasn't seen, or has forgotten, the lightning part of a storm. She hangs on to my arm, quaking as each bolt hits. And then, somehow, she is in my arm, her face pressed against my chest, while I hang on to the boat for dear life with the other arm.

"It won't hit us, the boat will stop it," I howl at her.

Water is coursing down the sides of the hollow we are in. Down below, the beach has disappeared under a wilderness of sinister yellow-gray breakers that are striking and tearing against the dunes, and throwing spray to mingle with the rain on us.

But by degrees, the wind changes from a wild whirl to a steady blow, driving the rain across us, and I am able to release my aching arm and rope the boat more securely.

That was, I think, my last chance to escape.

But I do not take it. That arm joins the other around the slender quivering Kamir, and she clamps her whole body against me. For warmth.

Her back is cold. I rub it to warm her, cannot resist fingering the pretty little fin, which makes her giggle. I rub, stroke, but the coolness seems to be in her skin. It feels thick, a pale green velour over soft curves. I try to concentrate on its interest, its prevention of dehydration. Yes, I see there are tiny pores, but how they function is beyond me. I am stroking rhythmically now, unable to keep from enjoying the exquisite forms of her back and flanks.

And oh! Warmth comes, but not the warmth I wanted. Her shivers have turned into unmistakable, sinuous wiggles under my hand. She is whispering something, her free hand feeling for my swim trunks. And, gods! Her silken loincloth seems to have come undone.... Tom Jared, what are you doing? Stop now, you fool. This is no girl, but a grown alien—a god-lost *fish!*

There is no stopping. I have only time to glimpse what seems to be an organ on the front of her lower belly, a solid mounded track running up to her navel, like a newly-healed scar. My body has taken me over, relieved me of the cold swim trunks, and is longing to press into her.

Only, where? Her crotch is as smooth as an armpit. I can only lay myself alongside the "scar" and squeeze our bodies together. "Yes," she says, "Oh yes." There is a feeling of clasping.

From there on I don't know exactly what happens. It isn't Human, but exciting beyond words, and finally, somehow, fulfilling. And at its height, a tremendous lightning bolt hits the beach....

Much later, I come back to consciousness. The rain is still drumming on our shelter, but the wind has abated somewhat, and the waves aren't quite so fierce. More water has drained into our hollow; we are lying in a puddle.

Kamir is asprawl, half under me and wholly wet. For a moment I fear I have hurt her. But she is only deeply asleep.

And I—I have broken Rule One, and the sky will fall on me. And I do not care.

"Kamir? Kamir?"

Answering smile, long, slow, and beautiful. Lazily the big eyes open their sea-blue pools.

"Are you all right, my dear?"

"Umm ..." Sleepy, obviously as fulfilled as I. Her lips move.

"What?"

"Never ..."

"Never what?"

"I thought—never would I know— Oh, you have been sent from the skies to rescue me."

Wild bells of warning—new ones—ring in my head. Does she assume I will stay here with her? Oh gods—I bitterly reproach my offending body, my weakness. But looking at her lying there, the mere thought of leaving gives me a pang. Can it be that I truly love this little alien? Oh gods! How wise are the Federation regs!

"Let me get you out of this water."

"Why? It's comfortable. . . ." As if daring greatly, she puts her hands up to my cheeks, the dainty wrist frills quivering.

"Tell me, 'Om Jhared: Do I still seem beautiful to you?"

"Yes . . . Oh, *yes!* But why do you ask? Don't you know you *are* beautiful?"

"But I am ugly, everybody knows that. My people say I am so ugly it is good when I leave!"

"No!" I protest. "But to me, and to the eyes of all my people, you would be considered wonderfully lovely."

"Ahhh . . ." She gives me an adoring look and a smile and next moment is fast asleep again, like a child. My mermaid.

There seems nothing better to do. I follow suit.

• • •

We wake in darkness. The wind has died, and the three little moons are rising, showing a sky of racing cloud fragments.

"Hungry!" exclaims Kamir, grinning.

"I too."

And we rise from our puddle and go up to sit on the dune top, now scoured almost flat by the gale. Below us the beach is emerging from the waves. It is chilly; a fire seems good, so I bring up the dry stuff we had collected and soon have a comfortable little blaze.

She is fascinated by my lighter. Soon she has satisfied herself that it uses the principle of friction, too, like her people—but what is it *made* of? What is this stuff, "metal"? Rock, coral, and shell are the hardest substances she knows.

So the evening starts, unexpectedly, with a lecture on metallurgy. Oh, if I could only find deposits of something, iron, copper, silver, tin! I rack my memory, can only remember something about manganese globules on the seafloor—or is it magnesium? There must be some metal available to these people, if only I could tell them what to look for. I dream of precipitating them into an Iron Age before—before I go. I wince.

As to my plastic gear, I can only describe to her a gross oversimplification of petrochemicals and polymers. She shakes her head worriedly.

"So much! You have so much.... But do you have music?"

I fish in my recorder pack and come up with a lovely piece by Borgnini.

"Listen. This reminds me of you." Which it does, especially the flute solos.

She cocks her head at the first notes. Then, seeing me lie back, she flops down with her head on my stomach to listen. I am diverted by the shining red silk of her pseudo-hair.

"Oh!" she exclaims once or twice. "Ah!" I think she likes it.

When the piece has drawn to its ravishing finale, she turns to me with glowing eyes. "Oh, you have beautiful music! I never—we never heard such sounds. But no voices?"

"Not in this one. They are what we call musical instruments."

"We must make some," she says determinedly. "You will show us how. Now, more!" She leans back again.

"I haven't much in this little box. But here is another from my homeland." I give her Brahms's Quintet for Clarinet in E.

And so the evening passes.... I am impossibly happy.

Before retiring, we drag the boat up to the top to sleep on, and spread out her loincloth to dry. It's more complex than it looks, with four small pockets. The fishnet goes in one. I concentrate on this to avoid looking at her body.

"You shall wear this now," she says shyly, patting the cloth.

"Me? Oh no."

"Yes. It is right."

"Why, what does the loincloth mean?"

"Well, first they mean that we are ripe. All my age-group are wearing cloths now. When all are ready, they go out to sea, to explore and to meet each other. When"—I think she says—"when a couple forms, they exchange clothes and return so, to let everybody know they are together. Of course I went out alone, this way where nobody will come, because I knew nobody would want me. I expected nothing. And I found you! Oh—"

In an exuberance of love, she pounces on me, and before I can protest, rolls me off the boat and around in the sand, nuzzling and kissing me. Strong little mermaid!

I catch her and roll her back and we play like puppies.

When we are both gasping with laughter, naked and sandy, we fall into each other's arms and let nature have her will. Blissfully, there are no insects here. We fall asleep once more, enmeshed in love.

Only, just as I am drifting off, I catch her whisper.

" 'Om Jhared?"

"Yes?"

"You will, won't you?"

"Will what?"

"Care for them. You will?"

"Them? What?" I force myself awake.

"Our babies."

Oh, gods.

"Kamir," I say gently, "I hope this will not make you sad, but there won't be any babies. Our physical beings, our bodies are too different."

She frowns. "You don't think there will be babies?"

"No. I'm sorry."

"Well," she says, with a return of her old mischief, "I think differently!" And she lays one hand on her abdomen, smiling, and lies back.

So do I, but not restfully. It has occurred to me that some Terran mammals, like rabbits, will give birth parthenogenetically if stimulated by saline water. What if, gods, what if she is right, and some monster is born?

" 'Om Jhared?"

"Yes?"

"Even if there are no babies, as you say, you will at least stay until I die?"

Oh, no—does she mean, spend my life with her? Gods, what have I done? "Oh my dear, do not talk of dying. Not now."

"Yes," she says musingly, "maybe you are right. But I think of it."

And I can feel a dark shadow on her mind.

"But why think of it? Please don't, my dear."

"Why? Because it comes so soon. Do you not know? This is my last season in the world now."

"Oh, Kamir. What's wrong? What's wrong?" I am bending over her, afraid of I know not what. "Tell me!"

"Why, because we love. Because I love with you. Is it not so with you?"

"Kamir, I don't know what you're saying. What is wrong?"

"Nothing is wrong. When you love, you die. The woman dies. The man lives, to feed the babies. Is it not so?"

"No! No! In my race, the females live long, whether or not they love. Longer than the men, often. Do you mean you expect to die because we made love?"

"Why, yes. We all do. Only I feared I would live forever, alone."

"Good gods ... But I am sure you won't have a baby, Kamir. We are too different. Like a—a crab and a fish, they can't have young together."

"And you are the crab?" She laughs playfully. "But no, perhaps you are right. We won't think of it. This is our happy time."

She snuggles down closer in the hammocky boat. "Sleep well, dear 'Om Jhared. Sleep well."

"Sleep well, my darling."

I lie sleepless, incredulous.

What horrible wrong have I committed in my selfish lust? Even if I call it "love," it led me terribly astray.

The little beach-life is tuning up its night song, but I am in no mood to appreciate it. A million unanswered questions are revolving in my head like rolls of barbed wire. What is this murderous process she believes will kill her? There must be a way to stop it. It can't be biological, the species wouldn't survive. Perhaps the people in the village make some lethal potion or charm they give the women. I could stop her taking it. Maybe they acquiesce in their deaths, by stopping eating, or something of that sort. I could stop that, too. There must be a way—I *must* stop it.

Eventually fatigue takes me and I lose consciousness, to dream of a terrifying great crab taking Kamir.

•   •   •

The morning is washed clean and clear, the barometer is high. Kamir gets up and announces she will go to the reef for fresh fish. I get out my scuba gear and prepare to go with her; I don't want us to be parted.

She is still nude, and as she stands, stretching luxuriously in the morning sun, I make myself inspect her.

She is a radiant figure, palest of green-whites in the golden sun, with that mop of fiery "hair." A faint flush suffuses her cheeks and lips and touches her body here and there. There is no other hair-like stuff on her; she is as smooth as a marble statue. Only, on her lower abdomen, there is this vertical thick welt I had glimpsed, like an old cicatrice. I see it is composed of two long lips, tightly appressed. Evidently their opening discloses the softness I had found. Closed, it is only a keloid-like ridge.

I find I, too, am being inspected. After a moment she comes close and touches me. Involuntarily I react, and she draws back, laughing and shaking her head.

"So different!" she says. Then, "Show me a picture of your women."

But I find I can barely summon up an adequate image of a Human female, so much has this little mermaid obsessed me. When I do, it seems, well, messy and strange.

"Hmm," she says. "So all are ugly, like me!"

"What is this 'ugly'?" I am becoming exasperated. "What about you is supposed to be ugly?"

"Why, I am so thin and bony, all over." She puffs out her cheeks and with her hands sketches over herself the outlines of a very fat woman. "I should be like this! Then you live long enough to help. Oh, but I see you don't want me to say that. Let's go to the sea."

So we run down the dunes and splash out until I have to stop to put on my gear. It all amuses her vastly. When I submerge, she circles me, swift as a fish, with her flared-out gills. I have trouble making her take my needs seriously; she tries to slip my mask off for a kiss, and I have to surface and explain that if she wishes to keep her lover, she must allow him to breathe. She sobers quickly, catching my serious feeling-tone, and after that we have no more trouble.

It is enchanting, down below, watching her herd little reef fish into her net. And I, too, sorrow when we come out and have to kill them.

I have an idea.

"Kamir, have you ever looked at yourself?"

"Oh yes. Mayrua keeps a polished shell. And sometimes, in very still water."

"Look." And I root out my little mirror. "Now you will see beauty."

She loves it, turning it to catch me, too. But she cannot resist trying to make a "fat" face.

I try to convince her, tracing my fingers over her delicate features. But she only hugs me.

"I may keep this? No one has seen anything like it."

"Certainly."

That reminds me. While she is tucking away the mirror, I try to ask her what her people call themselves. It's the same old situation, they are only "the people," or "us." Her particular settlement is "the Souls of Ema," after some legendary father, and a neighboring group is the "Souls of Aeyor," for a woman who made an extraordinary trip.

"But we must have a name for you. You don't want to let outsiders name you something like 'Homo Wettensis'?" (Or, gods forbid, Homo Pforzheimerana.)

"Homo Wettensis?" she mimics, giggling. "Why?"

So I have to explain about her world being called "Wet." That sends her off into paroxysms of laughter. But then she sobers. "Mnerrin."

"What?"

"An old word that means 'wet,' or 'the wet ones.' Would that not do?"

"Why yes, if your people agree. *Mnerrin* is quite fine."

"Oh, they won't mind. Very well; your Mnerrin asks, what shall we do today?"

"Well, would you like to explore inland? Or shall we look for some islands you haven't visited? I thought we might go in my boat, it will just take two."

She clasps her hands like a delighted child. "I'd love that!

Yes, there are islands there"—she points north—"that haven't been seen for lifetimes."

"Let's go see!"

So we launch and repack the boat, and set off. She is much pleased with our speed, only once or twice she puts her hands over her ears as if the motor's hum bothers her.

"How fast does it go?"

I show her, but she soon covers her ears and cries, "Slow, slower, please—I can't see anything!" I realize that she has been mostly peering down into the water, while my eyes are on the sea and sky.

"Look, there is a big fish."

I see a moving shadow of enormous size, perhaps three meters. And before I can protest, Kamir throws a last morsel of fish overboard. The shadow surfaces—a big tan shape with round eyes. As it spots the fish, a long beaked bill breaks the water and clamps down. I get a glimpse of big, sharp cartilaginous ridges inside.

"That thing could take your arm off!"

"Well, if you let it, maybe. But look!"

To my horror, she rolls overboard. I see a flurry and a swirl and the thing hurriedly departs.

Kamir jumps and flips back in, laughing. "See? I just popped it on the nose, I told you."

"Don't ever do that again, my crazy little darling. It frightens me for you."

She rolls over and cuddles between my legs, still laughing. "Well, your driving this boat frightens me for you! But there is our first island."

The new island turns out spectacular, an old volcanic cone with strange tunnels running into the sea, from former lava tubes. So Kamir must be shown my instant camera, and exclaims over the tininess of the images. She wants to sleep there, but I detect enough signs of possible activity to make me discourage this, and toward evening we push on.

The next island proves to be full of the bird-like creatures. I pick one up—they are perfectly tame—and fancy I can trace signs of its evolutionary course from fish, too.

Next day there are two islands covered with a multitude of flowers, and the day after that, one whose river and bay teem with bright-colored, harmless sea snakes. And some days later comes a highlight; some river fish are clambering out of water and up in the undergrowth in pursuit of butterflies. And the next day an oddly barren island; and the next day, and the next . . .

I am guiltily aware that I should be making a record of all this. But when I get out my recorder and start, Kamir is so amused at my solemn tone of voice that we get little work done. My only concession to practicality is to keep a route map of our travel; so far it has been due north, so that my little base camp and the lander—about which I refuse to think—are still straight south.

We junket on and on over the turquoise sea, sometimes stopping to dive at barely-submerged coral reefs that would tear the bottom off a larger boat. And when the spirit moves us, we make love, sometimes in a fit of passion, sometimes gentle as children.

It is the happiest time of my life.

Only, one day I notice that where Kamir's stomach had been elegantly flat, it now seems to have taken on a womanly curve. I put it down to the extraordinary number of little butterfish she eats, and forget it . . . or try to. The weather is halcyon beautiful. A few times we see storms in the distance, but they do not come near.

One very clear night we are camped on a beach like the one on which we met, with a small estuary and its group of papyrus-cenya in the center. Kamir finishes the handsome wristband she has been making for me from the tail of her loincloth, using for needle a splinter sliced from a cenya stem. (Regretfully, she has had to admit that we couldn't comfortably exchange clothes.) In lieu of my trunks I give her my identity bracelet; it won't do on her wrist because of the fin, but it goes nicely on her slim ankle.

When she sees the lettering, and I spell out my name, she frowns.

"I think this is something for Maoul," she says.

"Who is Maoul?"

"An old man, very wise. He made some of those land pictures you call 'maps.' These are something like that."

"Yes," I say, surprised. Bright little mermaid!

"And now"—she stretches out with her head on my lap, and hands me the binoculars—"you will tell me more, please, about those stars."

It is a topic we have just broached. I lament my star charts, left back in the lander; it is a perfect night for viewing, the moons are down for the hour, and the heavens are a riotous sight. I do the best I can; she is very keen and remembers well. Later we drift off to sleep, entangled in the binocular strap, with images of dark nebulae floating in our heads....

—And then I am suddenly awake. What's happening? All is still; too still, that's what waked me. All the night creatures are silent.

Something is on the beach.

I listen hard and catch a faint splashing. Correction, something is coming out of the sea, over by the river outlet where papyrus-cenya hide the view. The moons are just rising. I sense Kamir is awake and listening, too.

Can it be a giant crab?

But as I form the thought, the last thing I expected in this world happens—a light shines out.

It's not a torch, but a bright greenish glow. Then it begins to blink, rhythmically. Signals?

"Ahhh," says Kamir. "Wait one moment, my love. I go."

"Kamir, wait—"

But she is up and racing down the beach, toward the cenyas.

I wait tensely, straining my ears. Aha—a faint colloquy; of course, I remember, I'll hear little, these people are telepaths. Anger rises; who or what dares to intrude on us? Who can it be? I realize I know so little about Kamir; could this be a father? A lover? A pang of raw jealousy grips me, the thought that it might be another woman never enters my besotted mind. And I've forgotten, or never believed, Kamir's story of being unmarriageable. Can this be a *husband*, hunting her?

And then abruptly, without my hearing footsteps, they are beside me, two forms blocking out the moonrise. The stranger is taller and much stouter than Kamir.

" 'Om Jhared? This is Agna, my egg-mate."

What is she telling me? I get the image of a large object,

which crumbles or splits to reveal—no, not objects: babies. An image of a woman holding two of them.

"Your *brother*?"

"Yes, yes!"

Vast relief for me. I remember my manners.

"Greetings, Agna." But wait—has he come to charge me with violating his sister? Gods! No, he returns my greeting cordially, adding, "For three days I track Kamir. Now I find her here with you."

"Yes," says Kamir. "Agna, great happiness has come to me. 'Om Jhared is my mate."

"No!" says Agna, looking at me in astonishment. "But Kamir is so—so—"

I get an image of the unsaid word and push it away. So Kamir was being truthful about her "ugliness."

"In my eyes," I say firmly, "and in the eyes of my people if they could see her, Kamir is a very beautiful woman. Her appearance is so lovely that I was attracted to her at once. I only hope that I am not too ugly, as you call it, in your eyes."

"Never!" exclaims Kamir loyally, and adds with more realism, "He is so strange altogether that 'ugly' has no meaning. Oh, Agna, couldn't you tell? You followed a trail of happiness."

"Yes." Agna nods. "I was puzzled. Well, little sister, the sun of the seas seems to have smiled on you. Just when we gave up hope that you would develop, a mate comes from the skies!" He chuckles. "But I have come to bring you home. And 'Om Jhared, too, of course, if he will. The season of storms seems to have come unusually early this year. We should make the Long Swim now. And one has come from the Souls of Aeyor with very bad news."

"What news? What has happened? Aeyor is the campment near us," she reminds me.

"Later, later. You will have many questions, and I was not there when he came. Right now I need a bit of rest, and tomorrow early we will start."

"Oh, you are a tease, my solemn brother!" Kamir chides.

I am rather relieved that some Mnerrin are "solemn"; my little mermaid's unfailing merriment in the face of danger doesn't strike me as a survival trait. And I notice again what

I had felt with Kamir, the sense of this person's profound civility. And he must be very tired; he apparently has been swimming for three days straight.

"You have eaten?" I inquire.

"Oh yes."

"Then let us go back to sleep, night traveler!" Kamir laughs, flopping down on our boat bed.

"Right."

Agna's preparations are as simple as Kamir's were; he untucks the tail of his finely-decorated loincloth, sits down, and spreads it on the sand to protect his face and, saying, "Sleep well, little sister. Sleep well, 'Om Jhared," he lies back, face to the skies.

"Sleep well, Agna," we say.

I close my eyes against the bright, tricolored moonlight, and hold her close in silence. So our halcyon time has abruptly come to an end. I sigh, sad beyond measure. And what is this Long Swim Agna spoke of? It must be the seasonal migration Kamir had told me of; apparently the Mnerrin spend the stormy months at another island far to the south. I will, of course, go with them, somehow. Tomorrow I must calculate my batteries; perhaps I will have to return to the lander for recharge on the way....

My last thought, as sleep takes me, is the inflexible value they seem to place on what they call personal beauty. It is almost tangible to them—yet Agna was willing to accept my relative viewpoint. Civilized! ...

The nightly chorus is tuning up again, the three little moons ride high. What will the morrow bring? No—the day after; Agna estimated we were about two days' travel away in a straight line.... Out of the darkness comes a sleepy chuckle: Agna is laughing in his sleep. Kamir answers with an unconscious grunt, and I go to sleep.

• • •

The trip is dreamlike. Again I am struck by Mnerrin simplicity: next morning, after a quick breakfast and a pause to help me set a compass heading, Agna simply wades into the water and starts swimming. Through the pass, he turns due east, while Kamir and I pack up my gear and launch the boat.

It takes us a surprisingly long time to catch him up—those pale flashing arms really cover the distance, and he swims in a knife-straight line. Kamir has shown me how her red "hair" works as a direction-finder in the sea. Still it seems strange to find a lone swimmer heading so confidently with no land in sight. I wish I could take him on board, but the dinghy only holds two.

We match our pace to his and settle down, sleepy in the balmy air. Kamir, too, is saddened by the end of our happy days. But presently she is restless.

" 'Om Jhared?"

"What is it, darling?"

"If you would not be too alone, I want to swim for a time with Agna. I need exercise, and I'd like to see more in the sea."

"I'll miss you, my darling. But if you want to, go."

So she tumbles overboard, and after that we go through regular exchanges, with Agna taking a rest now and then. As we follow Kamir, I think of how my little mermaid must have been before we met—a small person swimming alone in the wide seas. She had seen the fires of the lander's retro-rockets, she'd told me, and come to investigate. Fearless little mermaid!

Agna proves to be pleasant company, with an inquiring and thoughtful mind. Like his sister, he has red "hair" and blue eyes, though his crest is darker and his eyes lighter than hers. His features would have been handsome had they not been so larded with fat.

Following my theory of the ultimately utilitarian base for standards of beauty, I ask him if the plumpness they value so has any purpose.

"Does it serve to warm you in cold water?"

"Oh, perhaps. But certainly it means long life."

"Long life? How do you mean?"

"For the female, after bearing young. And for the male, too. It helps with the feeding time. See me; I have just finished feeding five young, so I am thin. But I could not have fed my babies so well, had I been this thin at the start."

Complexities. I realize I have spent my time enjoying myself with Kamir instead of collecting data. Yet somehow I am unwilling to pursue the matter now, and am grateful when he says, reflectively: "Yes, I see what you mean. We have never thought of it like that—interesting! And thus you must have a different system, in which fat plays no part?"

"Yes, we do, although I'm not sure of the details of yours. But we regard fat as unhealthy. For us, *fat* seems to threaten short life."

His eyes sparkle with interest.

"So! How fascinating. Yes, a good theory! But look, there is our dinner. Kamir!"

Without pausing, she shouts back over her shoulder, "I see it! Do you think I am asleep?"

"A reef, thick with *emalu*," Agna explains to me. "A pity we cannot bring some back for the people, it is delicious."

"We could pile it in the boat," I suggest, hoping that "emalu" is not, say, a stinging jellyfish.

"No; it wouldn't keep," Agna says regretfully, and dives overboard.

Kamir, too, has submerged.

They come up with handfuls of a golden, anemone-like fuzz, which they devour like Human children into cotton candy. Emalu is, it seems, a fabulous treat. I get out my food-bars.

And it is fabulous, dining there on the sea with a pair of merpeople. At the moment, no land at all is yet in sight. I somehow hadn't realized, when Agna spoke of a two-day journey, that he meant two days and a night of simply swimming and sleeping on the open sea. Well, I'll be comfortable in the boat, and the weather seems settled. How will they do? I'm aware that there are a million questions I should be asking. But somehow it is difficult, conversing with two heads bobbing about on the ocean. The truth is, I'm unwilling to break the spell.

Their dinner over, Agna starts off again, and they swim till darkness. Agna calls for a conference and pulls out his light, which proves to be a small bundle of a lichen-like plant.

"Fish come to this," he explains to me. "I have to keep it in a dark pocket or I'd get no sleep! Tell me, little sister, do you wish to continue? I could lead with this light. But we have made good distance; I can feel home strongly. And there is a reef just ahead where we could have fresh breakfast."

"I feel it, too," says Kamir, who has been swimming with him. "I think we should stay here. I didn't get enough sleep last night, thanks to you." She laughs.

"Very well." Agna repockets his light and swims to a tactful distance. "Good night, little sister. Good night, 'Om Jhared."

"Good night," we call as Kamir climbs on board to join me.

We stretch out in the little boat and let the wavelets rock us to love and sleep.

But toward morning, Kamir nudges me awake. It's bright moonlight.

"Dear 'Om Jhared—I want to go in the sea now. To have a last sleep in the sea. Do you mind?"

"Yes, I mind. But go ahead, darling. Only don't go too far away."

"I won't. Oh, my sweet darling, my mate-from-the-stars!" And with a hug and a kiss she has gone into the deep water. I shudder with unknown fear. But she simply says good night again and turns over, gills open, to sleep in the sea. I see Agna's dark head floating, only a few yards away. Evidently there is no current here. I relax and try for sleep but it does not come. The image of my little mermaid slipping away from me into darkness haunts my mind. I watch her until the moons go down and I can no longer see.

● ● ●

Next morning we awaken still together, and the Mnerrin dive for their morning meal. Studying the horizon, I see, straight ahead, the kind of long, low cloud that means land. But the Mnerrin are scarcely interested; their senses had long told them it was there.

We set off as before. It is again dreamlike, but hour by hour the cloud grows higher, closer, until my binoculars show the island beneath, where the dream must end. Or change. But what a wonderful way to travel, I reflect, watching the two pairs of arms flash rhythmically. Living, sleeping, eating, *at home* in the sea. For all their Humanness, they are also aquatic animals. . . .

And I catch them mind-speaking each other as they go.

"See, Agna—new fish over there. Yellow, red, black tail . . . Will you remember it? I have at least twenty new ones to report."

"Yes . . . There must be a reef ahead," comes Agna's thought.

I am almost in a trance state when suddenly the unmistakable sound of voices singing comes across the water. We are arriving. I turn to my glasses and make out that we are coming to a large river estuary, surrounded by a low green swamp of delta, through which thread numerous streamlets. Behind the delta is the shore proper, a low bank running up to a plateau on which I can glimpse land vegetation, trees. And beyond that in turn rises a central mountain, green to its summit. A large island.

As we come closer I see that the swampy delta is full of small huts. And a column of smoke is rising from before a larger hut in the center. Most of the small ones appear in need of repairs, I see, as if no longer in use.

But most important, I see the people.

They are all on the beach, it seems, strolling or chatting in groups. One sizable group is lying down. And children are playing around them, seemingly all of one age. Babies, too, lie about doing Human-baby things, or are held in arms. All eyes are focused upon us; even through the glasses I can catch the gleams of blue. And I feel the feathery touch of mind-search.

I decide Kamir should arrive in style, so I bring her in the boat and put her up front with a paddle. As soon as we get closer I will hoist the motor and paddle her in.

The bay in front of the delta is quite narrow. Agna arrives at the reef and waves me to follow him through one of the many passes. Kamir is waving her paddle excitedly.

The mind-search and mind-greetings have become overwhelming. My mind-speech has much improved, so I send a formal greeting to the people, who respond in a babble. Evidently they have no formal spokesman.

"Whom shall I speak to, Kamir?"

"Oh, call to Maoul. That tall old man, there."

Agna is already wading ashore in Maoul's direction; we follow him in. And from there on, the afternoon is a genteel pandemonium.

Maoul greets us cordially, having received Agna's news. But everyone on the beach must receive it, too, and share it with others, and everyone must meet me and congratulate Kamir—with varying degrees of incredulity—and Agna disappears to go to his mate, who is one of the invalids lying down.

Finally he returns to direct us to his hut, and I make a fool of myself splashing through the swamp carrying my stuff, until someone points out that one walks in the little hard-bottomed rivulets, one of which, I now see, runs by every hut. By the time we get the boat and the gear up to Agna's terrain, after demonstrating everything to the crowd, dark is falling. And Maoul, it appears, has laid on a feast of celebration. They have caught a large fish to roast in cenya leaves, with various delectable fruits.

"Whoee!" Kamir laughs, plumping down on the boat after our last load. "That was fierce! Oh, 'Om Jhared, how I wish we were back alone with our islands!"

For me, too, the afternoon has been a melee of pale plump genial gentlemen in loincloths, eager children, ethereal invalids opening huge blue eyes at my strangenesses, and endless repetition by mind and speech.

"Me too." I hug her. "But what is the bad news Maoul started to explain? I got carried off to be shown to the ladies. What's the matter with the women, by the way? They're so thin. Emaciated. Have you had an epidemic?"

"Oh, no!" Kamir laughs. "It's just the birthings. Well, Maoul said that one came, wounded, from the Souls of Aeyor, the next encampment, to say that they had been set upon by terrible gold-skinned people, who tried to kill—yes, actually *murder*—all of them. Some have escaped by going in the sea—the gold-skinned ones do not swim, it seems—but the rest were killed. Isn't that terrible? What could such people be, how can it *happen*?"

I am shocked into sobriety. Oh gods, my paradise planet isn't all paradise, it contains others who are killers. Homo Ferox. Unless by chance this is an invasion of Black Worlders or other moral barbarians with high technology, out to conquer an attractive world?

But no, Kamir tells me. They are people of this world, only with strange tools to hurt and kill. And they have only the crudest mind-speech, and do not go in the water, as she'd said. The man who swam here—two days, with a bad spear cut in his side—said they had come from somewhere far, far to the west. "Where legends say we also came from," Kamir adds.

That would be the small continent Pforzheimer had seen, I figure. Perhaps it is still spawning out new races of Homo Wettensis, as a part of Old Terra once did. A dreadful parallel jumps to my mind; I push it aside resolutely.

"Kamir, I have seen such things on other worlds. I must talk with Maoul tonight. If this is what I think, you are in danger here. These goldskins will not stop with one encampment."

"Oh, no . . . Yes, you must speak with Maoul. And why don't you talk with Elia?"

"Who's Elia?"

"The man who swam here. He is lying in the big hut, ill with his wound. Maybe you can help him. Oh, 'Om Jhared, I showed your beautiful bracelet"—she points to her ankle—"to Maoul. He said they were pictures of sounds, and we should learn them and make one for everybody. *And* make a picture of important things, too. I didn't understand it all but he was very excited."

Fantastic. So I will end by having these people transcribe their speech into Galactic! I must see more of Maoul. Is he a lone genius, or is this the level of their intellects? Meanwhile, it's a good idea to talk with this Elia.

•   •   •

I do talk to Elia, and am not made happy. These goldskins appear to be journeying from island to island, attacking everything they meet. They cross the sea by large, ugly war canoes. And they have lost their flock, or herd of some kind of land animal, so that they're hungry.

"How did you learn all this?" I ask Elia. "I hid two days,

watching and listening, until I was able to travel," he answers. "Man-from-the-skies, I thank you for your medicines. The people here have been very kind, they even made a song in my honor. But the relief from pain is better still!"

"And I think that will end the infection," I tell him, putting away the universal antibiotic the spacers give us.

The feast that night is held in front of the hut in which Elia lies, where I had seen the cookfire; it is the only bit of hard ground in the swampy delta. All is very informal—we simply sit about on tussocks of grass, and the children pass us succulent-looking morsels of fish, beside which my food-bars seem very bleak. The invalid women, at whom I will not look closely, are helped to small portions of a soup made by their mates from the fish drippings. And I get my first good look at Mnerrin teenagers, who, like the children, seem to be all nearly the same age. Aside from the overweight, they are charming, most with rufous crests, plus a few blonds and brunettes, and all with the blue, blue eyes. As I sit there, the majority of the people are looking curiously at me between bites, and the impression made by those eyes is very striking. From dark to pale, from aquamarine to lapis lazuli to sapphire to crystal blue, all, all are as blue as if they carried a bit of the shining sea within their heads—as perhaps they do.

I think of a race whose eye color we will never know, and it motivates me to tackle Maoul. But first I must settle one question.

"Maoul, how does it happen that you are eating this large fish? Kamir gave me the idea that you do not kill, except the brainless little butterfish, and even those reluctantly?"

He becomes grave. "It was perhaps very wrong of us, 'Om Jhared," he admits. "But this fellow here was also eating our butterfish. And he began tearing our nets. All over the reef. He harassed us until Pamir hit him too hard on the snout. We call him *omnar*—and legend has it that omnars are very good to eat. And so it's proving!" He laughs—that universal Mnerrin laugh that seems to express the purest of happiness.

"Well, that makes my task easier. For I must explain that you have encountered another omnar—a land omnar, who will not stop with your nets, but will kill and perhaps eat everything, including you."

"You mean . . . the goldskins?" he asks dubiously.

"Yes, I do. The point is this. You and your people are very different from the great majority of races. In my life of traveling and learning of travels, I have never encountered a race who so hated killing. You have not even the words for what is the daily occupation of many peoples—war, aggression, fighting, invasion, attack. Here, let me show you." And I sent out horrible images, to him and the other men who were leaning to hear. I saw their faces change.

"How unspeakable!" Maoul exclaims with loathing. The others joined him. "Why do you show us such things?"

"Because you are in danger. I, too, hate what I have just shown, and so do most of my race. I thought I had come to the happiest world in the Galaxy when I found you. But now we must face the fact that you are not alone, that there is another people here, cruel and aggressive, who have found you. And they won't stop until they have attacked you and taken over your nesting site here."

"But there is plenty of room in the world. Why should they come here?"

"Yes. But people like that do not see it so. They want *all*. And maybe they want slaves—people to carry their burdens when they travel on land, or to paddle their canoes in the sea. Or they may want you who go in the sea to catch fish for them."

Maoul laughs. "If they make us go in the sea, we will leave."

"Not if they hold your children. Oh, they have terrible ways of forcing you to do their will."

"Hmm . . . You seem to know much about this." Maoul eyes me with a trace of dubiety.

"Yes, unfortunately. I told you, you are the only people I have met in a lifetime of traveling who are free of aggression."

Maoul ponders. "Well, it seems we must leave here and find another nesting place. But our women still live, yet are too weak to travel."

"Would you just give up your home to these intruders?"

"What else can we do?"

"You can fight. I can show you how. It means changing your way of life for a time, but that has been changed anyway.

Wherever you flee to, these predatory goldskins will find you again."

"How can we—what did you call it—fight?"

"What did they attack with? Spears—which are long sharp staves—or perhaps arrows shot from a bow? Like this?" I mimic shooting.

He shakes his head. "The, ah, spears, I think. And—" He lowers his eyes as if to shut out some vision too sickening to look at. "They came also with *fire,* Elia says." Maoul's voice drops to a whisper. "They burned huts—some with babies still in them."

"Oh gods. My friend, I am so sorry this evil thing has come to you. I believed I had found a world of peace, the most beautiful thing in the universe."

"What is *peace?*"

"What you have. How you live. No fighting. No killing. Harmony . . . When I leave, I'm going to petition the Federation to save you, to exterminate these gold-skinned aggressors."

"Oh no. That would be evil. This is their world, too."

"But they are destroying this world. . . . Maoul, when these goldskins come, you people will be like helpless infants before them. And they will come before you depart—they might be on us tonight, and you don't even have watchers out. Will you let me train the men in some self-defense so they may at least protect their women and children? And will you let me organize a watch? We have a word for such a leader and trainer of armed men: a 'general.' Will you let me be your general for this purpose alone?"

Maoul's blue eyes bore into mine, I can feel his mind searching me. And tendrils of mind-search come from the other men. I open to them, show them all I am. They must be right about this, sure of their choice.

"Very well, 'Om Jhared," Maoul says after a busy silence. "You have convinced me that we do face some trouble." The others nod. "We will call a council and you will show them such images as you showed me, and be our general."

"Gladly," I say, wondering at the same time what I have let myself in for. To transform a profoundly pacific people into a defense force in a few days? Obviously it can't be done.

But anything would be better than their present helplessness. I must try.

Maoul is pointing to my wrist. "Now there is another matter." He smiles. "Kamir."

She has been beside us, listening intently.

"We see you have, against all hope, found a mate," Maoul continues. "Our congratulations." He puts an arm around her, kisses her cheek. She smiles radiantly—my little mermaid bride.

"And you, 'Om Jhared, strangely are the father; father-from-the-skies. But Agna says you know nothing of caring for young babies."

"I did not think there could be young. We are so different—"

Maoul is laughing wholeheartedly. He places both hands along Kamir's belly so I can see. And I can no longer delude myself—it is the belly of a pregnant woman.

"Oh gods! Have I done something evil?"

"I helped you," says Kamir smugly.

"No," says Maoul, suddenly grave. "How can babies be evil? They are the consummation we all long for. But how will you care for them? What will you *do*? I fear Kamir will not be much help."

Agna speaks up from where he had been sitting beside an invalid woman. "I have been thinking of this, Maoul. They can of course have my hut and birthing-place—I will replace its roof, tomorrow. And I will help him feed them until we start on the Long Swim. Then maybe Donnia here—" He turns to a plump young Mnerrin who has been standing by us, his attention divided between Agna and me. "Donnia is also our egg-fellow," he tells me, meaning, brother to himself and Kamir.

"Yes," says Donnia. "Brother and sister, I will help. My mate—" he bows his head briefly "—has already gone. And you can see that I am far from drained."

"His babies did not live," Kamir whispers to me.

"Your sorrow is my sorrow," I say formally. "I—we thank you deeply for your help. As I said, I had not believed that two such different people could have young. And I don't know what may come; the results may be bad. But surely we need your help."

"Good, then it is settled," says Maoul. "Tell us, 'Om Jhared, why did you come to our world?"

"To rest," I tell them. "I was very tired after a long task, and your world looked so beautiful."

"And now you have another task," the old man smiled.

"Two tasks," I remind him. "Tomorrow I start teaching you how to defend yourselves against these goldskins. For tonight I will just say this: Remember, the eruption of these people is going to change all your lives, for a time at least. And you are going to have to prepare yourselves to hurt, to harm, to kill, other human beings, who seek to kill you. Think on that."

Looking and searching about, I see that my speech evoked mainly puzzlement. Gods, what have I undertaken? I must plan. . . .

• • •

At Maoul's council next day, I see that the children and many of the teenagers are absent. Maoul says that he thought such plans were not for children.

"To the contrary, it is important that they learn. They will have parts to play, and this problem may be with them all their lives." So they are brought, down to the smallest, who stare at me with huge blue eyes, so much like plump little Human kids, despite their straight-up small fins.

I start by repeating what I had told Maoul, and showing them images of war and of the goldskin's probable attack. They respond, as I'd expected, with horror and the suggestion that they at once go someplace else. I try to convince them that mere flight is useless, that the goldskins will pursue them, and that they may well attack before they are prepared to move.

"You would be simply laying this upon your children, and upon your children's children, if you fail to solve it now."

The mention of children turns their minds. These people are amazingly tied to their young—all of them, even the young boys, place great value upon babies, I find. Perhaps because,

I have noticed, they have relatively few compared with the other hominid races I know. I make a mental note to find out if the goldskin people are faster breeders.

I then outline my plan.

"When the goldskins attack us here, they will have learned from their last attack that you will seek to escape to the sea. So they will make sure to seize the beaches quickly, maybe even sending a separate party around the shore. If you attempt to flee that way, they will catch you easily. But tell me, that river"—I point to the line of papyrus plants marking the main stream to the estuary—"does it have a deep channel in the center all the way to the sea? Yes? Good. Then instead of going to the beach, you will make for the river. The problem is to defend yourselves and the women and children until you can all get there. One way is for the men to form a circle, with shields and spears on the outside, in which the children and weak ones can shelter. The goldskins will think you are making a final stand, and indeed, you can hold them off until all are assembled. But then you head for the river here, all in a group. That way you will fare much better than if you break and run individually; those who try that would be easily run down and killed." I show them an image.

The idea appeals to them, perhaps because of its symmetry.

"But the circle is no good unless we have shields and spears, and also warning of the goldskins' approach. So the first things we must do are make weapons, and set out a guard. The seasoned wood in these unused huts will do for spears. Every man shall make his own—I will show you how—and his shield. I have a spear-proof cloth, my tarpaulin, which we can cut up for shield covers. For the watch, I need volunteers among the boys with the best mind-hearing, four for the shore and four for the beach. And an older boy who will supervise them."

So I proceed to organize a watch, and a weapons sergeant. When I ask for something that would make a tremendous noise, they produce conch shells for the watchers to blow. And then I ask for a volunteer or two to go down the coast and keep watch on the goldskins' encampment at the lost village of the Souls of Aeyor.

A man named Falca speaks up. "It is my misfortune that I

cannot mind-speak well. But I hear well. So I will go and watch and listen. And maybe my young friend Kimra, who swims so fast, will come with me to bring word back if need be?"

Kimra, a relatively slender lad, jumps up with shining eyes. "Oh yes, Falca! Let us start now!"

I see that my message has been far more keenly received by the younger Mnerrin. So their pacifism is not some innate predisposition, but a matter of culture, of training. What carefully-wrought beauty I am destroying!

But I push the thought aside and proceed to set out our first watch shift, telling their sergeant to be sure to check on them at random, unpredictable times. And then I tear out suitable wood from a storm-wrecked hut, and give a demonstration of spear making. Strong knives are the bottleneck; their shell knives are too frail. I ransack my gear for extra knives and end by using my laser to prepare a supply of rough staves. As the first spears shape up in the hands of my future "warriors," I find another problem: I must dissuade them from weakening the spears by making handsome slim places for hand-holds, and wasting time on ornament and polish.

"I see that being a general is complicated," Maoul observes with a smile.

"Oh, it's an old, sad story. . . . But I have never met a people who were so far from war. I greatly fear for you."

That night about third moon I waken in Kamir's embrace and go as stealthily as I can to surprise our lookouts. I find, as I expected, two of them fast asleep. I rouse them roughly and give them a lecture on the sacredness of guard duty. The younger boy is nearly crying, but I ignore it—with difficulty. His eyes are so much like Kamir's. During the early morning I get the sergeant of the watch to repeat the same trick on the next shift.

• • •

Next day I vary the menu by arranging a drill. I get all the boys and girls to impersonate goldskins, and have them come down the coast onto the lookouts, who respond enthusiastically with horrific conch-blasts. The men come out of their huts and uncertainly form a loose circle near the riverside, into which the women, carrying babies, feebly come, and the smaller children. I see that some of my least-promising "warriors" will have to be spared to help the women take shelter and sort them out.

My remaining corps of potential fighters, while overweight, looks more promising. Like many fat men, they are light on their feet and supple, and like all Mnerrin, very strong. I explain how we will use the shields, held alternately high and low, and briefly impersonate a goldskin—whom I have as yet never seen—in coming at them. They tremble and make way, and I harangue them like a drill sergeant on the need to hold their places and protect the children behind. After I have harassed them into tightening to a respectable defense, we practice moving all together to the river and forming a corridor to protect the women and children going in the water. The idea of *protection* is, I find, the best spur.

Then we turn to shield making; a wicker frame covered with a piece of my best tarp held on with spacer's glue makes a pretty spear-proof defense, even if—which I can't find out—the goldskins have metal spear points. Against mere fire-hardened wood it is impressive, and gives my warriors confidence. They are not cowardly, but merely totally unused to the idea of war itself, of hurting and being hurt.

This becomes clear when we go on to practice actual combat. I sacrifice one of my two canvas ditty bags, stuff it with sand and moss, and hang it up to give them a target to thrust at. It is very hard to get them even to pierce the "skin." When I tell them to hit me, to make me fall down, their blows are mere taps. In desperation I pretend to fall; my assailant looks horrified, though I jump up and congratulate him.

But then comes assistance of a dreadful kind.

Young Kimra, who had been spying on the goldskins with Falca, comes swimming in one afternoon, broadcasting for attention. We gather round him as he wades ashore.

"The goldmen are definitely preparing for something," he tells us. "They have been holding conferences. Falca told me to tell you that. And—" he pauses. "We have seen several of the men they took prisoner. The golds have cut off their crests. Shaved them bald." He sends us the images.

"Now they can never escape," Maoul groans. But that did not seem to be all; Kimra is looking at the ground and biting his lip.

"What more?" I ask.

"And—I cannot say it. The children . . ."

"Yes, what about the children? What have they done to them?"

"They—they are *eating* them!"

"Oh, no!"

"Yes." The boy's lips tremble. "Yes . . . One night we swam in close—and saw. A child's body was hung up by their fire, hung up like, like *meat!*"

Maoul looks at me. "Is this possible?"

"I fear it is. You see, they do not regard you as people. And they lost their flock of some kind of animals."

"This must be stopped!"

Around us I can hear the report being whispered from man to man.

"We must go there!" Maoul declares.

"No," I tell him. "You could not equal them in fighting. You would only be killed. And then they would come here for your children."

"Can you stop it, 'Om Jhared?"

I have been thinking hard. "I can try. Tell me, is there an island nearby which is on the route of your Long Swim?"

"Yes. The Island of the Green Coral. It is small, but with good food."

"Then here is what we can do: there is one time when their camp will be little defended. That is when they start to come here. Find me a good swimmer, a boy too light to fight well. I will take him in my boat at top speed down to their camp. When the men leave to come here, I will go ashore with my fire-weapon and free the children and any other captives they have, including the mutilated men. Your boy can lead them all to the Island of Green Coral to wait for you. I will return here at speed and be with you when they attack."

"Can that be done? Let us question Elia closely on the distances by water and land."

"Spoken like a general."

As we go up to Elia's hut, I see a man attacking the canvas

dummy with his spear. He runs it right through. The horrible news has wrought a change.

Elia tells us that the plan is feasible. To get here by land, the goldskins must go around a range of foothills; it might take them as much as two days.

As we come away, the sergeant of the watch comes to tell us that his boys have sensed minds nearby in the dawn. But the trace faded soon.

"That will be their spies," I tell Maoul. "They will go back and report on this village, how many we are, and the lay of the land. Thank fate they didn't see our weapons; they will think we are just like the village they crushed."

So I must wait at least two days before trying my rescue raid. Young Kimra goes back to watch with Falca.

We spend the days improving our drill and solving last-minute problems. Such as, what if the goldskins attack the circle with fire? Torches? I set out big containers of water, with a delegate to keep them filled. But the prospect of torches is too daunting. In desperation, I give the fire-control sergeant my can of extinguisher and explain its use. But in future they will have to depend on water alone.

And I confer with Mavru, their quasi-official Healer, to set up the way to treat spear wounds—packing them with the water-moss, which seems, like a similar Terra sphagnum, able to suppress infection. We set up a first-aid station by the river.

Strangely enough, in those last hours of peace, I get to know the Mnerrin better than ever before. I stroll the beach, watching their recreations. Among the more expected sights—boys and girls playing ball—I find a man surrounded by onlookers. He is drawing circles and triangles in the sand and, with a knotted string, explaining what he calls "Relations." This seems to be their art of geometry and mathematics. I am startled to find diagrams that imply knowledge of the Pythagorean theorems. So these people are not just simple Polynesian-like paradise-dwellers! No, this beach is more like the Athenian agora, where men in simple lengths of cloth discussed the eternal verities.

"We plan to make a permanent structure of stone at storm-season home," one man told me. "And we are going to use Relations to make it beautiful."

I find that one of their carefully preserved possessions is a big shell straightedge, marked off in equidistant intervals. They have a standard of measure! The man who carries it across his back has found a friend who has promised to take it over in case he is wounded in the coming fighting with the goldskins.

Nor has Maoul forgotten his discovery of the Galactic alphabet on Kamir's bracelet. He has been talking it over with others. They get me to teach them the whole alphabet and begin discussing whether more letters are needed to "picture" Mnerrin phonemes. The agora, indeed!

For my part, I take time to teach the Relations enthusiasts about our system of written numbers. Typically, they grasp it at once, and start transcribing them onto their shell measure. They are especially interested in the concept of zero.

"With this, we can do many things!" exclaims Kerana, the Relations explainer. I wonder by how many centuries—or decades—I have speeded their mental evolution. I wonder about their minds; this is no case of an isolated genius, but of a group with high, though unexploited, mental capability. And they seem not to be in danger of the fallacy that brought Plato and Aristotle's deductive logic low, the fallacy of refusing experiment. No; they test out every step of their Relational logic.

I tell them the story of Aristotle's deduction that women must have fewer teeth than men, while refusing to count his wife's teeth. They laugh. I sigh, and wonder if I should expose them to Bacon's scientific method. I try.

But time is growing short. I have scoured the land that lies behind the beach, and on the last day discover a flint-like rock. I bring it to two men who have been doing shell knives.

"Look. I think you can chip this into blades which will be stronger than shell. Let me show you." Inexpertly, I flake out an edge. They assent with pleasure to trying.

Maoul has produced a youth named Manya to accompany me on the rescue party. On the last night I pack a few rations and emergency supplies into the boat, and we leave it secured to the beach, to start at dawn.

That last night with Kamir she is untypically thoughtful. I

think that the reality of all this has just come through to her, preoccupied as she is with her monstrously growing pregnancy. She has been lying lazily on the beach by day, sunning her vast belly, and smiling to herself, only distantly interested in my warlike activities. She is still enchantingly beautiful in a different way; my little mermaid has turned into a nature goddess.

"Darling, take this." I extract from my gear my last resort, a tiny close-action personal laser. "Defend yourself with it if I do not return in time. But remember, sweetheart, you must wait until your attacker is very close, almost within arm's length."

"I will kill for our babies," she says calmly. "And you are right to go to save those children. We Mnerrin, as you call us, do not have many. All are precious." She hugs me again, then pushes me away.

It is very hard to leave her.

But Manya and I get into the dinghy, and shortly the little craft is leaping through the green waters at its great top speed. In a couple of hours we are within sight of the other settlement's bay, a journey which had cost the wounded Elia two painful days. The birthing huts here are different, somewhat larger, and supported by a center pole. Falca and Kimra are still on the reef, invisible until we catch their mind-call.

We stop out of sight, where we will wait for the goldskins to leave, and hold conference.

Falca says he expects them to leave very soon. "And see, they are loading three canoes. I think it is as you said, they are sending a party by sea to cut off escape on the beaches."

"How many are there in all?"

"About ninety, counting thirty-six in the canoes."

"It is bad odds for our people. But I have a very powerful weapon which will kill many. I shall be busy!"

"Kimra told you about the children?"

"Yes. That is why I'm here." I tell him my plan. Falca sighs.

"That is a great relief. Last night . . . they killed another. It was all we could do not to rush ashore and assail them. Stranger, you are a good man. Kimra and I were going to try alone, but we had no place to send them. The mutilated men cannot guide."

"Manya here will take care of that. Meanwhile, you and Kimra are no longer needed here. You might as well start swimming home. But be wary that those canoes do not overtake you in the water."

"Good. I go. The children are in that large hut with two entrances, and so are the other captives. They are tied with ropes."

"I can take care of that." I show him my shark knife. "Fair travel, friend." He nods, and without more ado he and Kimra take off in long, flat dives.

And then we wait. It becomes clear that the goldskins' start will not be made till next morning; they are preparing for a feast. I make the mistake of giving my binoculars to Manya, and he sees the fresh-killed body of a child hung up by the fire. He chokes with fury, then weeps quietly. I take the glasses and try to soothe him as best I can.

"Oh, if only I had those long-range weapons you told us about! No—I would go to them, I will kill them with my bare hands. I would *kill!* I will kill! . . . We will return in time, won't we?"

"Yes, but you won't be with me, Manya. You will be leading the children and the mutilated men to safety on that island."

He heaves a sigh. "Yes, I forgot. But if there is a goldskin left ashore, I will kill him with my bare hands."

"Don't be rash, Manya. Those men are practiced fighters. One of them could destroy you. I will attend to the killing."

"Then I will kill their children!"

He seems to hear himself then, and looks shocked. But he continues in a grim voice, "Their children will grow into such as they. They have devoured our babies. Yes, I will kill them."

I, too, am shocked. What have I created? Or no, it was not me, but the circumstances, the irruption of the goldskins. The sight of one's children being butchered like animals is not to be reacted to in a civilized way. He is not to be blamed.

But what about me? I contemplate cold-blooded genocide. No, not cold-blooded; these Mnerrin are in a sense my children. My ideal of Human life . . . Grimly, I realize that I have fallen into every psychic trap that spacers are warned of. I love these people.

So be it. When I return, I will pull every lever, press every button known to me to obtain official intervention, to save this planet for the Mnerrin. It's just possible, especially if one or two of my friends are still in their offices. . . .

Twilight has come. We eat and settle for the night, thinking our different thoughts. This is, in fact, one of the few times I have had pause from my duties to reflect. Manya's slight form beside me in the boat reminds me of Kamir. What of her? What of my babies, if incredibly they are born whole and viable? Can I stay here with them? Could I endure this tranquil life, as a non-sea animal? I don't know. . . .

In any event, the need to get off-planet and do something for the Mnerrin will dominate my life for a while. After that, we'll see.

The fact is that my conviction that our mating would be infertile has been so strong that I still do not believe I am about to father little half aliens, if all goes well. I have never fathered others. What is this recurrent question: how will you feed them, how *are* they fed, without mother's milk, by non-mammals? I had vaguely supposed that they would eat fish, like the adults. Evidently there is something that I, helped by Agna and Donnia, are going to have to do. And Kamir—I shudder at the mounting evidence that somehow this birthing will mean her death. Surely those were older women, there in the village. Not my bright, vital little mermaiden! No . . . no . . . These concerns are for after the coming battle. . . .

Finally I sleep, and the balmy night goes by.

We rouse to dawnlight, at once aware that the camp is in motion. I check the glasses. Yes, goldskins are loading the canoes, preparing to cast off. We had better conceal ourselves.

We paddle in among some rocks that have tumbled to the sea, forming one arm of the bay shore. There we eat and watch.

This settlement is similar to the one I know in that it is in a delta around an estuary. Evidently these marshy places are proper sites for birthing and rearing the newborn. And there must be a limited number of them. By driving the Mnerrin from them, the goldskins could make it impossible for the

Mnerrin to breed. Idly, I wonder why the deltas are so favorable. Perhaps tiny babies are taught to swim in the little streamlets, before their gills are strong enough for the open sea? And I am still not clear as to what role fresh water versus salt plays in their lives. Really, it is shameful how I have simply *lived*, without collecting any respectable body of data!

At this moment Manya nudges me, and we hear the *chunk, chunk* sound of paddles. A long low dark canoe, gaudily bedizened, comes in sight. Six paddlers to a side. We crouch low.

It passes by, about fifty meters away, followed by another, and another. And then no more. Cautiously, we nose out of the rocks to where we can see the camp.

It is so still that we can hear voices. After we have waited about two hours, we hear a different sound, a kind of chanting. It takes on a marching tempo. And then we see a band of about fifty men tramping up out of the swampland, chanting and blowing on pipes. They gain solid ground and set off down the coast. My heart has sunk—fifty and thirty-six, more than two to one against the Mnerrin. My laser will have to do good work.

But now we have other work in hand.

We still avoid starting the motor, but paddle in to their beach. We beach the dingy and start at a crouching run toward the big hut Falca had pointed out. Women must be all about us in the camp, but we see none—until suddenly we come on a party of them right outside the hut. They have knives in their hands.

I notice only that they are brightly gilt, their hides like goldfish, and could be called handsome if your taste runs to eighty-kilo bodies.

Manya behind me is making an extraordinary noise through his clenched teeth.

I make a sweeping pass with the laser, and they go down like tenpins without making a sound, their throats burned through. Behind them the door to the hut is ajar. Had they been going in to murder another child?

Mind-cries are coming from the hut. I send strongly, "Friends come!" and Manya joins me. We step over the golden corpses and go in to a pitiful sight.

The hut is full of rails and posts, and everywhere are tied children, ranging from toddlers to teenagers. Some grown men, shaved bald, are tied up at one end. The hut stinks.

"Cut them loose, quickly." I have brought a spare knife for Manya.

"Hungry, hungry," comes the mind-cry, especially from the smaller ones, as we free them.

"You will have food soon," we send. But how? I shudder to think what meat we will find beside the cookfires. Still, surely they have already fed on it. And would their dead friends object to giving their flesh to save the living?

A spear clatters in at the other door, a woman dives back.

"You finish freeing them, I'll attend to the village," I tell Manya. "Can you guard the outer door?" I ask a bald man, who is rubbing his limbs.

"Yes."

I go out and start through the village like a dervish, burning everything that moves. From one hut I am greeted by a spear. Inside, a man obviously sick or wounded is clinging to the center post. Beyond him crouch two women and children. Mercy is not in me that day; when I leave the hut, nothing lives behind me.

At intervals I check back to the big hut, where Manya is leading the children out. They stare at the goldskin corpses. The mutilated men look nervously about. Their heads are covered with pink fuzz.

I have found a pot of meat stew simmering at a hearth, and basket bowls. I put it before the kids without looking too closely.

"Can you catch reef-fish, after what they have done to you?" I ask the men.

"Oh yes, if we can find our nets."

As luck would have it, a pile of their filmy nets, loincloths, and other belongings has been thrown beside another hut.

"Good. Now, when you have eaten enough, you and the children will follow Manya here to an island—I think you know it—beside the path of the Long Swim. The people from my settlement will pick you up as they go by."

"They haven't left yet?"

"No." And then I have to respond to the overwhelmin

mind-question coming at me from everyone, even as they begin to gulp food: "Who are you?"

"A friend from the skies, Tom Jared. I have been living with your people since I met a girl named Kamir and mated with her. Now, these goldskins are going to attack our village. I must return quickly and help them fight. I can carry only one. Is there a man here who can strike and kill? Kill goldskins? Our people need defenders." I send an image of a goldskin leaping at a Mnerrin.

To my surprise, amid the blank looks I had expected from most of the men, a younger one steps smartly forward. "I think I can do what you call fight, O friend from the skies. I have thought much during our captivity. Now I can kill. But I need things to strike with. Here!"

He bends down to the row of corpses and takes a strong-looking knife from a dead woman's hand.

"And now a long one—"

"We call those spears. Maybe we will find some in this big hut."

And indeed we find a cache of spears. But they are mostly slim, decorated things for rituals and dancing. Again to my surprise, my new recruit sorts out some that are sturdy and useful. This lad is an untypical mutation, in theory, maybe, a dangerous one. Right now I wish I had a hundred of him.

"Good. Now we go. I have fish in the boat, you can eat on the way. And you others had best be on your way with Manya, lest some goldskins catch you again."

I bid good-bye to them as they eagerly follow Manya to the water's edge. The men have found some rope, and start tying the smaller children on towlines to their belts. Always this care for the young! I cut short their curiosity about my boat.

"Later. No time, now."

The warlike lad's name is Sintana. His eyes shine as I direct him to help me tow the dinghy to deep water and hop in. When I start the motor and start skimming along the reef, he is visibly ecstatic.

"Now, I don't know whether we will overtake the canoes before they reach my village or not. So we must proceed with care whenever we cannot see a long way ahead. I want you to watch and listen with all your power for those canoes. I will have much watching to do to avoid hitting coral heads this close to shore. If you see or suspect a canoe, raise your arm like this and be ready for a quick stop, right? If you are *sure* that all is clear ahead, go like this."

Enthusiastic assent from Sintana. I gun up the motor to full speed, and we rip along at top speed toward my village. I want to keep close to the reef to avoid being sighted by the canoes ahead, but the danger from isolated coral rocks strings my nerves tight. Luckily, there is enough wave action to show where most of them lie. Avoiding one at the last minute, I nearly spill us. Sintana looks round questioningly, and after that I see him hang on.

He is radiating pleasurable excitement like a child, but looking him over, I see he has plenty of muscle to go with his combative spirit. A gods-sent ally.

It's getting dark. Each time as we round a shallow point, Sintana waves me on. Those canoes have really covered ground. I'm not afraid of their hearing my motor over their paddling splash—and even if they did, they would not know what it was. But where are they?

We approach the last point before our bay. Suddenly Sintana's hand goes up and we jolt to a stop.

"I think I hear minds from around the point. Maybe quite close."

"They could be holed up, waiting for the men on land to arrive. No more talking now."

At lowest speed we nose around the point. Presently we can see most of the bay, but no canoes.

"They're hiding right on the other side of these rocks," Sintana whispers. I listen, and fancy I can catch a crude mind-murmur.

"Can you paddle quietly?"

"I think so."

"Fine. Let's try to get a look."

We paddle the dinghy silently forward, about an arm's length from the rocks. Sintana's hand shoots up and I stop. Eyes glowing with excitement, he whispers, "I can see the bows of two canoes, in a cove in the rocks. I don't know where the third is."

"Sintana, get down low in the boat. I am going around fast

and fire my weapon at them. But we will be within spear-throw. Make sure they do not hit you. And *do not throw your spear*, you will need it later," I add, knowing what the excitement could do to such a boy.

"And your part is to keep watch for that third canoe. Got it?"

"Yes." He is reluctantly crouching down.

"Get farther down. The air will be full of spears, and I must fire over you. Can you *stay* down?"

"Yes."

"All right. Hang on, here we go!"

I slam the lever to high, and we round the point in a great roostertail of spray. In the cove behind the point are two canoes full of goldskins—good, I had feared some might have gone ashore. I fire as soon as I'm in range, zigzagging as I come at them. Screams, barely audible over the motor and spray. I roar in as close as I dare, and then twist the dinghy into a hair-raising U-turn, firing all the time. Spray splashes over the canoes, but I can see goldmen struggling up, lifting their spears. I turn again and make another pass, managing to laser every standing man.

But Sintana is in my way.

"Get down!"

"The third canoe! Look out, look out!" he yells.

I glance back and see the third canoe, come out of nowhere, rushing straight at me. I turn and fire. Luckily, from dead ahead, the spearmen are blocking each other. But they are also shielding each other from my fire. I whip around fast and slice in close to the gunwale, doing slaughter—and then I'm out of the little cove, heading for the reef. Luckily, moons are up.

But that's as far as we go. The feel of the dinghy warns me—I see two spear shafts sticking from the pontoons. Oh gods. I turn toward the beach, weaving between the rocks at the start of the reef, and just make shallow water as our craft collapses around us. No one is in pursuit.

Sintana and I jump out. I wrestle the motor from the sagging folds and hand it to him while I rescue the batteries. Thus laden, we struggle ashore, towing the half-submerged dinghy. Sintana, I'm glad to see, still has his spear. A cool boy.

At that moment a fearful hooting hits our ears from the delta beyond. The watchers have sighted goldskins and are blowing their conches.

I hate to leave my wrecked dinghy to the attentions of any survivors from the canoes—it is my only link to the lander—but there's no time to do more than throw a couple of armfuls of brush over it. We start for the village at a run.

As we near it, I see splashing in the shallows. A Mnerrin family has forgotten the drill and is heading straight for the sea. Ahead of me two goldskins, shining in the moonlight, race after them, spears lifted. They throw before I can get the range; the man of the fleeing group goes down into the water. The children stop, trying to pull him up, but the goldmen are upon them, I manage to pick one off, but the other is too close to the children.

He whips out something silvery—it's a rope, he is tying them up. He starts out of the surf, dragging them behind him, screaming.

We pound after him, Sintana in the lead. I see his spear-flash, and the goldman goes down. By the gods, my Mnerrin has killed! We cut the children loose and tell them to follow us.

"No, Father Pava is out there!"

"He'll be all right. Come." I know that if Pamir has survived the spear, he will be safer under water than on shore.

We run on.

Most of the goldskins are still coming down the bank onto the delta. I can see the main hut now, see that my Mnerrin have actually formed a protective circle. Women and children are still being thrust in.

I identify us by mind-call.

"Quick, there is time to start for the river *now*!"

"But Pava's family are not here."

"He ran to the sea and got caught. I have his children. Here," I tell them, "get in behind these men."

The leading goldskins are upon us. I fire, pick them off. Others are circling, trying to get between us and the sea.

"They are after the children! Quick, to the river! All together, go!"

The circle starts off at a wobbly trot, the men in the rear having a hard time to shepherd the children and fend off goldskins, who are now arriving in force. I fire, fire till no more are in range, wishing that I were within the circle firing out—too many times I have had to hold fire to avoid hitting Mnerrin. And then another shining rank of goldmen is upon us.

The next hour is collapsed in my mind into a montage of firing, running, firing, running. The goldskins catch up with the Mnerrin circle before they reach the river, and there is wild spear-jabbing, hand-to-hand combat. Children's skrieks fill the air.

At last they reach the river and form a corridor as I had taught them. Children rush down it, women hobble after, babies in arms, and fling themselves into the deep channel, followed by the men. Goldskins rove the banks, searching futilely for some shallow place where they can get at their prey. I lurk behind, picking them off as I can. I do not think many of them are clearly aware of me. Finally when they pause at the beach, I have a clear shot at a mass of them, and wreak scorching havoc. Sintana is busy chasing stragglers.

There is a moment's lull. I stand up to look—and am jolted by a blow. A spear shaft in my shoulder. But moments later I am aware that Sintana is by me, having dispatched my attacker.

"Pull this out of me, Sintana."

He does so, surprisingly gentle. I watch the ripples that mean Mnerrin are reaching the sea, gritting my teeth.

"Is there much blood?"

"Some."

"Pack that moss in the hole." I cut off a length of rope and make a sling for my arm. Fortunately the spear doesn't seem to have hit anything vital.

"Where are the rest of the goldmen?"

"I don't think there are any more standing," he says with quiet pride. I can see in the moonlight that he is bloodied all over and has a different spear.

"You have been busy. Are you wounded?"

"In the leg. A little."

We go through the moss-packing routine. He has a fat shaft broken off in the big muscle of his thigh.

"That will hurt worse later. How do you like war?"

He grins and sighs together. "I think—too much!"

"Yes, it is like that. . . . Now, if you can walk, we must find my light and check all the wounded goldskins."

"And kill them?" He makes an eager motion with his spear.

"Yes. All except two whom we will tie up for questioning."

Then I feel free to do what I'd been desperately longing for. I send out a focused mind-call to the Mnerrin hiding in the water.

"Can you hear me?"

"Yes." A head surfaces just inshore of the reef.

"I think it is all safe now. But wait until dawn to come ashore. And—*is Kamir safe?*"

What must be her head surfaces, too, and I receive a sending of such love and longing that I can scarcely resist going to her. "Till daybreak, darling. Now I have work to do."

"Always work!" Her laugh, my mermaid's laugh, rings out over the water, piercing me with sweet memories. I sigh, and turn back to the job.

Sintana and I go first to the pile of goldskins I created on the beach, and then start searching systematically through the marsh for gleams of gold. Their shining skins are a great liability.

"In future we will not be able to assume all is over so soon. They will learn to take us more seriously, and arrange a second wave of attackers to come in just as the Mnerrin think all is safe."

We also come upon three Mnerrin dead and two wounded, men whom I don't know well, and three children who have been stabbed. To my amazement, a dark figure is there, bending over a child. I hold my fire just in time, as the mind-signal comes.

"Mavru! What are you doing here?"

"I swam upriver and waited," he replies. "I thought I might be more needed here."

"And you are. Wonderful. Mavru, meet my young friend from the lost village. He has worked hard in your defense."

The two Mnerrin greet warmly. I go in search of my medical supplies to help Mavru, and we resume our search of the marsh.

Long before we are through, Sintana is weary of killing the wounded. His battle fever has ebbed; only when a "corpse" surprises him by striking at him does it return briefly. This, I think, is a good lesson for him.

We save out two captives who seem in fairly good shape, and tie them up far apart so they can't communicate. As I'd been told, they seem to have no mind-speech except a sort of alarm call, and a threat-sending, a hostile blare.

When the moons go down we rest and eat. Mavru joins us.

"Their bodies are different from ours," he says. "I think I will cut up one or two and find where the vital centers are. Do you think that's a good plan, 'Om Jhared?"

I agree, and warn him about the dangers of handling cadavers. "You must wash your hands scrupulously. I, too, would like to see."

Sintana meanwhile has been questioning the nearest prisoner. He has picked up a few words of their tongue, which sounds barbarous in contrast to the Mnerrin's.

"I asked him why they ate children," he reports. "He only shrugged and said, because they were hungry. So I asked him why they did not catch fish. He seems not to understand. I think anything connected with water is entirely strange to them. I remember there was a great fuss about who was going to go in the canoes."

"And that reminds me," I tell him. "We must go and try to salvage those canoes and fix up my boat."

"Why do we want those ugly canoes?"

"First, to keep them out of the hands of any more goldskins who come here. And, most important, I think our people can use them on the Long Swim. They could transport the wounded; some will take a long time to heal. And babies could go in them, too."

"Oh, good idea. Hey, it's like you said, my leg hurts more."

"I'm sorry. But we have a job to do."

We check the other prisoner, who glares at us mutely, and hike down the beach to where the dinghy lies. It's untouched, thank the gods, and the repair kit, like all my supplies, is fastened inside. The spacer's gooey stuff really works well, but will take an hour to dry.

We leave it and climb over the headland to where two canoes float aimlessly in the little cove. A moon is rising again; I can see the glitter of bodies inside. The third canoe is only a prow sticking up. Its former contents are floating about.

"We have to go through the check again," I tell Sintana. "And then we have to fish those corpses out so they won't foul the sea. We can put them on the rocks up here, maybe the crabs will eat them."

Sintana shudders. "Parts, anyway ... I didn't know, when I volunteered to fight, that it included cleaning up the battlefield!"

"It includes whatever it includes," I tell him grimly. But I am suddenly dead tired, and my shoulder is on fire. I have been running on pure adrenaline. Do we really have to do this task? And my boat will take strength to pump up ... The first pink light of dawn is in the sky.

"I have a better plan," Sintana says. "Your people here have been idling in the sea all night." He goes back up on the headland, and I hear him send out a mind-call.

To my astonishment, three heads pop out of the water below us almost at once.

"No need to shout," comes a young voice. "We followed to see what you were up to. Hello, 'Om Jhared, I'm Pelya! What do you need?"

We tell them, and soon, to my great pleasure, three sets of strong young arms are hauling dead goldskins ashore and up the rocks. The goldmen are short and compact, heavy-boned.

"How many of you in the sea are wounded?" I ask Pelya.

"Three. And Pava's mate got a spear through her arm. She was very weak, you know. She died soon after we got to the bar."

"Oh, I am sorry."

"Yes ... But you did so much. We boys have been thinking. We will have to train ourselves to do this thing, to do fighting. War. Some of the older men think it is all over. but we don't agree. . . . But 'Om Jhared, just *why* do the goldskins attack us?"

"I don't really know, except that it is their nature."

But later, when we have pumped up the dinghy and are leading the procession of canoes back to the village, I tell them what I fear.

"I'm afraid that what I have seen on other worlds may be happening here. Somewhere far to the west there may be a great many goldskins, so that beaches and food are in short supply. They would be fighting over them, and the losers may pack up and come east, looking for new homes. If that's true, it means there will be more coming, and more after that, without end. I think they have more babies than you, so the pressure will go on and on. I hope to the gods this isn't true, that this was just a wandering band, but as I said, I have seen this thing before. That is why I am going to appeal to the power of the Federation to help you. But that will take a long time. Meanwhile, you are wise to try to help yourselves. . . . We can question the prisoners, and it might be good to send a couple of scouts back along their trail to see what we can find out."

"I see," says Pelya, and the other boys agree. For once they do not laugh.

Nor do I. In the growing light I can see the Mnerrin coming ashore. There is old Maoul, there is Agna, and Donnia, helping Kamir. I can already sense tendrils of contact, carrying gratitude to me. I hope there are not to be speeches, I am dead. And all too keenly I realize that I have now broken all the Federation's Rules of Contact. I have interfered massively with the Mnerrin's life-ways, and I have taken a decisive part in a war. . . . So be it.

• • •

"Wake up, 'Om Jhared! Kamir is giving birth!"

It is Agna's voice. I come to, groggily.

We are in Agna's birthing hut. Kamir is lying beside me on the crude bed, which is covered with moss and hay. She is on her side, curled around her vast belly, her hands pushing at it as though trying to push it away from her. Agna is beside her, doing something. I hear Kamir whimper.

Gently, Agna takes her hands and pats them.

"Here," he says to me. "Hold."

I take the hands. Kamir's eyes open and meet mine. With effort, she smiles. "Don't be afraid, darling. This is normal."

Normal? I am looking for some sort of opening, some birth canal through which the babies will emerge. There is no sign of anything like that. Instead, Agna's hands seem to be working on the "scar" or line I had seen, running around her abdomen. He is kneading it, carefully pulling it apart. I see that the scarlike line is starting to separate, like long, threadlike lips.

"In a moment now," he tells Kamir. "You can push."

Kamir puts her hands with mine up on her great belly. It is hot, hot. Then she pushes at it again.

Suddenly, with a dreadful caving-in feeling, her whole belly, containing the fetuses, starts to *separate* from the rest of her body! It tips forward, away from her, as the scarlike "lips" open. Agna is furiously working at this line, pushing his hands under her. She whimpers again. I see that the lips are actually a deep separation line, circling her whole belly, from ribs to pelvis. Oh gods, what is happening here?

Slowly, deliberately, yet too fast for me to follow, the fetal mass tips forward farther, revealing a deep cleavage. It tips, separates farther yet, and then rolls over, away from her, onto what had been the outside of her belly. Agna steadies it. Kamir gives a series of loud sighs, and then rolls away from it, onto her back.

"Whew! That feels better."

But I have a horrifying look at the shell of her body left after the fetal mass tore loose. From diaphragm to hips it is *empty*, covered by a rapidly thickening gel membrane. Through it I can see, under her ribs, a dark mass pulsing: her heart. Below that, by her spine, I can see the great cords of nerve and blood vessel running along her backbone, inside her empty flanks, to her hips and pelvis. Nothing more.

Agna is looking, too, as the membrane becomes opaque.

"See? Almost no fat at all. My poor little sister will not live long."

"Why?" But the answer is before me. Stomach, intestines, digestive organs, all are gone, taken away with the fetus-bearing mass of her belly. She has no means of taking in food. A fast-sealing tube end that must be her esophagus is visible near her heart. I can only hope that her kidneys are left, so she won't die of thirst.

I am squeezing her hands so tightly I must be hurting her. I relax them and make myself kiss her face, despite the ghastly display of her body. She strokes my hair with trembling hands.

"I'm fine. See to the babies."

The babies? Dimly I am realizing that this is no catastrophe, but a natural process of parturition. Or rather, it is a catastrophic process, deadly to the mother. But the babies are alive, the fetuses; through the gel of the torn-away side I can glimpse aqueous forms moving vaguely. Clearly they are too young for independent life. A great placenta lies on them, with coils running to each fetus—there are three. And there must be some sort of secondary heart with them, there is the throb of circulation.

Indeed, this mass that has torn itself loose from Kamir is almost a primitive animal in its own right, with organs it has stolen from Kamir.

To me it is a monster, which has mutilated and killed my mermaiden, my girl.

But Kamir is gazing at it with fond eyes. Her babies.

I make myself look at it. It is a globular mass about half a meter in diameter, lying on what had been the outside of Kamir's abdomen. All the part that had been inside Kamir is covered with this gel membrane, now fast thickening to opacity. Agna is bent over it, inspecting and feeling it all with tender hands. He points out a circular ring, or tube, set in the "top."

"That is where we feed the babies."

Oh gods; it is the remains of Kamir's esophagus, leading to her stolen stomach. I begin to shake with delayed horror, scarcely noticing that Donnia has come in, and is offering to me, of all things, a great bowl of butterfish, cut in pieces. When I see it, I am revolted at his apparent callousness.

"Fathers first," says Agna. He and Donnia each take some and begin to chew.

Then I am even more revolted by the understanding of what they are doing. They are taking food for the fetuses, substituting for their mother's missing mouth. Preparing it for digestion by her stomach, somewhere inside that monstrous package. Grimly I force myself to take some and begin to chew. A vaguely consoling thought comes to me: many Terran birds feed their new-hatched chicks like this.

Weakly, Kamir demands some, too. Now that her huge pregnancy has gone, I can see how thin the rest of her has become. Her limbs are no longer slender, but bone-thin, and her beautiful face has been fined to where it seems all great dark blue eyes. But how short a time ago it was that we played and tussled with each other on our magic isles! What a terrible thing I have wrought on my little mermaid, what evil I have done! Yet she seems strangely content, her eyes are luminous with joy when she gazes on the dreadful lump that contains our babies. Mysterious are the ways of instinct! Something in her makes her accept happily the shortness of her life for its irrational reward.

Agna is speaking to me. "Empty your mouth into this, new-father." He grasps the tube opening on the monster and pulls it free. I realize, for Kamir's sake, I must.

It would have been appalling were it not that the fetus-monster has an oddly attractive smell. Organic, but very sweet and clean. A lure to feed it, I think. Well, it works.

After I have fed it in this strange fashion, Agna and Donnia follow suit, and last, Kamir. "Are there three?" she asks.

"Yes," says Agna. "Lucky you did not make more. It will be a job to feed these, they also have no fat."

"I wonder what they will look like," Kamir says dreamily. She is sinking into sleep. Yet she turns to me and hugs me, with a momentary return of her old strength.

"Oh, my darling strange one, I am so happy! Never did I think I would have babies to watch over. Never! And you came from the skies and gave them to me." She kisses me again.

"But—" As I look at her exquisite young face, my heart feels as though it will burst then and there. How can she be so truly happy? Wait; is it conceivable she doesn't know her fate?

"I hope I will live to see them. I must. I *will*." She sinks back, blue eyes brave with resolve.

She knows, all right.

Agonized, I watch her drift smiling into sleep. Donnia is

nudging me, holding out the bowl of fish. I turn to my detested duty. I am very tired.

• • •

I wake to morning light.

Kamir is beside me. The monstrous baby-package is still there.

"Hello, my darling. How you slept! Do you know you fell asleep in the middle of feeding our babies? Fighting must be very tiring."

"Yes."

"I did some!" she tells me. "A goldskin came at me, and I burned him with the little weapon you gave me! But he was so strong. And falling down, he kicked me where the babies were. I was afraid he'd injured them. Then Agna came and helped me run away, to the men. And oh, I was so glad when you came back."

"I was too."

"Agna and Donnia have gone for more fish. See how the babies are stirring? That means they're hungry."

I see signs of movement within on the fetus-package. Gods, what appetites!

"Tell me, darling. How long will they stay like that?"

"Oh, twenty, thirty, forty days, it varies. I think ours will come out sooner, because they were with me so long. That's why I think I can live to see them."

Twenty days? Is that the span of our time?

"Don't talk about dying. If you die, the sun of my life will go out."

"Oh, don't *you* say that, although it is beautiful. If things were the other way round, it's how I would feel, too. When you were so long in coming, I feared the sun of my life had gone out."

And we have more private things to say, until Kamir pushes me away, with "Friends come!"

"I think it is that fierce boy, what's his name—Sintana. And old Maoul."

There is a knock on the hut wall. Even I can pick up Sintana's mind.

"Greetings, all."

They come in and sit on Agna's log. I see that Maoul is actually carrying a spear.

I congratulate him again on having got the Mnerrin to form their circle.

"It *was* a task," he admits. "I only wish Pava had heeded."

"People panic and forget. He thought the way looked clear—he forgot that goldskins can run faster than a man with children."

"Listen, 'Om Jhared," Sintana interrupts. "We have got some news out of our captives. They say there are no more goldskins on this island, or nearby, but there are many many more very far to the west. That sounds like your theory."

"Yes. I was never more sorry to be right. Did you ask why they eat your children?"

"Yes. They say they had a group of somethings, and they ate them. But they died, from drowning I think. Animals about so high." He put a hand about a meter from the ground. "And I think they have come on others like us and taken their children, too."

"A flock or herd of meat animals . . . This is common on other worlds. It seems clear they don't regard you as people, but as a sort of food animal. They might get the idea of taking a group of you captive and eating the young."

Maoul's face is a mask of fury, but he says nothing.

"We're not people because we don't fight, is that it?" Sintana asks.

"Something like that. Did you ask about their own children?"

"No, but he saw one of our women die and seemed to understand. He said their women do not die like that."

"Hmm . . . A real mutation. That fits, too. A higher birthrate."

"Mutation?" asks Maoul.

"A word we use when some of a group of beings become quite different. It usually starts with one or a very few, and the new form spreads because their offspring survive better."

"This sounds interesting," Maoul says. "I wish we had time to talk of it now."

I laugh. "You are learning bad ways, friend. In the old days you would have gone ahead and discussed some topic no matter what practical matters called you."

He laughs, too, somewhat sadly. "I feel I have aged ten years since day before yesterday. But what must we do with these goldskins now? Kill them, as Sintana says?"

I'm glad he's said it. "Yes, I'm afraid so. You can't take them on the Long Swim, and if you let them go, they will certainly make their way back to the main goldskin group and lead others here. That way they gain chieftaincy.... If you are revolted by killing them, would you rather I did it?"

"No," says Sintana.

"I am revolted," says Maoul. "But I will do it. It is right."

"Then will you let me give you one last lecture about this?"

"Speak on. Your last lectures saved our lives."

"I'm very glad. You know I feel one with you. Your pain is mine, too. Listen: *It is very hard to kill helpless men—or women—in cold blood.* And they will be talking, pleading, promising anything, to save their lives. They will promise not to bring others, to stay and wait for you, to work for you. They may claim they are not like the other goldskins, but that the others made them attack you. They may claim they can guide you to somewhere, that they have secret weapons. They may fall down and clutch your ankles and beg for mercy. They may tell you that they have young children to care for—anything! They may swear they never ate of the children's meat. Remember, to them, a promise made to an enemy need not be kept, lies told to an enemy or an inferior do not count. They will be talking and acting solely to save their worthless lives. What you must keep in front of your minds is that they have eaten your children and got caught trying to kill more. Then strike! Close your ears completely, and strike! And beforehand, send away any softhearted one who might be fooled."

The two men think this over for a moment.

"It seems very difficult," says Maoul. "What if we took them by surprise, while they are sleeping?"

"No, that is not the best way. And *you* would be surprised at how quickly they woke up and read your intent—because this is what they themselves would do. No; you should be brave and tell them, and ask them if they have some supernatural entity they pray to. Tell them to do so now."

"I have heard of such a thing," says Maoul.

"If you need more, remember that it is as necessary to kill them as to stamp out sparks of fire nearing your hut. Do you think your resolve will hold?"

Maoul sighs, straightens up; Sintana takes a deep breath.

"Thank you for warning us, 'Om Jhared. I think we can do this thing."

"Good. It will be harder for you, Maoul. Sintana has already had a taste of it. But to you, maybe this saying from my land will help. We have had wars and fighting, too much, as I told you. And one of our wise men said, 'They who live by the sword must die by the sword.' You have met Homo Ferox, who lives by the spear. That was their choice. Now they must die by it."

"Yes." Maoul nods gravely. "I see."

Kamir has been listening wide-eyed. "How many evil things you know, dear 'Om Jhared," she says. "Oh, Agna and Donnia come."

Then Maoul shakes his head, as if to chase out dreadful thoughts, and says in his normal tones, "But I have also come to tell you that we must leave soon for the Long Swim. Only two of the women yet live, and the star we call the Wind Bringer has appeared. The season of storms will be on us if we don't go soon. So we will be leaving you, man from the skies. What will you do? Will you come with us?"

"I was expecting this," I tell him. "I know you are late. I don't dare come with you, the call from my ship may come at any time now. When it does, I must go with all speed back to the island where I left my camp and the little sky-ship that will take me up to them. I can take Kamir and the babies. But someone will have to come with me and take over the babies when I leave. Of course, I will give him the boat and anything else I have that would be useful to you."

Agna and Donnia, who have come in with baskets of butterfish, join us in time to hear all this. Conscientious fathers, they are already chewing. Donnia speaks up.

"I can go with him, Maoul."

"And I," says Sintana unexpectedly. "Every day I am with

him I learn. But I can't make a swim alone, like this." He taps his still nearly bald head.

"I wish I could stay with you, 'Om Jhared and little sister," says Agna. "But I must go to relieve the friends who are caring for my five little ones."

"I shall be delighted at your company, companion-of-battles."

"Well then, that is settled," says Maoul, rising. "You will await your signal, while we leave, I think, on the second morning."

"Are you taking the canoes?" I ask as they leave.

"We're thinking about that. Right now I have this evil job to do," says Maoul, and they depart.

We go back to feeding the baby-monster. Just as I have contributed my mouthful to the sweet-smelling sac, Agna pushes past me.

"Hold a moment, let me look."

Gently he rocks the baby-sac until he can see beneath. I notice a bluish-black discoloration at the bottom, where the membrane joins with what had been Kamir's skin.

"How long has this color been here?" he demands.

No one knows. Kamir has struggled up to look. "What is it, Agna? What's wrong?"

"Trouble." He tips the big bundle up so we can all see the bottom on which it has been resting. The evil-looking purplish color is heavy there, with yellowed streaks in it. "I think that is about where the goldskin struck you."

"Yes," says Kamir. "Oh, I feared he had harmed them! We must get Mavru."

"I go!" says Donnia, and ducks outside. We can hear him break into a splashing trot in the stream.

When Mavru comes and sees, he looks grave.

"One of the babies is, I fear, dead. I must cut it away lest the trouble spread to others. 'Om Jhared, I need the sharpest possible knife. May I borrow yours?"

"Yes. And I'll clean it as thoroughly as I can first." My shark knife takes a keen edge and will stand heat.

Mavru calls for an armful of moss and washes his hands thoroughly in the stream outside. Then he produces a packet of long, slender thorns. "I have dipped these in your cleaning solution," he tells me. "They are for sewing."

He turns to the fetal package and carefully turns it over to show the discolored side. This had been the outside of Kamir's belly; it looks eerie to see her navel there. Mavru is studying the stains, figuring where to make his cuts, as carefully as any surgeon of a technological culture. There are no magical passes, no shamanism.

When he is ready, he slices into the mass with delicacy and boldness, beyond the farthest stain of blue, and continues around to the side, folding back the skin. The characteristic sweet odor of the babies fills the hut, but it is mixed with the sickening smell of infection.

Kamir winces in sympathy as he cuts, but says nothing.

The exposed mass of flesh and organs looks a healthy pink. I can see a tiny pink foot through the membrane enclosing it. Mavru gropes deep into the sac with both hands now. I find myself feeling queasy, and quickly turn my head away. When I look back, Mavru has pulled out a nasty-looking length of stained purple and yellow gut. He drops it into the waste moss and reaches in again. Exposed now is a discolored fetal sac. He palps it carefully, and mutters, "Dead." He sighs, and with one quick gesture pulls and flips the fetus out and onto the moss, its umbilical cord tight.

Mavru pays no more attention to it, but goes into the wound with his knife, cutting the cord far in, and cutting away all infected tissue. Very little of the dark purple blood flows. I notice he is careful not to contaminate the knife by cutting into infection. He seems to know the anatomy of the fetal sac well.

When he has finished, the hollow he has made where the dead baby was is clean-looking, with only the ends of a few thorn-sewn vessels sticking out. Mavru inspects it with care, then bends down and sniffs thoroughly. Satisfied, he asks me, "A dusting of your wonderful powder now?"

"I think so, yes."

He takes the antibiotic flask out of his loincloth and dusts sparingly. Then he takes up clean moss and carefully packs the wound, pulling the skin back as far as it will go and fixing it with thorns.

No advanced surgeon could have done better with the tools at hand.

At last he turns away from his completed task and, with the point of his knife, slits the discolored membrane off the discarded dead fetus.

I gasp.

Lying there on the moss is what appears to be a Human baby boy, an infant almost ready to be born. There can be no doubt that I have fathered this child; it is no parthenogenetic alien, but Human in every way that I can see. My son. My almost-son . . . What about the other two?

Kamir is staring, too. "Oh, what that goldskin did," she mutters through clenched teeth. "Oh, my little stranger baby! How beautiful! He is—was—just like you, dear 'Om Jhared. What about the others? Are they all right?"

"I believe so," says Mavru. "I think we caught this in time. And they are like us, by the way; Mnerrin, if that is to be our name. I had a good look at both their feet and they have our fins, as this poor little lad had not." He touches the dead baby's Human toes.

"Are they to be girls or men?" Kamir asks.

"Oh, I couldn't tell. But one is decidedly larger."

I have pulled myself together. "Healer Mavru, all our thanks. Now tell me: on most worlds, it is customary to pay healers, or give them a present. What may we do for you? Of course I will send you my good knife when I go, but there must be something else."

He starts to wave me away, but checks. "Well, if you are serious, would it be improper to ask that you give me this dead baby to study? I want to compare it with our own. And it might help me if ever I have to deal with more Humans."

"Gladly," I say. "And you will, of course, bury him with a little marker or whatever is appropriate?"

"Yes. With a marker saying it is the first Human child born of Mnerrin."

"But—" says Kamir. "Oh, but . . ." Then she seems to reconsider. "I guess it's all right, Father Mavru. Only . . ."

"I know," says Mavru compassionately. "I know. I thank you very much. And this will solve what might be a problem for you."

It would indeed. I had been thinking that.

When he goes out, taking the baby, Agna and Donnia hurry in to resume the feeding. I hold Kamir quietly for a while to comfort her—and myself.

• • •

That evening Agna and I take a few minutes off to go down and join the conclave on the beach. The Mnerrin habitually gather here to watch the sunset and chat. Agna leads me around to the five men and their children who have been caring for his young. The babies are all appealing plump little Mnerrin, three girls and two boys, one of whom can already swim strongly, as Agna demonstrates.

Old Maoul is here, too, earnestly debating something with several men.

"They are deciding whether to take the canoes," Agna tells me. "I think we will. Normally the babies swim, fastened to their father, but that of course slows us down. If they were in a canoe, we could travel faster. The two wounded men and Elia could go in them, too. But some of the older men are afraid that this will change our way of life too much."

"I can understand that. . . . Hello, Sintana. How goes it?"

The young man has a worried look. " 'Om Jhared, do you know any way to keep those canoes from tipping so easily? That is one of the objections to taking them. I thought that if they had a down-thrusting wood piece below, it would stabilize them, but I don't see how to do that."

Inventive boy. "That's what we call a keel. It would indeed stabilize the canoes, but it would also hit rocks, if it was long enough to do good. But there is another way, which we call outriggers." I smooth off a spot of sand and draw him a picture.

"I see. But there isn't time to build these, 'Om Jhared."

"Well, can you produce two long logs each and some rope? I'll show you a quick and dirty version." I make another sketch, showing a canoe with a log loosely lashed on each side. "The idea is that the logs must be loose enough to float when the canoe is loaded. It will slow down the paddling a bit, but you will be surprised at how hard it is to tip.... Want to try it?"

"Absolutely! I knew I could count on you, 'Om Jhared!"

I reflect that it is best I leave before my meager store of information runs out. Meanwhile Agna is looking wistfully at a group still deep in their study of Relations.

"I used to love that," he says. "But now I am so rusty."

"My case too," I tell him. "Tell me, what are those men playing at? It looks like a game I know."

"Oh, it's an old game we all love. Legend has it that the other man who came from the skies taught it to our forefathers. Do you really recognize it?"

"Yes, I think it is a game called 'chess,' only the pieces are carved a little differently."

"Yes, 'chess,' you say? We call it 'Shez'! It must be the same. So some legends are true!"

But I have something else on my mind.

"Agna, Donnia says that you know the straight-line direction to the island where I left my sky-ship. Can you show me? Then I can set my instrument here. It would be much quicker than retracing my steps."

"Yes, I do. Don't you recall, when we first started home with Kamir, you showed me where you'd come from? Let us go in the water, I'll give you the line."

We swim out, and Agna submerges for a few minutes. When he comes up, he has one arm pointed west-southwest. I set my compass pointer.

"You must have thrown something in the sea there," says Agna disapprovingly. "I could sense alien stuff in the current."

"Yes, I fear my ship must have sprayed exhaust when I landed. And it will again when I take off. I'm sorry—I hope it will dissipate soon."

"Oh, it's almost gone," Agna concedes.

"The island is such a small, flat one, Agna. Do you think this line will really carry me to it? At least, near enough to see it?"

"Yes," he says firmly. "If I were swimming, I'd say, seven days."

"Good enough." Then something inside me lurches, as if a

curtain were rent. "No, *bad!*" I blurt. "*Agna, I don't want to leave!*"

He looks at me with affection. "I know. I, too, will miss you. But speak to Maoul of this. I am not sure you know your own mind."

"Yes. I will," I say, near to weeping.

When we get ashore, I confide my feelings to Maoul.

"I know, I know," he tells me. "You are sending sadness all about. But tell me: if you go, you *can* return, can't you?"

"Yes."

"While if you stay here, if you refuse this sky-ship, no other may come for you, right?"

"True."

"And if you go, you may be able to help us against the goldskins? And in other ways, Mavru says?"

"I can try. I can always do something, even if only to send you weapons and supplies."

"You could not do that if you stay here."

"No . . . Oh, I see what you mean. If I truly love you and want to help you, I should go. . . . And I should take the course which is not irrevocable, which again means I should go."

"That is my thought."

I sigh deeply. "Then it is my thought, too. Thank you, Father Maoul. . . . But oh, I shall miss this world so."

He, too, sighs. "It has been for you a happy time, out of your real life, which we cannot imagine. But for us this is real life, with all its good and evil."

I see what he means, and bow my head. To me, this is still a dreamworld, though the people are real. I have not been truly into life here, as I would have to be if I stayed. As I would have to be if I come back to stay. Dreams must end.

"You are wise."

He shrugs this off. I see Agna looking at me anxiously. It is time to go back and feed.

And just then, in the midst of everything, I hear a loud, familiar sound from the hut. Everyone looks up.

"What is that?"

"A beep from my transponder. That is, a signal that the ship which will carry me away has come into your sun's system. I now have only a few days to get back to that island. If they have to wait, they will charge me money, and I can only pay for two days."

"Pay?" asks Maoul.

"A system of portable value we use for returning the favors of people we may never meet again."

"Legend says," Maoul tells me, "that the one who came here before tried to explain something of this. To us it sounded unharmonious."

"Unharmonious" is a term they use for, roughly, *uncivilized* and perhaps inhumane. It amuses me to hear our great economic system so brusquely—if perhaps justly—dismissed.

I bid Maoul good night and return with Agna to the hut.

That night Kamir faints for the first time.

● ● ●

The last day passes quietly. I cannot bring myself to start until the Mnerrin leave.

I watch them making up sea-proof packets of their scant possessions and, one by one, placing them in the canoes. They consist primarily of a few small looms and supplies of thread, a musical instrument someone has been working on, some pots, several large pieces of cloth. I reflect on how little of their rich life would remain for archaeology if anything happens to the Mnerrin themselves.

When it comes to the spears and shields, the canoe-paddlers object. "There will be no room left for the babies and the wounded men." In the end a few are taken.

I watch a burial party taking the body of the last woman up into the hills. In the past I have avoided looking at such scenes, though I knew they went on. But now I wonder how soon I may have to undertake such a grim trip myself.

Kamir is all over her fainting fit and says she is looking forward to traveling again. I marvel at how she can do with no food except the clear broths we make for her. She drinks more water than before; perhaps it has some richness in it. I would give an arm for an intravenous feeding rig. There will be one on that big ship. I have wasted hours trying to figure how I could get it to her.

The last night there is much singing. Kamir asks to be taken to the beach. I pick her up, almost weeping to find how light she is. She who only weeks ago had been my strong little mermaid, rolling me in the sand. . . . Now she scarcely weighs as much as the canteens I bring with us.

On the beach I pack moss around her poor knobby knees and hips, and prop her up where she can greet all. The Mnerrin are kind to her, particularly Sintana and his friends, who rally her about "fighting like a man."

The singing rises around us, sweet and true. Kamir joins in, surprisingly strongly. I hold my face up to the moons and wish I could howl like a hound. Dreamworld or not, I love these people, love Kamir. Even love my dead son, and the other two. . . Of that last night I shall say no more.

The next morning there is a surprise—one of the rare fogs has closed in. It makes no difference to the Mnerrin's plans. The canoes are loaded; I see the fathers of toddlers tying them to the thwarts. The first shift of paddlers is in place.

And then they simply walk into the sea. Many turn to wave at us and for the last time I get the impact of so many blue, blue eyes. Then they are gone under sea and into the fog, leaving only the dark shapes of the canoes.

The paddlers dig in rhythmically, and the canoes, too, fade and vanish into the white wall.

It is very lonely on the beach.

But it is time for us to go, too. Donnia and Sintana carry the boat to the beach and return for the sac of babies. I am astonished to see how they have grown in the last days; the skin now seems almost too small for the full-size infants within. I carry Kamir down and arrange her in the stern beside me. The babies, and a big pot of fish, go in front, where she can touch them. It has been arranged to stop every hour for feeding, since I can do little while driving the boat, and Kamir is so weak.

Then the two Mnerrin wade out into the bay. I follow, expecting them to want Agna's heading once they are past the reef. Instead, they simply submerge briefly and start off, straight on target. Wonderful instrument, those guide-hairs! Even Sintana's fuzz seems long enough to give him some help.

Then we set off behind them, much as we had arrived,

except that different arms are flashing ahead. And Kamir lies dying at my side. We settle into the dreamlike trance of travel over the blue sea, and the mists gradually clear.

• • •

And that's about it.

On the third day there is a tear in the babies' envelope and the whole skin looks dry and different. Kamir is excited; her eyes glow, she seems to be keeping herself alive on sheer will. But she can't speak. "I will see them!" she whispers to me.

On the fourth morning it is difficult to feed. Donnia says that the babies must come out. He grasps the edges of the torn skin and pushes it down. It peels away; a shriveled placenta comes with it. As we tear it loose, the two babies roll out on the moss. One is exposed, I see it breathing, but the other is still in its fetal covering. I cut it free quickly, and the baby takes a great gulp of air and begins to cry—the immemorial infant squall. It is a Mnerrin baby, and so is the other, a girl and a boy.

Kamir tries to crawl toward them, her eyes burning hungrily. "Wait, darling," I tell her. We swab the babies off, and put them in her arms.

"They're perfect," Donnia says.

But after a moment her head falls to one side. She has fainted, I hope, and take her in my arms. She breathes for a minute or two; that is all. She is dead in my arms, with the babies in hers.

Gently we take them from her and feed them. To me they seem sturdy little things, but Donnia says they are thin. "We have work to do."

There is an island nearby, a pretty one with a mountain. We take Kamir's body there, up above the dunes, with a headstone on which I inscribe words too emotion-laden to repeat here.

And we continue. . . .

After a time it becomes clear that my batteries will more than hold out, so I suggest that both men get in the boat. Thus burdened, our progress becomes something of a wallow, but still much faster than swimming. On the way, I teach Donnia and Sintana to drive it.

And so we arrive, on the morning of the seventh day, at the small island I had left a lifetime ago. The little space-lander is just as I left it, my camp is untouched. As though on signal, my transponder beeps again that evening, signifying that the ship is taking up an orbit above us. I signal her and arrange a rendezvous at dawn my time.

Then I busy myself with a quick check and turn to giving away everything I can possibly spare. The lander's big batteries will recharge the boat and the laser; I estimate their battery lives at years with a little care. My best knife I send to Mavru via Donnia, along with the big medikit. The laser is for Sintana and the little one for Maoul. Everything else—blankets, lenses, a small microscope, emergency cook pans and all—I heap on them.

"Use your judgment. Something nice for Agna—and this waterproof drawing pad and stylus for the older man who does Relations. God, I wish there were more."

"It is ample," says Sintana. His eyes are on the lander, I sense that both are anxious to see it go up.

But there isn't room for them to stay on the island, with the exhaust. So I bid them farewell and send them out in the boat. They seem reluctant to have me leave. As they motor out I catch a last gleam of blue.

Waiting to lift, I allow myself to think of what has haunted me, ever since the goldskins' coming:

On ancient Terra there was once another race of Humans. They were big-brained and, some think, unaesthetically formed. They flourished for a time, leaving few signs in the stone records except their bones and a grave lined with flowers. We call them Neanderthals.

And then came Cro-Magnon, our direct ancestors, and after that Neanderthal was seen no more.

What happened no one knows, whether some interbred, or whether they were wiped out in one of our first acts of genocide. (We left no living close relatives.) What thoughts Neanderthal thought, what intellectual discoveries he made, no one will ever know. They were strong; the fact that they disappeared at Cro-Magnon's advance must have been partly a matter of temperament. Perhaps they were noncombative.

Have I been seeing the start of just such a tragedy? I have no illusions about the Mnerrins' ability to defend themselves against Homo Ferox. Their wonderful artifacts of song and thought reside in their minds, their art of Relations is literally written on the sands. If they go under, no one will ever know that here men were following the thinking of Pythagoras, in a wholly different technological contest. But they do not need the technology, except now, for self-defense.

No. No one would ever know—any more than we will ever know the color of the eyes that looked out from under Neanderthal's shaggy mane. Perhaps they were clear, and filled with compassion and the growing light of reason. We cannot know. We have, I fear, killed them. And I fear, I greatly fear, that those lost eyes were a brilliant blue.

• • •

Now I have made my record. To you who hear it, I beg, allow yourselves to imagine how it was. To be moved. To help! Surely the Federation could spare one small party to sort this out, to transport the goldskins to another planet. To save what can never be replaced of peace and beauty, of mind.

THE TOR DOUBLES

Two complete short science fiction novels in one volume!

☐ 53362-3 A MEETING WITH MEDUSA by Arthur C. Clarke and $2.95
  55967-3 GREEN MARS by Kim Stanley Robinson — Canada $3.95

☐ 55971-1 HARDFOUGHT by Greg Bear and $2.95
  55951-7 CASCADE POINT by Timothy Zahn — Canada $3.95

☐ 55952-5 BORN WITH THE DEAD by Robert Silverberg and $2.95
  55953-3 THE SALIVA TREE by Brian W. Aldiss — Canada $3.95

☐ 55956-8 TANGO CHARLIE AND FOXTROT ROMEO $2.95
  55957-6 by John Varley and — Canada $3.95
  THE STAR PIT by Samuel R. Delany

☐ 55958-4 NO TRUCE WITH KINGS by Poul Anderson and $2.95
  55954-1 SHIP OF SHADOWS by Fritz Leiber — Canada $3.95

☐ 55963-0 ENEMY MINE by Barry B. Longyear and $2.95
  54302-5 ANOTHER ORPHAN by John Kessel — Canada $3.95

☐ 54554-0 SCREWTOP by Vonda N. McIntyre and $2.95
  55959-2 THE GIRL WHO WAS PLUGGED IN — Canada $3.95
  by James Tiptree, Jr.

Buy them at your local bookstore or use this handy coupon:
Clip and mail this page with your order.

Publishers Book and Audio Mailing Service
P.O. Box 120159, Staten Island, NY 10312-0004

Please send me the book(s) I have checked above. I am enclosing $_____
(please add $1.25 for the first book, and $.25 for each additional book to cover postage and handling. Send check or money order only—no CODs.)

Name _____

Address _____

City _____ State/Zip _____

Please allow six weeks for delivery. Prices subject to change without notice.

THE BEST IN SCIENCE FICTION

☐	54989-9	STARFIRE by Paul Preuss	$3.95
☐	54990-2		Canada $4.95
☐	54281-9	DIVINE ENDURANCE by Gwyneth Jones	$3.95
☐	54282-7		Canada $4.95
☐	55696-8	THE LANGUAGES OF PAO by Jack Vance	$3.95
☐	55697-6		Canada $4.95
☐	54892-2	THE THIRTEENTH MAJESTRAL by Hayford Peirce	$3.95
☐	54893-0		Canada $4.95
☐	55425-6	THE CRYSTAL EMPIRE by L. Neil Smith	$4.50
☐	55426-4		Canada $5.50
☐	53133-7	THE EDGE OF TOMORROW by Isaac Asimov	$3.95
☐	53134-5		Canada $4.95
☐	55800-6	FIRECHILD by Jack Williamson	$3.95
☐	55801-4		Canada $4.95
☐	54592-3	TERRY'S UNIVERSE ed. by Beth Meacham	$3.50
☐	54593-1		Canada $4.50
☐	53355-0	ENDER'S GAME by Orson Scott Card	$3.95
☐	53356-9		Canada $4.95
☐	55413-2	HERITAGE OF FLIGHT by Susan Shwartz	$3.95
☐	55414-0		Canada $4.95

Buy them at your local bookstore or use this handy coupon:
Clip and mail this page with your order.

Publishers Book and Audio Mailing Service
P.O. Box 120159, Staten Island, NY 10312-0004

Please send me the book(s) I have checked above. I am enclosing $_____
(please add $1.25 for the first book, and $.25 for each additional book to cover postage and handling. Send check or money order only—no CODs.)

Name _____

Address _____

City _____ State/Zip _____

Please allow six weeks for delivery. Prices subject to change without notice.

THE BEST IN FANTASY

- ☐ 53954-0   SPIRAL OF FIRE by Deborah Turner Harris $3.95
  53955-9   Canada $4.95

- ☐ 53401-8   NEMESIS by Louise Cooper (U.S. only) $3.95

- ☐ 53382-8   SHADOW GAMES by Glen Cook $3.95
  53381-X   Canada $4.95

- ☐ 53815-5   CASTING FORTUNE by John M. Ford $3.95
  53826-1   Canada $4.95

- ☐ 53351-8   HART'S HOPE by Orson Scott Card $3.95
  53352-6   Canada $4.95

- ☐ 53397-6   MIRAGE by Louise Cooper (U.S. only) $3.95

- ☐ 53671-1   THE DOOR INTO FIRE by Diane Duane $2.95
  53672-X   Canada $3.50

- ☐ 54902-3   A GATHERING OF GARGOYLES by Meredith Ann Pierce $2.95
  54903-1   Canada $3.50

- ☐ 55614-3   JINIAN STAR-EYE by Sheri S. Tepper $2.95
  55615-1   Canada $3.75

Buy them at your local bookstore or use this handy coupon:
Clip and mail this page with your order.

Publishers Book and Audio Mailing Service
P.O. Box 120159, Staten Island, NY 10312-0004

Please send me the book(s) I have checked above. I am enclosing $_____
(please add $1.25 for the first book, and $.25 for each additional book to
cover postage and handling. Send check or money order only—no CODs.)

Name _____

Address _____

City _____ State/Zip _____

Please allow six weeks for delivery. Prices subject to change without notice.

have always been famous. For what purpose, then, can our rulers want a weapon like the photon-director?

We know. We are not naïve.

But uncertainty about the final handling of the ones wielded by Sayari Snow and Master Gordon still plagues us. It is impossible to demand of Our Shatira Anna any sort of clarification.

Gabriel Elk, however, has clarified a point that used to deprive me of sleep. Why a place like Stonelore? Why the agony and the frustration to which he yearly subjects himself?

"Because one day I am going to make them weep, Ingram, one day I am going to make them weep." Until that day, despite the old man's and Bethel's undoubtedly justified reproaches, they will continue to be maskers to me. Not Mansuecetrians; maskers. But they will weep, that day will come—I'm certain of it. And when it comes the citizens of this island nation will cremate the dead when they die, and I, since I have no talent for dramaturgy or sculpture, may become the first living actor in all our history.

Nevertheless, the day is coming when they will weep.

No thinking, I told myself, *deeds only!* With that, I leapt down into the reivers' blind. Blood pounded viciously behind my eyes, rudely insistent. A face turned toward me, a face unlike any I had seen in Ongladred.

The Shattered Moons poured light over the features of that face and over the whole of the shape squatting to its left. It was the face to the left that had the rifle; I saw the barrel glinting too late. That figure I should have attacked first—not this unarmed one, not this odd, glowering mask rising up out of its own off-balance surprise to confront me.

I could feel my fingers gripping the haft of my knife— was dimly aware of the knife itself sweeping up in an arc to my ear, the blade quivering briefly a forearm's length from the face beyond it.

Then, not wanting it to be the way it was happening, wanting a less terrible portion of the Pelagan's anatomy for a target, I pulled my knife down into his face— stabbed once—then drew back as the reiver screamed, clutched his fearful wound, and rolled away.

(An image of the dead horses flashed into my mind.)

My weapon clattered into the rocks.

The Tor SF Doubles

A Meeting with Medusa/Green Mars, Arthur C. Clarke/Kim Stanley Robinson • **Hardfought/Cascade Point**, Greg Bear/Timothy Zahn • **Born with the Dead/The Saliva Tree**, Robert Silverberg/Brian W. Aldiss • **Tango Charlie and Foxtrot Romeo/The Star Pit**, John Varley/Samuel R. Delany • **No Truce with Kings/Ship of Shadows**, Poul Anderson/Fritz Leiber • **Enemy Mine/Another Orphan**, Barry B. Longyear/John Kessel • **Screwtop/The Girl Who Was Plugged In**, Vonda N. McIntyre/James Tiptree, Jr. • **The Nemesis from Terra/Battle for the Stars**, Leigh Brackett/Edmond Hamilton • **The Ugly Little Boy/The [Widget], the [Wadget], and Boff**, Isaac Asimov/Theodore Sturgeon • **Sailing to Byzantium/Seven American Nights**, Robert Silverberg/Gene Wolfe • **Houston, Houston, Do You Read?/Souls**, James Tiptree, Jr./Joanna Russ • **He Who Shapes/The Infinity Box**, Roger Zelazny/Kate Wilhelm • **The Blind Geometer/The New Atlantis**, Kim Stanley Robinson/Ursula K. Le Guin • **The Saturn Game/Iceborn**, Poul Anderson/Gregory Benford & Paul A. Carter • **The Last Castle/Nightwings**, Jack Vance/Robert Silverberg • **The Color of Neanderthal Eyes/And Strange at Ecbatan the Trees**, James Tiptree, Jr./Michael Bishop • **Divide and Rule/The Sword of Rhiannon**, L. Sprague de Camp/Leigh Brackett • **In Another Country/Vintage Season**, Robert Silverberg/C. L. Moore* • **Ill Met in Lankhmar/The Fair at Emain Macha**, Fritz Leiber/Charles de Lint* • **The Pugnacious Peacemaker/The Wheels of If**, Harry Turtledove/L. Sprague de Camp*

*forthcoming

MICHAEL BISHOP
AND STRANGE AT ECBATAN THE TREES

A TOM DOHERTY ASSOCIATES BOOK
NEW YORK

Grateful acknowledgment is made to Houghton Mifflin Company for permission to to reprint lines from "You, Andrew Marvell" from *Collected Poems of Archibald MacLeish 1917–1952* by Archibald MacLeish.

AND STRANGE AT ECBATAN THE TREES

Copyright © 1976 by Michael L. Bishop

All rights reserved. No part of this book may be used or reproduced in any manner whatsoever without written permission except in the case of brief quotations embodied in critical articles and reviews.

A TOR Book
Published by Tom Doherty Associates, Inc.
49 West 24 Street
New York, NY 10010

Cover art copyright © 1989 by Brian Waugh. Used by permission of the Luserke Agency

ISBN: 0-812-55964-9   Can. ISBN: 0-812-50204-3

Library of Congress Catalog Card Number: 75-25075

First Tor edition: January 1990

Printed in the United States of America

0 9 8 7 6 5 4 3 2 1

To Jeri

*And strange at Ecbatan the trees
Take leaf by leaf the evening strange*

Archibald MacLeish

PART ONE

i

I went with the old man because Our Shathra Anna's foremost minister had bade me watch his every move. For ten days I had been at the old man's side, and uncomplainingly, though not very congenially (though this was changing), he had accepted my presence. The old man's name was Gabriel Elk. He was sixty-three years old. He was universally acknowledged a genius, perhaps the only bona fide one in all of Ongladred, indeed on all of our ruthlessly harsh planet, Mansueceria.

And on the night with which this account begins Gabriel Elk and I were going into Lunn, our capital, to buy a dead masker.

The city lay before us as ominously quiescent as an unstruck gong. I had been living—these past ten days—with Gabriel Elk, his wife, Bethel, and his son, Gareth, at Stonelore, the neuro-theatre he had built nearly seven kilometers outside of Lunn. Now we were coming back into the city under the cold light of the Shattered Moons, and I was glad to see Lunn's majestic squalor again, the unbroken rows of four-story dwellings, the canyonlike alleys, the ever-visible lemon sheen of the dome under which Our Shathra Anna resides and toward which nearly all the dirty alleys lead: the Atarite Palace. As an aide to Chancellor Blaine, as a very minor doer of the sort of work Our Shathra may not sully her hands with, I was going home again—even though Gabriel Elk and I would not set foot within several city squares of the domed palace. We were going among the poor, "the Mansuecerians themselves," Gabriel Elk would say, and our way was through the torch-lit sidestreets.

We were walking our horses. Their hooves clacked on the stones, their eyes were round with a mute claustrophobia, their nostrils quivered with the pungent smells of packed-in humanity. But we met no one in the streets. It was the time of the Halcyon Panic (hence, my assignment to Elk, whom the Magi feared as a potential demagogue), and at night everyone stayed docilely indoors—everyone but those with state business and, of course, the maddeningly uncoercible Gabriel Elk, who had come on business of his own.

"Do you know where we are?" I asked him, a bite in my voice.

He halted his shaggy animal and looked at me. The old man's eyes were a pale green, his face as heavy as carven marble, the jowls giving way only slightly to his sixty-three years. Great white sideburns framed his cheeks, and his hair fell in bearish curls over his forehead and neck. "On Earth my sixty-three years would be seventy-five," he had told me when I was first assigned to him, but he carried himself with an intractable agelessness. In this alleyway in Lunn he looked like a statue that has willed its limbs to move, that has broken out of stone into life.

"I know where we are, Ingram. This city was mine long before you entered either the service of Our Shathra or the elitist gangs of Chancellor Blaine. Some say the Chancellor got his roan tooth by sucking blood up through it, and, from what I see, a bit of that blood is yours, Master Marley. You're as bumptious and ticky as a person of power."

"I work for persons of power, Sayati Elk." Against Blaine's wishes, Our Shathra Anna had given Gabriel Elk the title *sayati* in his fifty-sixth year, after the construction of Stonelore and the presentation of the first series of neuro-dramas. In the seven succeeding years Blaine and the Council of the Magi had agitated quietly for the revocation of Elk's royal dispensation to assemble the people and for the nationalization of the formidable power complex he had built in the upland arena.

"So you do, Ingram, so you do. And in your own way you also are a person of power."

"I do what I must—to insure that the Halcyon Panic doesn't break out roaring in the throats of our within-doors maskers."

"And I do what I must, Ingram, to insure that when the 'maskers' come out to Stonelore they perceive an order in things which the universe and the Magi of Ongladred don't always choose to grant them. The order is there, it inheres, and I'm the man who reveals it to them."

The Shattered Moons moved in a yellow band beyond the in-leaning rooftops, a monochrome rainbow in the night sky. Only the brightest stars were visible behind it, and it was hard to imagine that Ongladred was an island besieged, that the culture we had twice before built up over six thousand years as colonists on Mansueceria was in danger of collapsing again, collapsing completely.

The street was silent; my voice echoed in it. "And so to give the maskers order, you've come tonight to buy a dead man."

"Not exactly, Ingram. I've come to buy a dead woman, a beautiful girl killed by reivers. And the order I try to give the Mansuecerians, the gentles, is a glimpse of the order inhering outside themselves—for inwardly they're disciplined, Ingram, they're more serene, more in control of the animal in themselves than you or I. Only artists have to rage, artists and rulers."

"Our rulers don't rage, Sayati Elk."

"No, they simmer, Ingram. The worse for them." His horse, a woolly beast, lifted its head, whickeringly barked. The old man pulled the horse's head down and began walking again. The stones rang. Shadows wrapped themselves around us like voluted capes. "My sense of direction never faileth," he said after a while. "Look there."

We had come to a side-canyon, a narrow crevice between two rows of maskers'-houses perpendicular to the alley by which, on the city's southeastern outskirts, we had originally entered Lunn. There was no room for our horses here. But I looked where Elk was pointing and saw a green-gowned figure on a third-story balcony on the lefthand side of the alley, a figure stooping beneath a pair of conical lanterns to see us. But for this solitary revenant and those two lanterns, the "street" was unhaunted, dark, and coldly daunting.

The Halcyon Panic had begun to play in me; I wanted no part of Sayati Elk's sinister purchase of a dead girl.

"Come on, Ingram," he said. "We'll tie our horses here." He wrapped the reins of his animal around a stone gutterspout; I did likewise. Our footfalls reverberating in the night air, we walked through the alley between the maskers'-houses. There was a balcony across from the one on which the stooping figure stood, and it seemed to me that it would require very little effort to step from the lefthand balcony to the righthand one, three stories' worth of darkness gaping beneath that step.

"Who's up there?" I asked.

"Josu Lief, the father of the dead girl. Or so I'd guess."

The man on the balcony called out. Before he called, I had not been certain that he was a man; the gown had confused me. It was mourning garb. Under him now I could see that the gown and his shaved head—he was newly bald—were his only concessions to "grief." The Mansuecerians are immune to it, genetically serene, philosophically spartan. "Sayati Elk?" Gentleman Lief called out. Then: "Please come up, both of you." A serene, spartan voice.

We entered the bleak doorway. We climbed the corkscrewing stairs. We let Josu Lief usher us into a three-room apartment where the rest of his family, dressed in forest-green mourning gowns and sitting in the candlelit central chamber, awaited us. There were introductions. Lief's wife wore her hair cut short, as did the two female children. Josu and his young son were bald from the razor. They accepted the news that I was a minor official of Our Shathra Anna's oligarchy with utter blandness; they were maskers, and I was a nouveau Atarite, programmed to rule. Gabriel Elk was of them, but different; a throwback in whom the primeval aggressions still roiled, still threatened eruption. The old man was the bridge between the Lief family and me.

"Where's Bronwen?" Gabriel Elk asked.

"Through here," Gentleman Lief said, and led us out of the central chamber into a sleeping room where there were six pallets on the floor. The girl lay on the pallet on which she had undoubtedly slept while alive: Bronwen Lief, eldest daughter of these anonymous maskers. One family amid a city full of similar families, all of them de-beasted, shaped in their genes toward a civilizing harmony. On them had been founded the state of Ongladred; only rulers and artists raged, and we Atarites so seldom as to suggest an innate serenity akin to that of the maskers.

"Will you accept my price?" Elk asked Lief.

"I accept it, Sayati Elk."

"Good. The money has already been credited to you. It's there for your use. Three days from now, bring your family to Stonelore."

"And she will perform?"

"A special performance, for the Lief family and some privileged others. Not a neuro-drama, but a kind of reading."

"Will she later act in the dramas?"

"Such is my hope."

The three of us looked at the dead Bronwen Lief—her father with an expression predictably neutral, in which there was neither pride nor remorse nor pity nor anything paternal in a strictly Atarite sense; Gabriel Elk with quiet appreciation; and I, the outsider, with an awareness of terrible loss. For Bronwen Lief, arranged on her pallet in her white death-gown, was an image that called up evocative names: Helen, Guinevere, Ligeia. She was beautiful, but there was something in her young face hinting at the ability to betray; in a Mansuecerian, a masker, that look disconcerted, it slept in the corners of her mouth like an incongruous smirk, an anomaly of character. As a dirt-runner I had long ago learned to recognize such telltale glimmerings under men's false, placid exteriors. But Bronwen Lief was a masker girl, and a corpse, and the candlelight made her flesh resemble porcelain.

Gabriel Elk said: "I'm very pleased, Gentleman Lief. She's beautiful; she's what I'd hoped for."

"Our thanks, Sayati Elk."

I said: "How did she die, exactly?"

The two older men turned their faces toward me. Josu Lief, I saw, could not have been more than forty; even with a shaved head he was a handsome man, with full lips and dark eyes. "I have told our friends, in a fall. But there's more, as Sayati Elk knows. Last night she went with a young man, the one selected for her, to see the bonfires by the eastern channel, the bonfires holding off the sloak—"

"You let them go?" I said. "At this time?"

"Bronwen did as she wished. It wasn't for me to permit or hinder her, either one. She had a good life, Master Marley."

"And a short one. What happened on the coast with her young man?"

"Laird and she was walking in the rocks, looking toward the Angromain Archipelago where your renegade ancestors kill each other and catch fish, Master Marley. They was thinking on the cycle of the sloak and the barbarians way out to sea there. Bronwen's young man says they spoke of the bonfires on the beach and of living to oldsters in Lunn, such things as that. Then they saw an empty boat, just a pinnace, beached in a rocky place between two of the bonfires. No sooner had they seen it than they heard voices, men speaking in accents not of Ongladred. The men surprised them, a party of three or four thick-bearded Pelagans on a raid of some sort. The Pelagans ran at them, pushed Bronwen and young Laird from the rocks, and leapt to the sand. It was a short drop, Laird says, but Bronwen must have twisted her neck. Laird fell into a gravelly place and broke his leg. He shouted so the bonfire tenders on both sides come running, you know, but it was too late. Out to sea the Pelagans went, oaring it like madmen or fiends—and Bronwen was dead. And so she came home to us, and we dressed her like you see her. In her deathgown."

"And Laird?" Gabriel Elk asked.

"He's on the mend, I'll wager."

ii

We went back into the apartment's central chamber. The women sat on straightbacked chairs, doing something to the patterned quilts in their laps. Lief's son, his bald head shining, was on the floor marking a piece of paper with a stylus; he was about six.

"At least your boy won't be called up," Elk said. When the Halcyon Panic broke, military service for men between the ages of fifteen and fifty would be obligatory. Unless one were an Atarite (and in many cases, even then). I knew that inductions had already begun. Josu Lief confirmed me in my knowledge.

"They tapped me two days ago," he said. "I go in five days." And he would, too. Docilely, he would take off his mourning gown, don a warrior's breeches, and cover his shaved head with a leather cap. Then off to the Lunn garrison for his assignment. The masker, the gentle, would become a soldier—pacific in his innermost soul, but ruthlessly obedient in war.

"Then Gareth will be touched soon, too," Elk said, and genius or no he could not keep the regret out of his huge, corrugated brow. Unlike the serene Gentleman Lief's, his feelings toward his children—his child rather, now his only son—ran deeper than stoic affection. After all, Gabriel Elk was a mistake, an artist; in all things he raged, he harkened to a gong inaudible to maskers and Atarites alike.

We sat down. Gentlewoman Lief left her chair, went to a cabinet in the apartment's kitchen, and returned with three cups of *haoma*. This is a mildly intoxicating drink distilled from the bullcap fungus and banned at court; the maskers believe that it induces righteousness and piety rather than drunkenness. Curious, I sipped what was given me. Simultaneously sweet and tart, the haoma seemed to transfuse warmth through the lining of my stomach, into my veins and marrow, like a flow of heated blood. While Gabriel Elk and Gentleman Lief talked, I nodded and tried to heed their words.

"When will the Halcyon Panic break?" the old man asked.

"Not yet, Sayati Elk, not yet."

"Your neighbors?"

"They continue calm. There's talk of the sloak, and of the Pelagans, and even of the rupturing of the sun—but no one screams in his sleep, no one's yammering of Ongladred's death. Our Shathra Anna watches over us. She's a wise-eyed lady, wise in her watching."

Gentlewoman Lief smiled at her husband, the girls continued sewing, the boy colored his scrap of paper without heeding his father's visitors at all. At court, a young official's death would have kept us from secular activity for at least a day or two; here, it required all my haoma-ridden powers to remember that Bronwen Lief lay dead in the next room. Haoma. No doubt Josu Lief had had the examining physician administer an undiluted extract of the principal drug in this beverage to his daughter's corpse, as a temporary preservative. And here I was, embalming myself in a maskers' drink. Bronwen's face, her ambiguously smiling face, floated into my mind, into my sight. I gripped my chair.

Unaffected, Gabriel Elk was standing. The other people in the room began rising, too. I heard Josu Lief say, "Do you want me to bring her out to Stonelore tomorrow, Sayati Elk?"

"Have you a blanket you can spare?"

"I've finished this quilt," Lief's wife said. "You may take it, if you like. For Bronwen."

"Good. I'll wrap her in it, and Marley and I will take her with us now. There's no need in your carrying her out there tomorrow, Josu."

I was standing now. Someone took the cup out of my hands. Josu left the room. He came back with his daughter wrapped in the quilt. I noticed that the silken quilt, a series of cream-colored squares, was embroidered around its hem with blue flowers, the kind that grow on the cliffs above the Angromain Channel. Bronwen's face was not covered; her black hair fell over Josu Lief's supporting forearm. I watched as the father gave her into the arms of Gabriel Elk, even though by rights I ought to have been the one to carry her.

"Remember," the old man said. "Come three days from now." Then, turning to me: "Ingram, let's go." I managed to get to the door, and to open it for the burdened-down old codger. The stairwell yawned beneath us. The family, but for Lief's son, crowded into the opening. I stood with my back pressed against the open door, cold seeping up to me from the street.

"The Light stay with you," Gentlewoman Lief told Elk, "and the Lie die." That was their religion, the whole of it, conveyed in two gently spoken imperatives. The woman said nothing at all to her dead child, though I half expected her to. The girl had gone to the Abode of Song—despite the fact that maskers never sing during their lifetimes. Singing is an activity that lies outside their stoic code; indeed, outside their very natures.

Gabriel Elk was on the stairs. I looked back into the Liefs' main sitting room and saw the six-year-old boy standing there with a piece of paper dangling from his hand. He raised his blond, boyishly thin eyebrows a little.

"Goodbye, Bronwen," he said.

I reeled toward the stairwell, grabbed the railing there, and clumped groggily down the steps behind the old man and the dead girl he carried. In the cold street we found our horses and rode toward Stonelore and Elk's rock-capped residence. Bronwen Lief, wrapped in a quilt embroidered with blue flowers, lay doubled over the old philosopher/

playwright's saddle, wedged between the pommel and his paunch, deprived of dignity. Lunn faded behind us, and the Shattered Moons danced. Our horses climbed powerfully into the dark of the countryside. Immersed in wind, my head began to clear.

iii

Even though Stonelore lay seven kilometers beyond Lunn, to the southeast, it was easily accessible by a road running from the capital to the fishing village of Mershead on the Angromain Channel. In the spring the maskers set up produce stalls and vanity booths along this road, and did a good business among the travelers and fishermen going between Lunn and Mershead. Since it was in the spring that Elk presented his three neuro-dramas of the year, he had no difficulty attracting maskers to fill his circular stone amphitheatre. But, on the night we rode back from Lunn with Bronwen Lief over Elk's saddle, the equinox was still a good Mansuecerian month away; consequently, the Mershead Road was deserted but for a company of lately inducted maskers, carrying antiquated Yorkley rifles, marching toward the beaches. (The Halcyon Panic had had its subtle grip on Ongladred for the whole of the winter.) A few of these men hailed us civilly as we rode by, then the darkness loomed up again, and abruptly Elk goaded his horse off the road and into unmarked country—a stony shortcut to his home in the rocks.

The ground, covered with short grass, seemed to swell up beneath us, the horizons to expand. I imagined that at any moment we would ride into peril; our horses would plunge from the sea-fronting cliffs, the withdrawing tides would carry us to the barren archipelagoes where our enemies lived out their hatred for us. —Instead, the horizons contracted again as chunks and blocks of stone began to rise up around us.

Finally we rode into the rock-walled upland arena in which the Stonelore amphitheatre had been built. The amphitheatre was white under the Shattered Moons, its broad plastic cap gleaming dully. To the left of the amphitheatre was the energy unit that provided the power for both Elk's house and the animation of the delicately programmed actors in his neurodramas; it squatted in the dark like an outsized toadstool.

In Lunn a similar but differently constituted unit powered the heating and cooling systems in Our Shathra Anna's palace, as well as the glass flambeaux in the corridors and bedchambers. Solvent from his early literary activities, wealthy from his share of booty taken from the Pelagans during the midcentury skirmishes in which he had served as a commander, Elk had bought the components of the energy unit with his own funds; then he had engineered its design and construction, engaged in covert talks with a Pelagan minister, and acquired enough fissionable material to keep Stonelore running for three hundred years. Later he had admitted—openly—making a reciprocal arrangement with a representative of the barbarians that Ongladred had held successfully at bay during the undeclared, midcentury hostilities.

Those days were gone. Elk was past the age of conscription, and he lived and worked beyond the means or the capabilities of the citizens whom his work "enlightened." Only Our Shathra Anna and the wealthiest of Atarites could challenge his lifestyle. Several days before, I had asked him about this. "How can you, one of the people, justify the way you live, Sayati Elk?"

"I don't have to *justify* anything, Ingram. Our Shathra Anna gave me the title by which you address me, and Stonelore grew up around me as the result of the efforts of my hands and mind. I dwell here, but I don't look upon a single pebble of this site as 'property.' "

I laughed. "You're just a caretaker?"

"No, I'm a creator. Transient as they are, Stonelore and

the neuro-dramas are my gift to the civilization of Ongladred."

"A civilization now threatened," I reminded him.

"Exactly, Ingram. So I create the harder. A social order promoting social order, and nothing more, isn't civilization at all; it's a machine for maintaining the status quo. The Mansuecerians live as they must, the Atarite Court rules as it must—but I have to give shape to voices and forms lying outside your experience or muffled so close to you that you're blind to them."

"Why? In these times, to what purpose?"

"So that you can experience them. And so that I can live." He had started to say more, but bit his heavy lip and turned away.

Now we guided our horses to the right of the amphitheatre and dismounted in front of the house carven out of the rear wall of the upland arena: Grotto House. Gareth, Elk's son, came out to greet us; he took the horses and led them to shelter in a stable down from Grotto House. (The stable was an anomaly; it was made entirely of wood, and it could not be seen from the environs of the amphitheatre.) Holding Bronwen, I watched the boy go. He was sixteen, very nearly the child of his father's dotage—except that Gabriel Elk was a long way from senile garrulity; he struggled to contain his natural affection for the boy.

Gareth was his parents' last child. Two older sons had died in separate accidents, one drowning in the Angromain Channel, the other apparently the victim of a thief or Pelagan raiders, very like the dead girl in my arms. This was years ago. A daughter lived in Lunn, married to a masker with no more fire in him than any other of their kind. She did not like to come out to Stonelore. As for Gareth, he had his father's heavy face, and he was trying to grow a beard. It was coming out thin, red, and lugubrious-looking, but he persisted in a standing refusal to shave. Too, he had some of his father's spark: already he had shown himself skillful at hacking boulders into strange, sinuous shapes. Sculptures, he called them, although it wasn't always easy to tell of what. He said they were supposed to be trees, artwork designed to suggest the possibilities of growth.

"Come inside," Gabriel Elk said. "Before you drop her."

My arms *had* begun to ache. We passed through a heavy wrought-iron gate that blocked the entrance to Grotto House, a gate with old Spanish scrollwork in the iron; and then I followed the old man into the foyer of the rock house. Illuminated panels made every wall glow, and two rough corridors led out of the foyer to right and left. "Where do you want her?" I asked.

"In the programming room."

Bethel Elk came out of the righthand corridor to greet us. She took her husband's hand and said hello to me. She was as tall as I; her arms were bare in a pale-yellow gown. Without self-consciousness she also wore a thin wire brace as additional support for her back, which she had long ago injured in a fall. She was a Mansuecerian, but it was rumored that her father had been an Atarite. How else account for the saucy cast in her eye, a look heightened rather than dampened by her age?

"The girl's beautiful," she said.

"Aye," Gabriel Elk said. "So I bought her. Now if Master Marley'll escort her down to the programming room—"

"Tonight?" the woman said. "Let her lie in a bedchamber."

"I'm going to work tonight," Gabriel Elk said. "Haomycin doesn't hold forever, my lady, and we have company in three days. Go on, Ingram."

I said: "Surely you can begin in the morning and still get done."

Elk grinned; his sideburns stood away from his smile like white wings. "Ingram's on orders to watch me," he said, "and he's too tired to do it. Don't worry, Ingram, I'm not going to sneak off while you're sleeping and file for citizenship among the Pelagans. Take Bronwen down the hall. Then go to bed."

"Fine," I said. Alone, I went down the corridor to the left, all the way to its end, then halted in front of the elevator there. The door slid open. I stepped in. Humming, the elevator dropped us three or four meters to the programming room.

I carried Bronwen Lief into this chamber, placed her on a table, opened the silken quilt away from her, and stared at her gowned body and her noncommittal lips. Still, the ability to betray was there even yet; in death as well as in life she could betray. In the programming room, amid support consoles, minicomputers, oscilloscopes, and Elk's privately engineered neural-surrogate equipment I associated Bronwen Lief with everything that was then threatening Ongladred's civilization: the barbarians of the Angromain Archipelago, the mythical sloak, Elk's own wayward genius, and, damn me for thinking it, maybe even the inflexibility of Atarite rule. Somehow Bronwen Lief was all of these things; somehow she embodied all the intangibles of the Halcyon Panic.

Weary, I left the programming room, found my own bedchamber on the upper level, and slept until the sun was high.

iv

All the next day I saw nothing of Gabriel Elk. However, there was a tunnel running from the programming room to the comp-center beneath the Stonelore amphitheatre, and I was certain that the old man, laboring alone, was preparing both the corpse of Bronwen Lief and the comptroller room itself for the special performance two evenings hence. I was of Our Shathra Anna's intelligence service, the Eyes and Ears of the Court, but I'd begun to trust Gabriel Elk—more, to respect him. He was too busy, too unconcerned with our petty preoccupations to try to elude me.

At midday I threaded my way through the rocks to the stable. In the barren paddock I found Gareth and the Elk family ostler, a middle-aged masker named Robin Coigns. He had been sleeping when we arrived from Lunn the previous evening, and Gareth's father had chosen not to disturb him. Gareth, as usual, was chiseling at a block of stone on a split-rail table, and Robin was grooming Gabriel's horse, pulling out long strands of kinky sorrel hair. The other animal was beneath the wooden awning, eating.

I entered the paddock. "Hello, horsesweat," I said to Robin.

Blandly, the ostler grinned. Gareth was too busy to do anything more than nod. His chisel glinted in the anemic sun; splinters flew away from his gloved hands. This statue, this "tree," was going to be as convoluted as any he had ever made. I shielded my eyes and looked into the sun, into feeble old Maz.

"Well, Robin," I said. "What do you think? Is Maz going to nova, blow up in Ongladred's skies? Everything else imaginable is supposed to happen when the Panic breaks."

"Maz won't blow," Robin said. "I'll expect the sloak first."

"Do you believe in the sloak?"

"It's been ver-i-fied, hasn't it, Master Marley?"

"Postulated, not verified."

"Well, Our Shathra Anna says there's geo-logical ev-i-dence."

"Some." I was always amused by the gullibility of maskers, particularly uneducated ones like the ostler Robin Coigns.

Gareth looked up from his work. "I believe in the sloak," he said. His wide face glistened with sweat; his patchy beard outlined his jaw with a moist, plastered redness. "And Father believes in it. As Robin says, there's evidence to support its existence—at least in theory."

"In theory," I said. I had heard all the arguments before. *Sloak* was the masker name for an apparently chimerical sea creature that no one had ever seen. No one had ever seen it because it dwelled kilometers off the coast of Ongladred, on the very bottom of the ocean floor: a millimicron-thin membrane of otherwise immense proportions cloaking the sea bottom all the way to Mansueceria's equator, where the planet's waters supposedly became too warm for so sensitive a monster. Legend had it that the sloak, which moved in slow, vaguely peristaltic undulations, thickened itself consciously every two thousand years and pulled its bulk over the entire surface of our island. Then, like a huge dappled eye, it lay basking, breathing, for a year or more, in the dull sunlight of our world—after which it returned to the marbled green depths of the Suthward Trench.

An unhurried, rhythmical departure, no doubt.

"Two previous civilizations on Ongladred died," Gareth said. "Died seemingly at the height of their glory; died without suffering human conquest. And Father says that it wasn't so terribly long ago—during or after the creature's last cycle—that the Angromain Archipelagoes were settled by fleeing Atarites. Only enough people survived on Ongladred to begin again. Ours is the third civilization of colonists so threatened, Master Marley."

"The sloak is an explanation only if you have no other," I said. "There's firmer evidence for two periods of mild glaciation. Why not accept these as the means of destruction you're looking for, Gareth?"

"Glaciation from the south!" the boy said heatedly. "Why accept the illogical? I prefer the sloak, Robin's sloak."

"The sloak it was," Robin said. "The sloak it was."

"And if the cycle holds true," Gareth said, "this is the year." With his chisel, he made several chips of stone fly.

"The more immediate threat to Ongladred is human, Gareth—the Pelagans. They're real, they're avaricious, and they've finally begun to demonstrate the unity to undermine us. Before, their own divisiveness kept them manageable."

"Ten thousand years ago, on Earth, the threat was always human," the boy said, chiseling, his brow furious. Then he halted, looked over the block of stone on the table, fixed me with his blue-green eyes. "And you, Master Marley, see a threat even in my father. That's why you've come to Stonelore. That's why we bed and feed you, one of the Eyes and Ears of Our Shathra."

"I do what I must." It seemed that I had used these same words a hundred times before. Ingram Marley, a dirt-runner, a spy with no cover. Robin Coigns finished grooming Gabriel Elk's horse and led it under the shelter; he began pulling the wire comb down the flank of the other animal, tactfully out of earshot. Aswim in a welter of ambiguous loyalties, I watched him.

"And so does my father," Gareth said. "He also does what he must, but you've placed him among the potential dangers to Ongladred. In reality he is in himself the culmination of what that civilization ought to stand for. Does the Atarite Court know what it's doing, Master Marley?"

"Do you question Our Shathra Anna?" I was ashamed to frame this response, but I didn't know what else to say to the boy; therefore, subtle intimidation.

He would have none of it. "Not Our Shathra Anna. She alone among you may understand what Gabriel Elk represents. It's Chancellor Blaine and the Magi of the Atarite Court whose wisdom seems to me suspect, Master Marley."

"How suspect, Gareth?" Then I asked him something else, before he could answer my first question. "Will you disobey your conscription order when it comes, as it surely will?"

"If Ongladred requires men to defend her, I will aid in her defense." The boy was indignant; his voice quavered. "My father fought for this island, and so will I. I, too, am an Elk, Master Marley."

"Your father's a man of influence. Will he let you go?"

"He would have to, wouldn't he? In everything, he obeys the laws of the island. Besides, he knows if he attempted to hinder me, I wouldn't be stopped; I would go without his consent." The boy's stare fell away from me, a gratifying respite.

Robin Coigns came back, his currying unfinished. He sat on a bale of fodder between Gareth and me; I was leaning on the paddock rail. Robin said, "They say all civi-li-zations die, Master Marley. It's the nature of things. En-tro-py, you know, all of it running down. But it seems to me, one way or the other, it can be fought, you know. So I'll fight it, too."

Apparently he had heard the last part of our conversation. I asked, "Are you of induction age, too, horsesweat?"

"Forty-nine," he said. "I'll go with Master Gareth. The top and the bottom of their numbers, we'll be. Youth and sagassa-ty."

Gareth laughed. I was grinning, too.

"Oh, I'm not worried a' tall," the ostler went on. "My father always said that at the third coming of the sloak, the Parfects would return, too. To watch over us, you know. They dropped us here six thousand years ago, he said, and they'd come back if things went too swackers, like they're starting to do now. Why, it's my opinion, Master Marley, that the Parfects are cruising a ship out there among the Shattered Moons right now, orb-it-ing, you know—watching over us Mansuecerians, the People Accustomed to the Hand. And maybe over you ruling Atarites, too, for governing us good like you have."

"Those are comforting notions, horsesweat. But I'm afraid

your sloak and the hoped-for return of the Parfects are cut from the same mythical cloth; they cancel each other out. We're left with the Pelagan threat, and no mitigating circumstances."

"And don't forget the peril posed by my father," Gareth said.

My grin faded; then I saw that Gabriel Elk's son was baiting me, prolonging the moment of uneasy jocularity that Robin Coigns had given us. In the same spirit I said, "I won't. You keep reminding me. The children of geniuses ought to voluntarily slit their throats as soon as they're cognizant of their heritage—a gash in the Adam's apple. Otherwise, they begin to take themselves too seriously."

"You don't like my stone work, Master Marley? My trees?"

"You'd be better off petrifying driftwood. Wouldn't take so long, and the results would be about the same."

"That's a hit," Robin Coigns said. "That's a hit."

We talked some more, then went back through the garden of rocks to Grotto House. Bethel gave us haoma, biscuits, and jerky for a midday meal, and sat down to eat with us herself. It was the first time since I had been there that she had served haoma. The old man did not appear; it was doubtful that he had even slept that night. I thought for a moment of Bronwen Lief, of her disquieting beauty. Then I put her out of my mind and enjoyed the company of the Elks and Robin Coigns, the company and the food. The haoma began to work in me as it had done the night before in Lunn.

Afterwards I excused myself and retired to my bedchamber for a nap. I didn't see Gabriel Elk at all for the remainder of that day. Nor did I see him the next. Nor the next—until late afternoon.

V

The Magi at the Atarite Court had determined that if we on Mansueceria converted our system of time-keeping into Earthly terms, it would be the year 12,500 A.D. Of course, this was an approximation. We measured time not in this long-ago-discarded way, but in terms of how many Mansuecerian years had passed in the reign of our current shathra. The winter and spring of the Halcyon Panic were preternatural seasons in the Year 35 of Our Shathra Anna, and ensconced in Gabriel Elk's house at Stonelore I wondered how many more years she would reign. I hoped it would be many; she was an estimable woman.

As Robin Coigns had said on the morning after Elk's and my return from Lunn, there had been colonists on Mansueceria for six thousand of our years. We had been brought from Earth in starships conceived and constructed by a neo-human species whom our earliest records had always referred to as the Parfects—principally because Earth's last men had considered them free of all human vices, cleansed of the quasi-mythical taint of Original Sin. It was the Parfects who had saved mankind from ultimate extermination in the terra-cotta city of Windfall Last in the Carib Sea; who had redeemed us genetically, providing for two contrasting but complementary types of individual (the stoically disciplined Mansuecerians, or "maskers," and the more aggressive, more emotional Atarites); and who had then delivered this population of half a million to the rugged heartland of Ongladred, on a planet more than eight hundred light-years from Earth. Another chance. Yet another chance, in an isolation even more splendid than that the ambient sea had insured at Windfall Last. Then, the early records and later legends unanimously agreed, the Parfects themselves had left us, gone back to turn all of Earth into the gardens of Adam's first paradise. As for man, he had the rocks of Ongladred—and another chance.

And for six thousand years, despite two major collapses, we had maintained ourselves entire; more, we had managed, with very few exceptions, to maintain our genetic heritage as well, the People Accustomed to the Hand and the People Touched by Fire alike. Together, we had survived. Now Atarite barbarians from the sea-blasted, storm-scoured archipelagoes in the Angromain Sea threatened all we had built together, and there were rumors in the land of the coming of the slow, ravening sloak and the imminent explosion of woe-beset Maz. It was the Year of the Halcyon Panic, as well as Year 35 of Our Shathra Anna; a self-conscious calm prevailed.

Late in the afternoon of the third day after our return from Lunn, Gabriel Elk emerged from his seclusion and greeted me in the open courtyard in the center of his house. My ankles crossed, I had been sitting on a stone bench watching Maz drop mauvely down the sky. "How have you been faring, Ingram?" the old man said. His green eyes looked tired; his great, winged sideburns were unkempt, and I could see the previously muted resemblance between him and Gareth. For the first time, I could see it clearly.

"Well," I said. "And you? Are you done?"

"Done. I had to be. Tonight the Liefs are coming, Ingram, and some others."

"What others, Sayati Elk?"

"Be patient, and see." He stood in front of me for a moment, casting his long shadow over both the flagstones and my legs, then turned and went back into the house. I had to pull myself up and follow. I felt uneasy. I could sense all the diverse strands of my anxiety preparing to knot themselves together.

There was no supper that evening, no haoma to share. Bethel met her husband in the foyer, took his hand, nodded vaguely at me. Then we left Grotto House and walked across the sandy arena which the Stonelore amphitheatre completely dominated. Instead of entering Stonelore, however, we took up sentry positions in one of the natural doorways in the rock wall overlooking the Mershead Road. The wind blew balloons of sand out over the grass, Gabriel and Bethel talked in low voices, and I waited. Just waited.

At last the Liefs came, man and wife, distant figures walking on the low road; they had walked the seven kilometers from Lunn. Even after we saw them, it took a good while for them to reach us. Maz had set, and when they arrived the five of us stood in the twilight like liquid ghosts.

"Hello, Josu," Gabriel Elk said. "Welcome, Rhia. Tonight you'll see your daughter reanimated, given a kind of life again. Bethel will take you into Stonelore and show you your seats. I'll follow in a while. There are others whom I'm pledged to greet."

The Liefs went off with Bethel in the liquid dusk, toward the amphitheatre. When I looked after them, I saw Stonelore's broad circular cap glowing a soft yellow-orange. In response to my questioning look, Gabriel said, "Gareth's in the comptroller room. Tonight, he does my work." We turned again to the Mershead Road. Overhead, the Shattered Moons were scarcely visible, as milky as a thousand clumsily shaped pearls floating between Ongladred's strong rock and the heavens' weak stars.

At last we saw the vehicles on the roadway, and I knew that our visitors were Our Shathra Anna, her Chancellor, and some Atarite retainers—guardsmen. Two chariots preceded Our Shathra's equipage, and torches burned in the hands of the men in the chariots. The sound of the horses' hooves grew steadily beneath the sound of the wind, and Gabriel Elk and I watched as the chariots separated from Our Shathra's carriage and circled off in different directions, one halting about fifty meters from the gate in the rocks, the other undoubtedly taking up guard on the other side of the upland arena. The equipage, however, proceeded on up to us, black and silent, its matched horses caparisoned and haughty.

Gabriel Elk, waving his arms, directed the vehicle to the steps at the base of the amphitheatre. Robin Coigns had appeared from the darkness to help our eminent visitors get out and to show the coachman where he might shelter himself and his horses during the neuro-performance.

"Sayati Elk," Our Shathra Anna said.

The old man bowed, as did I. The carriage drew away from us. Arngrim Blaine, a tall, ascetic-looking man in his sixtieth year, smiled at us. Even in the failing light his roan tooth was visible, a translucent reddish-black canine pointing upward like a knife. Long ago he had had it scrimshawed with his initials (it was rumored), but over the years these had either faded or worn away (if they ever existed). He was a well-meaning, narrow-principled man. "Hello, Ingram," he said. "Sayati Elk. I'm happy enough to greet you, but not at all convinced that this trip was merited. Stonelore has always seemed a frivolous waste to me, and now more than ever."

"Arngrim has no taste for the arts," Our Shathra said. She wore a black cloak that fastened at her neck; although she smiled, there were grey circles under her eyes.

"Neither did Cyaxares of Mede," the Chancellor said. "Nor Walpole of Augustan England. Besides, Ongladred wasn't made for art."

Our Shathra Anna said, "With which man do you compare yourself, Arngrim—the Median king or the English minister?"

"The minister, Lady. The other would be presumptuous." He bowed.

"Art is an enrichment granted those cultures deserving it," the creator of Stonelore said. "Or inflicted on those attempting to repress it."

Our Shathra Anna looked at Gabriel Elk. When she spoke, her tone was liltingly sharp, ironically humorous. "Blaine is irritated because he can't rule in all things. Most of all, he can't rule me. I've come to see your entertainment, Gabriel, because I may not be able to come again."

"The season's dangers ought to have dissuaded us from coming tonight," Blaine said. "Two chariots! An inadequate guard, Lady."

"Then I love the lady for the dangers that she's passed," Gabriel Elk said. "And I welcome you both. Let's go inside." He didn't bow; his gallantry derived from conviction. Taking Our Shathra Anna's arm, he escorted the lady up the stairs to the wide illuminated portal of the amphitheatre. Chancellor Blaine and I trailed them up the steps, two serving-men, each as much a dirt-runner as the other—a situation which I found satisfyingly amusing.

Two of Gareth Elk's tree-sculptures flanked the wide door.

Inside, Elk led us to a glass booth on the theatre's highest circular tier, a booth reserved for Ongladred's Atarites and Atarite retainers. The top of the booth was open, and even though we were on Stonelore's uppermost level, the ceiling arched over us like a miniature sky, utterly out of reach. Our chairs were velvet-upholstered wingbacks set so that we could look comfortably down into the neuro-pit. Across from us, in the preliminary dark, we could discern Bethel Elk and the Liefs sitting poised and expectant on the continuous stone tier. Otherwise, Stonelore was empty—but sentient, immense, and brooding. Gabriel Elk had infused it with something of his own character.

"Those are my actress' parents," he said. "I felt that they should be here, too, if they wished to come."

"Of course," Our Shathra said.

"I hope," Blaine said, "that they're maskers in every sense, inured to feigned emotions and resigned to their daughter's death. This sort of thing can undermine even the stolidest personality, Sayati Elk."

"It hasn't yet, Chancellor. Tonight, in any case, a reading only. The neuro-drama doesn't undermine anything; it offers release, purgation, for a people manufactured to think they don't require it, but subliminally craving it in any case. The neuro-drama illuminates our oneness, it strengthens the social order you represent."

"When it's comprehensible, perhaps," the Chancellor said. "Mostly, at Stonelore, it criminally drains energy reserves." It was not impossible to admire the roan-toothed old pragmatist; even genius left him unabashed, wittily clawing.

Gabriel Elk answered him angrily: "The reserves are mine,

not the state's! And the drain is far from criminal since the law refuses to permit human actors. Stonelore is a compromise with that law, Chancellor Blaine—a law of Atarite urging which you capably championed before the Magi. Perhaps you remember?"

"Very well, Sayati Elk, very well."

Our Shathra Anna leaned forward in her engulfing chair. "May we begin now, Worthies? These things are past argument and I've come for intelligent entertainment, not debate."

"Certainly, Lady." Gabriel Elk left the booth.

Chancellor Blaine turned to me. "Well, Ingram, what can you say for yourself? It seems you've been enjoying a vacation from the Court, a holiday at Stonelore."

"Shame," Our Shathra said. "You wanted him to come out here, Arngrim. Now you scold him for doing your bidding."

I said, "Anyway, I don't believe the old man is a threat to Ongladred; he'll precipitate no early break in the maskers' steadfastness, Chancellor—nor will the neuro-dramas planned for after the equinox."

Blaine asked, "What *does* Sayati Elk have planned, Ingram?"

"I don't know," I had to admit. "I'm not even sure what we'll see this evening, but Gabriel Elk's neither a fool nor an apostate."

"Thirteen days out here, Ingram, and you don't know what the man's planning. You're arguing from faith." Blaine's roan tooth seemed to slash at me. "When the Halcyon Panic breaks, when the maskers give themselves over to fear and misdirected anger and other inutile emotions, you'll find Ongladred's biggest fool and darkest apostate coexisting in the same skin, Master Marley: *yours!*" The Chancellor's thin lips drew together firmly, hiding the red-black canine.

"Melodrama," Our Shathra Anna said. "Your own fears betray you into rhetoric, Arngrim."

"I hope so, Lady," Blaine said, immediately calm again. "But I see no reason to court disaster. The neuro-drama is a folly, a corruption of masker and Atarite mores, that I can't comprehend your fondness for. In times like these, Lady, your protection of it—forgive me—seems almost perverse." He looked at me again. "In the meantime, Ingram, I think your mission at Stonelore is effectively at an end. Tonight you'll come back to Lunn with us."

"Very well," I said.

vi

Suddenly the neuro-theatre was plunged into absolute, impenetrable darkness. There was music: a single, stringed instrument playing mournfully. The sound—not loud, but resonant and golden—seemed to issue from everywhere at once. "At last," I heard Our Shathra's voice say, "the *folly* commences." Then a battery of incredibly bright lights threw their stinging yellowness into the sunken arena of the neuro-pit, Sayati Elk's "stage." Even yet, however, the blackness obliterated everything else in the Stonelore amphitheatre; we could not see Elk's wife and Bronwen's parents on the tier opposite us.

Then Gabriel Elk stepped into the light. As he spoke, he turned so that all in the theatre could hear him, even the phantom maskers whom he apparently imagined to be in the tiers above him. His foreshortened body, his monstrous hands, his upturned, expressive face all had a sharpness of focus intensified out of the realm of nature. Ageless he was, ageless and transcendent. Turning slowly, he spoke; and, without amplification, his voice reached out to us like a wave breaking. "My performer tonight is the corpse of Bronwen Lief, a girl killed by the Pelagans four days ago. I bow to her parents, for allowing me to buy her." He bowed in their direction. "What she will perform is not of my composition; indeed, it is not even of our tongue, and I have decided to let her speak it as its ancient poet, now forgotten, set it to paper. The strangeness of the language will be no stranger than the strangeness of our times. Ultimately, all languages are vehicles for the same remorseless, unending reaching out—even to the moment of man's extinction."

On that word he walked out of the neuro-pit, into the ambient dark. But he didn't return to our booth.

We were left staring into the neuro-pit. Then a section of the floor about three meters in diameter withdrew into the bowels of the amphitheatre; when it returned on its pneumatic lift-shaft, Bronwen Lief was standing on it—her supple body clad in a white Etruscan stola, her eyes reflecting back at us the disquieting glaze of her deadness. The music began again, livelier than before but still mournful. Just as the girl had no soul, the music now had no body; the thin plucked notes slipped away into the air. Perhaps Gabriel Elk intended for the music and the girl to complete each other, to make the whole human being out of an empty shell and a disembodied noise. I didn't know. This was the first time I had ever seen any sort of performance at all at Stonelore: Arngrim Blaine enforced his own prejudices among the Eyes and Ears of Our Shathra Anna, and except for my assignment to Elk as a dirt-runner I might never have been permitted to receive the old sayati's special brand of "enlightenment."

The performance itself both bewildered and moved me. I saw a corpse behave as no living masker ever had, even under Atarite command in war.

Bronwen Lief, a dead girl, danced.

Maskers never danced—nor did Atarites, even though the range of emotions conducive to dancing lay well within our psychological compass. It was against the law. For the same reason that dancing was against the law, living human beings were forbidden to be actors.

As products of the Parfects' genetic engineering, the population of our planet reflected their unanimous verdict as to what qualities a reasoning creature ought to have. Out of the maskers the Parfects had bred avariciousness, aggressiveness, xenophobia, lust, and even a degree of the inclination to fear. At the same time the Parfects had recognized that survival in a new and hostile environment depended, at least in part, on these very "vices." Hence, they had engineered a second, smaller group of colonists to guide and administer to the first; these were the original Atarites, people in whom the dangerous dross of the animal, the primeval recourse to fang and claw, still had a bit of play—but subordinated now to the need to build, command, and protect.

The Parfects had even tried to program into our ancestors' genes and blood the elementary knowledge that the two groups were dependent on each other; that the seemingly irresistible urge to interbreed would lead to ruin; that the similar tendency for the People Accustomed to the Hand and the People Touched by Fire to go their separate ways, to take their own evolutionary roads, would have to be subconsciously, intuitively, fought. In all of this, the Parfects had perhaps demonstrated the extent of their own limitations. Still, we had managed to survive. Renegade Atarites had established themselves long ago on the islands of the Angromain Archipelago, and for several generations on Ongladred there had been more liaisons between ruler and ruled than were wise (my own grandparents were an example); but even so threatened and picked at, our civilization stood.

In Gabriel Elk's neuro-theatre I watched the dead Bronwen Lief go through the motions of a choreography programmed into her but seemingly motivated from within, from a *human* source. Of course, that source was Sayati Elk himself (and Gareth, too, for he directed some of the girl's movements from the comptroller room). The old man had turned technology into a kind of aesthetic, he had tried to infuse spirit into what was essentially a mechanical operation—not because he wanted to, but because he had to. The neuro-theatre was a compromise with the laws of Ongladred, a compromise that the old man could not have been entirely happy with. I was moved by Bronwen's dance because her programmer had come so close to accomplishing the impossible. She moved with genuine grace; her garment followed the flow of her limbs like a ghost counterpointing her motions. But, in reality, it was Gabriel Elk's vision, his need to communicate, that was flowing down there under the withering brightness of Stonelore's lamps.

Bronwen Lief was the vessel into which he had poured both vision and need. Because she was a corpse.

The law said that no human being could be an actor, no human being could take part in any sort of performance contrary to Mansuecerian nature. For uniformity's sake, the law included Atarites. The relatively high incidence of interbreeding between the two groups during the last century had made the law seem reasonable to many. An actor, after all, is one who constantly assumes roles requiring him to abase or repudiate, if only momentarily, the genetic characteristics given to him by the Parfects. One becomes something other than himself. Drama derives from conflict and emotion—excessive and aberrant emotion, according to men like Chancellor Blaine. In a society like Ongladred's, these men felt, such "artificial" emotions posed a very real danger to the persons acting them out; the audience for these spectacles was also in some danger of corruption, but a few of Our Shathra Anna's most influential Magi had deterred the closing of the neurotheatre by arguing that it might be a healthy outlet for the subconscious turmoil of the ordinary Mansuecerian. Or maybe this was the rationalization of Our Shathra herself, who was a sympathizer, who enjoyed a slightly illicit entertainment. And so the issue of Stonelore balanced on the horns of the fuzzy moral ideologies of these two factions: One could attend Gabriel Elk's dramas, but one could not perform in them.

The dead, however, were exempt from the non-participation law. No stigma attached to the reanimation of corpses for actors; in Ongladred we had developed an almost callous disregard for death and the attendant luxuries of mourning, burial, and lingering memory—or at least the maskers had, out of both necessity and the hope for survival. Therefore, Sayati Elk reanimated the dead. He poured his vision and need into the only vessels the state would allow him, striving always to touch and transfigure. This he did for an audience that almost invariably sat mute and subdued to the end. That his audience again and again came back to be silently worked upon was his incentive to continue—that, and his obsession with a dream, and occasionally Our Shathra Anna's reaction, whether approval or pique.

Tonight she approved. "Beautiful," she said.

Mansuecerian dancer, Atarite applause—except that Arngrim Blaine made a sighing noise. He shifted his thin body in its chair and his lacy clothes rustled. I ignored the Chancellor. Leaning forward, I tried to catch every nuance of Bronwen Lief's performance.

Then it was over, or at least this preliminary part of it was. She came out of her last graceful pas seul into an equally graceful walk. Then stopped. She turned her eyes up to her parents, then faced in the direction of our booth and looked up at us. They were still dead, those eyes, still empty and glasslike.

The lute continued to play.

When she finally spoke, her voice was deeper than seemed right—but melodious. The ancient language in which she spoke came naturally to her lips and mesmerized us with its accents; we forgot our inability to understand and simply listened. From somewhere in the dark, his voice coming rich and assured after each line Bronwen delivered, Sayati Elk translated the forgotten poet's words.

The poem dealt with time, and with the inevitable crumbling away of empires, and with the poet's awe in the face of their passing. It dealt, too, with the nearly inconsequential prospect of his own death. A fluid poem with few pauses, and a headlong surging toward its final lines.

In Elk's translation we heard them:

> *And here face downward in the sun*
> *To feel how swift how secretly*
> *The shadow of the night comes on . . .*

Bronwen Lief folded her hands and let her head fall to her breast. And that was all; the show was over. A dance and a reading, with very little room for the sort of *emoting* Chancellor Blaine took exception to. Sayati Elk had programmed the girl and cautioned Gareth to underplay the "entertainment"; in everything but the subject matter of the reading he had aimed at conciliating my roan-toothed superior. Less than twenty minutes had gone by since the dimming of Stonelore's house-lights and the flaring of the great lamps around the neuro-pit.

Brevity had always impressed Arngrim Blaine.

vii

But afterwards, in the tapestry-hung dining chamber of Grotto House, we discovered that the poem's subject had not impressed him, except negatively. There were six of us around the great stone table there, and places for two more. Those two were for Gabriel and Gareth, acting now as our stewards, moving between dining chamber and kitchen with platters of food and decanters of vintage haoma. A silent masker woman, the cook and scullery maid Maria, helped them with these labors. Our Shathra Anna and Bethel Elk sat at opposite ends of the table, each as queenly as the other. To the right of Our Shathra, Chancellor Blaine voiced his objections to the reading while the Liefs remained humbly noncommittal.

He was saying, "I can only assume, Mistress Elk, that your husband chose the piece we've just heard for its elegant pessimism. He must have had to rummage long and hard through your library—until he found a microchip whose very shape and color suggested the defeatism of its contents. A tasteless choice, considering the dangers besetting us now." He sipped the haoma from his cup, a small illicit pleasure.

"Or an appropriate one," Bethel Elk said.

"No. He might as well be a propagandist for the Pelagans.

Suppose that this were given on the first night after the equinox. How would our maskers—" Blaine's lips tightened; he began again. "Forgive me. How would our *Mansuecerian* citizens react?"

"Why not ask the Liefs, Chancellor?" I said.

Husband and wife continued silent, Rhia smiling and Josu bland under his leather mourning cap.

Blaine went on: "You see, they can't yet formulate their reactions. But I believe the effect of a presentation like the one we saw tonight is bound to be insidious. And the neurodramas themselves are a thousand times more disquieting than Bronwen Lief's recital. Eventually, the people's faith in Our Shathra and the Atarite Court will be sabotaged." In the glow of the dining chamber's candles, his roan tooth glinted with carnelian highlights.

Gabriel and Gareth came in with baskets of potato bread. They were enjoying themselves. The old man smiled at his wife.

Our Shathra Anna said, "Arngrim is maligning your choice of material, Gabriel. Says you'll sabotage Ongladred and me with barbarian propaganda."

It was the boy who answered her. "Father will respond to that after we have eaten—if the Chancellor leaves anything for us." He and the old man went out again, and, surprisingly enough, Blaine smiled—wanly.

Then the Elks, father and son, returned and took up their places at table with us. Gabriel spoke to the Liefs: "Well, what did you think? Tell me how you felt seeing Bronwen as you saw her." Unlike Chancellor Blaine, he genuinely wanted their reactions; I could see him preparing to take mental notes.

"I don't know, Sayati Elk," Rhia said. "She wasn't our girl, that one down there."

"Her voice, it was different," Josu volunteered.

"Getting the voice right is very hard," Gareth answered. "Father has to coordinate the neural impulses from the electrodes in Broca's area of the brain with the programming of the lungs, vocal cords, and lips."

"Why don't you just use a recording?" Blaine asked. "It seems to me you've made things unduly complicated for yourself, Sayati Elk."

The old man glanced at the Chancellor. He said nothing. He returned his gaze to Rhia and Josu. "Bronwen didn't sound like herself?" he asked.

Josu said, "No, sir. Not exactly—but it could've been that old sort of talk she was speaking in."

"Maybe it was the talk," Rhia said. "That different language."

"Which supports my contention that your choice of material left a good deal to be desired," Blaine said. "The language itself, Sayati Elk, alienated the Liefs from their reanimated daughter, whereas the moany business about every civilization crumpling into shadow certainly wasn't designed to send either Our Shathra Anna or me away from Stonelore happily whistling your praises. A bad choice—from a diplomatic point of view if not an artistic one, Sayati Elk."

"It's spoiled your digestion, not mine," Our Shathra told Blaine.

Suddenly there was a silence; a stillness descended on the dining room of Grotto House. Eight people stared at one another over the baskets of potato bread, over the decanters of haoma, over the silver platter of roast mutton and the bowls of bread pudding. A silence and a tenseness. Then Arngrim Blaine raised his cup and sipped. By this simple movement he directed our attention to him. Looking over the rim of his cup, he spoke to Gabriel.

"Is Ongladred going to die, Sayati Elk?"

"Probably. One day."

"Soon?"

"*Soon* is a relative term, Chancellor Blaine. On what scale do you wish me to apply it?"

"Bronwen Lief's performance in Stonelore suggested that collapse is inevitable. I'm supposing that you selected the piece out of some rational, therefore comprehensible motive? What motive? To frighten us? To warn us? To suggest that resistance to fate is foolhardy? What, Sayati Elk? As for my definition of *soon*, do you think Ongladred will die during our lifetimes?"

"It's conceivable."

"Is it inevitable?"

"Even its death isn't inevitable, Chancellor Blaine. Societies fall when their leaders fail."

A pause; a darker tension.

Blaine's mouth was open slightly; a thread of spittle lay across his discolored tooth. He sipped more haoma. Then he said, "Who do you see as failing first, Sayati Elk? The Atarite Court in Lunn or the wolfish Pelagan captains across the Angromain Channel?"

Gareth Elk, the boy, said, "Whoever is least flexible, Chancellor Blaine; whoever is least adaptable." It was a thought I had had before, but never voiced. Blaine himself, though capable of a quick and witty range in conversation, was not otherwise known for his readiness to abandon old ways, old prejudices. The boy, I felt, had inadvertently given voice to our most basic fears about Ongladred's time of trials—the suspicion, even among Atarites, that our leaders had lost the quality of vision.

Then Our Shathra Anna said, "We may have as much as a year before the Pelagans put us to the test, perhaps as little as three months. Right now they're content for reivers and fear-strikers to harass, to steal, and"—here she nodded at Rhia and Josu Lief—"to murder when surprised in these pursuits. Invasion is not yet. We have a little time to mobilize. Even so, Gabriel, you ought to remember one thing in particular."

"Yes, Lady?" he said.

"That you must include yourself among that group of leaders who may fail or not fail in the attempt to preserve Ongladred."

"I, Lady?"

"Come, come, Gabriel. You're too old to play coy. Just as Arngrim and I are"—she inflected her next word self-consciously—"*political* leaders, you're an intellectual leader of our island."

Chancellor Blaine almost smirked. "In other words, Sayati Elk, you have a responsibility nearly as great as ours."

"Sometimes," Bethel Elk said, "Gabriel views his efforts at Stonelore in a Promethean light; against a hostile array of gods and vultures, he labors alone for the redemption and advancement of humanity."

"Oh, no," the old man protested, grinning. "Not alone. The gods and vultures I don't dispute, but I've always had help—you, Gareth, and lately even tight-lipped Master Marley there. The labor's almost always been *intellectual*, though," he continued slyly. "I wouldn't presume to put my foot in *politics*."

The meal went better after that. I studied the ornate woolen tapestries on the walls; I enjoyed the haoma, the food, the less sensitive drift of our talk. It was difficult to believe Stonelore's relative isolation from the Atarite Court, the belligerence of the inhabitants of the windy archipelagoes, the nightmarish threat of a creature called the sloak. Candles flickered. The evening drew to a close, as did my own residence at Grotto House. Oddly, I regretted this fact; I didn't want to go back to Lunn.

Then Our Shathra Anna said, "Arngrim, you'd better tell the Elks of Gareth's conscription."

Talk ceased again.

Chancellor Blaine said, "The gist of it is that Gareth and your ostler—"

"Robin Coigns," Bethel said.

"Yes. Gareth and Gentleman Coigns must report to the Lunn garrison in two days. Our Shathra wished this message to come from me personally, Sayati Elk, not from an induction-runner."

"Two days!" Bethel said.

"That's very little notice," her husband added.

Our Shathra said, "The message was to have come a day or two ago, Mistress Elk, but we hoped that hearing it from our own lips would make the news less distressing. I'm sorry the notice is not more, though. Sincerely sorry."

Josu Lief put his arms on the table. "You'll be reporting, Master Gareth, when I do, it seems."

"That's fine with me," Gareth said. "The hardship's not mine, but Father's. He'll have to do all the work, virtually all the work, in the neuro-theatre by himself. Mother can't work in the comptroller room; her back won't let her."

Gareth's comment seemed to be a serendipitous clue for Chancellor Blaine; quickly he interjected: "Sayati Elk, we can offer you the command of a unit of recently inducted men—a naval unit—if you choose to accept now. You will hold it for a year, or until this crisis is past. Should you accept, spring performances at Stonelore will cease to be a problem for you. Gareth's absence won't be felt here."

"Certainly it will be felt," Bethel said.

Blaine qualified this comment: "I meant that your husband's work in the neuro-theatre wouldn't be impeded by his absence."

"Because there wouldn't be any work in the neuro-theatre," Gabriel Elk said. "I'd be captaining a contingent of young Mansuecerian seamen against the Pelagans—at sixty-three. Stonelore would close."

"Regrettably," Blaine said.

"I refuse." Gabriel Elk turned to Our Shathra Anna. "Lady, was this proposal of your own devising? Am I to understand that you wish me to close Stonelore and hobble off to war?"

"You are far from hobbling, Gabriel. But no. The proposal originated with the Chancellor himself."

"Who believes," Blaine said smugly, "your intellectual leadership can be put to good military use, Sayati Elk. Since survival depends on leadership."

"I refuse. I'm too old for conscription. I've served."

"Our Shathra Anna," Gareth said, rising, "I'd like to go tell Robin."

"Please. Go ahead."

As the boy left, Gabriel Elk said, "In any case, we've nearly finished. When you return to Lunn, Lady, I humbly request that you let Josu and Rhia share your coach. The roads are dangerous at night."

Our Shathra agreed, and in another twenty minutes our entire company was outside, in the shadow of Grotto House, under the motionful brightness of the Shattered Moons. The Stonelore amphitheatre loomed up before us like an immense round starship, promising us Earth. It was cool. We saw Gareth and Robin Coigns walking toward us across the upland arena, Our Shathra Anna's equipage rattling along behind them like a circus cage of noisy blackbirds. Somehow, the equipage struck me as an evil thing. Above the caparisoned horses the driver snapped his long whip; apparently they had not been unbridled during the whole of the long evening. A second time the driver snapped his whip, and a third.

In front of Grotto House, Josu Lief crumpled to his knees in the dust and then pitched forward on his face.

If I hadn't seen the spark of uncanny red in the rock spires opposite us, I would have supposed the man had fainted—but the three successive crackings of the carriage driver's whip had concealed the report of a rifle. The second shot had no such fortuitous cover, however, and the burst of fire from the rifle muzzle seemed terrifyingly brighter than the first one. The report and the ricochet were deafening.

"Get down!" someone shouted. "Get back inside!"

I fell to the ground and rolled. I saw the three women—who had come out last—duck back into the deep well of Grotto House's inset entrance. Gabriel Elk and Arngrim Blaine scrambled into the rock garden to the entrance's right. I rolled again. On my stomach once more, I looked up. Gareth and Robin Coigns, caught in the open, ran for the protecting curve of the amphitheatre; the carriage rattled after them, horses whinnying.

Another spitting of fire; another shot. Everything was noise and moving bodies.

At last I found some cover for myself, a crevice on the side of Grotto House leading down to the stable.

"Gareth!" Gabriel Elk shouted. "Gareth!"

"Here, with Robin!" the boy answered from the portion of Stonelore's wall out of our concealed enemy's sight. "We're all of us whole."

viii

For the first time all evening I was alone with my thoughts, blood revving through my temples, roaring in my ears. The Shattered Moons buckled, flowed, shifted in their myriad orbits. I tilted my head back against the rough wall of my hiding place and watched them.

I, Ingram Marley, dirt-runner and spy.

For three hours I had been subsumed in the personalities of people more important, more powerful, than I. Now, through this violence, I had been given back to myself. The gift wasn't entirely appreciated. Involuntarily my shoulders pulled up against my neck, my palms flattened against cold stone.

I wondered how long the lot of us had to live. If the armed men in the rocks had got past Our Shathra Anna's chariot guard, who remained to save us? Only ourselves: Gabriel Elk and son, our effete Chancellor, Robin Coigns and the coachman, and one member of the Eyes and Ears of the Atarite Court. Stonelore and Grotto House lay too far away from either Lunn or the Mershead Road for us to count on accidental reinforcements—although if the court party were too long in returning, the Magi would dispatch a contingent of horsemen.

Two, three, four more shots sounded in Stonelore's arena. Could they be heard on the Mershead Road? Maybe. As dull, echoing *pings* over the sounds of wind and sea. It wasn't likely that anyone would follow them up.

Frozen in place, I felt my own impotence in the face of a reasonless, impersonal hostility.

Then the hostility took on a distinctly human character: there was laughter from the rocks opposite us. Gleeful, self-assertive laughter which even the wind couldn't drown with its gusting.

Then two more shots, ricocheting away.

Then still more laughter and a voice crying out, "Ilk! Ilk! You surrender!" After which the old man, from his hiding place with Blaine, shouted an obscenity. There was disconcerting silence then; no shots, no braying laughter.

Several minutes passed.

Finally the voice in the rocks began taunting us in a dialect both lilting and guttural, a dialect which I knew as Pelagan but which I had never learned. Our attackers—how many murderers peered down on us?—were men from across the Angromain Channel, reivers, thieves, fear-strikers, danger-drinking barbarians. I thought of Josu Lief lying face down in front of Grotto House. In less than a week these randomly operating Pelagan agents had killed two members of the same family. And one of them, drawing down on us with a stolen rifle no doubt, was alternately laughing and spewing out streams of incomprehensible invective.

After a time I realized that the hidden reiver was declaiming poetry at us, venomous couplets in his own tongue. He wanted Gabriel Elk, Ongladred's only literary giant, to suffer these insults in a form that mocked the old man's genius. And so he railed away at us like an actor, disdainful both of Sayati Elk and of the Atarite law that had indirectly given rise to the neuro-theatre. More than likely, Chancellor Blaine was chewing his upper lip with chagrin, his roan tooth on the verge of breaking flesh. How must he feel, in a situation in which he was as powerless as I?

"Ilk! Ilk!" the reiver called out; then regaled us with brusque, barbarian couplets.

For answer the reiver got three bursts from a handgun and a bit of bravado from Arngrim Blaine. "You'd better get out while you can!" his thin voice shouted. "If you don't go now, you'll not make it!"

I couldn't see around the crevice containing me, I was afraid to look out—but apparently the old Chancellor had taken the handgun from beneath his cloak and fired in anger. Gabriel Elk, beside Blaine in the low rock garden, translated his message into the Pelagan dialect and added a severe-sounding message of his own. I realized then that my own fear was greater than Chancellor Blaine's, that it was my own weakness that had imagined *him* chewing *his* lip. I was afraid because we were pinned down in Stonelore's arena. Still, we were not automatically doomed to end up like Josu Lief, wavy pencils of blood outlining our chins and discoloring the ground.

In my belt was a knife, a dagger with an elaborate haft. Almost every Atarite or Atarite retainer carried one like it; mine, like most of the others, had never been used. I curled my fingers around the haft and edged away from the crevice's opening, my back still making contact with stone. Rock encased me. Then the crevice funneled out and the night sky seemed to flood in on me. A tattering of wind slipped through a smooth-worn hole in the granite passageway, and later two separate, fancifully carven windows looked out on the narrow path leading down to the stable. I pulled myself up and crawled through the larger of these.

On the path, I ran.

Almost at once I came to the fenced-in paddock in front of the horses' shelter, a stable without walls. Despite the moons and the attenuated starlight, it was dark here; every shape appeared distorted, angular, unreal. Above me, in the Stonelore arena, I heard more rifle fire, echoings of deliberately hysterical laughter, and the mocking lilt and clack of the reiver's "poetry"—all of this noise incredibly tinny with distance. It was a temptation to go on down the path, find my way to open country and tall grass, and circle back to Lunn. *To bring back help,* I said to myself more than once; *to bring back help.*

Instead, I opened the paddock gate and walked between

bales of fodder that Robin Coigns had left out for his animals. Maybe he had come down here during our entertainments at Stonelore and Grotto House and carried a bale or two back to the arena for Our Shathra Anna's horses. If so, he hadn't returned to the paddock for a while.

One of the distorted shapes that I nearly stumbled over was not a bale of fodder; it was Gabriel Elk's round-eyed, woolly gelding. I knelt. A reiver had plunged his knife into the animal's breast and then ripped the blade upward toward the long, vitally muscled throat. The other animal, the one I had ridden to Lunn, had been dealt with similarly.

How many Pelagans had done this? What had happened to the chariot guard? Alone, I almost wished myself back with the others.

The smell of recently spilled blood, warm and salty, commingled with that of dry fodder and the horses' last, scarcely cold droppings. These things daunted me. I trembled with nausea and the night's chill. I heard Chancellor Blaine's handgun again; he could not have many shots left, unless he also wore ammunition under his lace cloak.

Why had the Pelagans not placed men on both sides of the Stonelore arena? Had they done so, those of us emerging from Grotto House would have had very little chance of getting either back inside or to cover. Maybe we had come out before they expected us to. Certainly they had been busy up until that moment. The chariot guard must have purchased a little time for us. After slaughtering the guards and our horses (our transportation down from Gabriel's Elk's citadel), the reivers had crossed back to the other side to see what they could do with Coigns and the unsuspecting coachman. There could not be too many of them; otherwise they would have worked in several concerted, simultaneous assaults rather than in cautious stages. Like me, the Pelagans were amateurs—infinitely more daring and bloodthirsty maybe, but not inherently more competent.

I stopped wondering; I stopped thinking.

If I managed to get onto the roof of the stable shelter, I saw that I could pull myself from there to the top of the rock wall into which Elk had built Grotto House. The rock wall, though broken in one or two places, inscribed a rough circle around the Stonelore arena.

So I climbed. I stacked several bales of fodder, then attained the shelter's roof. Then I fought the wind and the dizzying sky and clambered onto a rectangular ledge projecting out over the roof. From there, up to the rugged dentition of the rock wall itself.

Using hands and feet alike, I edged my way between these granitic, Brobdingnagian teeth, through the sudden drops, and over a few treacherous flat surfaces—toward the chattering Pelagan who had murdered Coigns' defenseless horses and the masker Josu Lief.

Something very ancient had come awake in my blood.

At one point I realized that I was on the roof of Grotto House. A useless realization. The rooms lay embedded in the stone under me like fossils buried in strata geologically unapproachable. The tapestries in the dining chamber; the electric wall panels in the foyer; the sound of women's voices. I wasn't a part of those things anymore; I was alone, moving stealthily toward some indefinable but necessary end. The Shattered Moons accompanied me.

Halfway around the wall I did something stupid: I stood full up and looked down into the arena.

I saw Gareth and Coigns huddled beside the amphitheatre, Our Shathra Anna's equipage a tangle of reins and shadows and jittery horses in front of them. The ostler and Elk's son were gesticulating madly at the coachman; he was slumped down in front of his seat, warily keeping his head low. As I watched, they managed to attract his attention and communicate to him their wishes.

Then, in rapid succession, these things happened: The coachman nervously jumped down from the equipage. He threw open the door on the side away from me. Gareth and Coigns rushed out from the wall and hurdled into the coach, which began angrily rocking. The coachman, shielded by the amphitheatre, slapped at the flanks of the gaudily accoutred horses, shouted at them, tugged at bridles. First a lead animal, then one in the second rank, reared in their traces; then all four of them plunged forward together, yanking the carriage out of its angry rocking. The coachman jumped back out of the way and sidled to safety along the base of the amphitheatre's wall.

Rattling and churning, the equipage jounced toward the opening by which the Liefs and the Court Party had originally entered the arena. The two men inside had not a bit of control over where it went or at what speed, they simply kept their heads down.

One of the reivers fired at the departing carriage. I saw him silhouetted on the wall's rim, upright among the rocks. We were almost on eye level with each other, though fortunately he didn't look my way. Fascinated, I remained where I was. I thought I could see another Pelagan crouched beside the first, staying out of sight: the profile of a hawklike head.

Because of the intervening bulk of the amphitheatre itself, the man with the rifle had only a moment to stop the carriage, that moment when it burst into view again on the other side. But by then the matter was out of the reiver's hands. Although not in full control of the situation, Gareth and Coigns had escaped. Our Shathra's horses, ears flattened and manes floating, hurtled toward the Mershead Road.

A shot from Arngrim Blaine's handgun reminded the armed Pelagan that he couldn't take aim with impunity. He slumped quickly out of sight, so quickly in fact that I thought he might be wounded.

I waited.

It was several minutes before the more articulate of the two Pelagans began taunting Gabriel Elk again. "Ilk! Ilk! You surrender! That coach going off, it means nothing!" Then the mocking couplets, a singsong of scorn. Arngrim Blaine responded; the old man translated. The old man shouted words that carried a taunt of their own. Back and forth, this colloquy of deprecation—and I began moving again.

No thinking, I told myself; *deeds only.*

In another ten minutes I had worked my way over a broken stretch in the wall and back into the gnarled rock. The voices of the Pelagans came to me more and more clearly; when the poet wasn't shouting his insults, I could hear their exchanged whispers and even the irregular breathing of one of the men. At last I could see them. I hugged a spire of rock behind their natural blind and tried to still the revving of my heart. Looking out over the grassy highlands surrounding Stonelore, I saw no sign of the chariot guard who had supposedly taken up his watch there. The Pelagans had so thoroughly dealt with him that the landscape might have cracked open and swallowed him, chariot and all.

No thinking! With that, I leapt down into the reivers' blind. Blood pounded viciously behind my eyes, rudely insistent. A face turned toward me, a face unlike any I had seen in Ongladred.

The Shattered Moons poured light over the features of that face and over the whole of the shape squatting to its left. It was the shape to the left that had the rifle, I saw the barrel glinting too late. That figure I should have attacked first—not this unarmed one, not this odd, glowering mask rising up out of its own off-balance surprise to confront me.

I could feel my fingers gripping the haft of my knife—was dimly aware of the knife itself sweeping up in an arc to my ear, the blade quivering briefly a forearm's length from the face beyond it.

Then, not wanting it to be the way it was happening, wanting a less terrible portion of the Pelagan's anatomy for a target, I pulled my knife down into his face—stabbed once—then drew back as the reiver screamed, clutched his fearsome wound, and rolled away.

(An image of the dead horses flashed into my mind.)

My weapon clattered into the rocks.

As I had done a few minutes before, I stood there upright and exposed, stupid in my immobility. The other Pelagan, his odd face somehow managing an expression utterly incredulous, began to rise. He brought his rifle up, a rifle that had been throwing off sparks and noise for over thirty minutes now, and all I could do was remark the clumsiness of his effort and the way the barrel shone so prettily. Would this thing kill me?

Then a shadow eclipsed the second reiver, knocked the rifle out of his hands, and bobbed nimbly out of harm's way. Old Robin Coigns, alias Horsesweat, had jumped into the blind and disarmed my would-be assassin.

A moment later Gareth Elk followed Coigns out of the darkness, and the three of us stood there looking down on the disarmed Pelagan. The one whom I had stabbed lay off to one side, dead or certainly dying, his face mercifully twisted away from us.

No one spoke. There was the almost peaceful sound of heavy breathing, together with a misleading glut of peaceful white moonlight. I was empty of whatever had moved me so violently to this place. A malarial dizziness still ran through my blood, but the infection itself was gone.

I looked at Robin Coigns, I looked at Gareth Elk, I looked at the disarmed Pelagan. They in turn looked at me.

ix

Back in the Stonelore arena we tried to piece the situation together.

Someone had wrapped poor Josu Lief in a blanket; the women were inside Grotto House, Our Shathra Anna and Bethel Elk senselessly comforting the dry-eyed, almost unperturbed Rhia.

In the arena, I had my first real opportunity to look at the man we had captured. He was bound. Too, since he had proven annoyingly voluble on our trip back to the arena in Our Shathra Anna's carriage, he was gagged as well. Gareth had used the man's shredded undertunic for both the binding and gagging. Now the Pelagan sat in the dirt beside the luminous amphitheatre while Coigns and the coachman tried to calm the horses, and the rest of us huddled together beside the dust-covered equipage, assessing and reassessing.

"Just look at him," Arngrim Blaine was saying. "He *isn't* a man. How can you argue that he's a man?"

"Despite his looks," Gabriel Elk said, "he's a man very much like you, Chancellor Blaine." He paused, then added sardonically: "Or me. But perhaps more like you since the people of the archipelagoes were all originally derived from

Atarite stock, and I have to confess a background predominantly Mansuecerian. Nevertheless, Chancellor, the man's a human being, not an animal."

"Look at him, Sayati Elk! Look at him!"

I looked at the Pelagan captive. The Chancellor was overreacting, as I had overreacted to my first glimpse of the face of the reiver I had killed. It was easy to see that our captive belonged to our species, although certain minor differences in physiognomy and anatomy made it possible to *pretend* an evolutionary breach had occurred.

Sitting in the dust, his knees drawn up to his chin, his head balanced sullenly there, the reiver was demonstrably human. His dark eyes followed us with the same pupil-bright disdain with which a minor court official might regard a nouveau Atarite like Ingram Marley: I knew the look. It was made bearable now by the fact that he directed it against all of us— Gabriel, Gareth, Blaine, Coigns and the coachman, as well as me. In the Pelagan's eyes, we were the subhumans, the creatures not deserving the name *Man*. He lifted his head from his knees and threw it back against the amphitheatre's wall.

These physical distinctions existed: The captive was darker than any of us; his hair hung straight and black over his forehead and ears. His upper eyelids had a tuck in them, an epicanthic fold, Gabriel said. In fact, the old man told us that the Pelagan's appearance would have once been termed at least quasi-Mongoloid. Contradicting this assessment, however, was the reiver's abundant body hair, a sparse, ravenlike down over hands, arms, and face, though so thin on our captive's face that only the moonlight and my own proximity made this hair visible; on the man I had killed this facial down had seemed more horrifying, the sort of animalization of human features that Blaine was now insisting upon. Earthly Mongoloids, Elk said, had very seldom had a great deal of hair on their faces and bodies.

Finally, our captive had a purplish patch of skin on his throat, distinctly visible now because his head was back.

"All the people of the Angromain Archipelagoes don't look like this one," Chancellor Blaine said. "I know they don't, I've had distasteful dealings with a few of them before."

"The man I killed had similar features," I said. "Face, body hair, all of it."

Gareth affirmed this. We had left the dead man in the rocks, not wanting to sully Our Shathra's carriage any more than was needful. "He even had a mark on his throat like this one."

"From what I've heard and seen," Gabriel interjected, "this type—this quasi-Mongoloid type of individual—isn't at all uncommon in the archipelagoes now. I've had dealings with the Pelagans many times, Chancellor—more often than even you have, I'd imagine—and I've seen men resembling this one more than once. The Pelagans esteem men like him," nodding toward our captive, "because they seem to be particularly daring and resourceful. Many like him are in positions of leadership."

"Do they also esteem them murderous and cruel?"

"Life in the archipelagoes is not entirely like life in Ongladred, Chancellor; values differ."

"Obviously."

"There weren't many Asians among the final population of Windfall Last," I said. "Were there?"

"No," Gabriel Elk said.

"Then why should a people who look like Asians—the tuck in the eye, the dark hair, the yellow-brown skin—suddenly appear out in the Angromain?"

"It hasn't been all that sudden; it's been incremental, Ingram—though what the precise origins of people like these are, I don't know. Maybe the Parfects *engineered* an Atarite heritage into the genes of some of those penultimate Asians in Windfall Last." Gabriel Elk, something of an engineer himself, here pronounced the word with a deliberate nasality. "The descendants of some of these individuals were undoubtedly among the Atarites who fled Ongladred a millennium ago. Ironic, yes?"

"How do you mean, ironic?" Blaine asked, visibly peeved.

"Many of the oldest Earth civilizations were Eastern. Now, out here, eight hundred light-years from our spawning place, Oriental physical characteristics are asserting themselves again."

"But altered," I said.

"Yes," the old man agreed. "Altered. As everything alters, as everything changes—except ourselves." Nobody said anything to that; the comment had a self-consciously sagely ring to it that Elk usually avoided. Moreover, the Parfects' grand experiment on Mansueceria didn't altogether support the concept of an unchanging and unchangeable human condition. Long ago, for our own good, we had been "engineered." No one could dispute that.

We were all beginning to feel the length of the day, the late-evening cold, the after-numbness of fading shock. We moved around in the arena's dust; we watched Coigns and the coachman soothing the sweaty-flanked horses, currying them with rags, talking to them; we tried to shake ourselves back into reality with random gestures and banal resolutions.

The reivers had murdered the chariot guards, just as I had earlier assumed, and the chariots' horses had more than likely pulled the empty vehicles all the way back to Lunn. This was something none of us had come to grips with yet. As was the death of Josu Lief. Coigns put the dead masker, wrapped in a borrowed blanket, into the equipage—on the seat opposite to the one on which Chancellor Blaine and Our Shathra Anna would ride.

Blaine raised no protest.

Then we all came back to our captive, the Angromain barbarian who had taken part in, perhaps even masterminded, the night's surreal carnage. The women remained in Grotto House, waiting for us to do something, regal in their patience; and at last all our movements came to revolve around the sullen, insolently watchful Pelagan who had very nearly killed me up on the rock wall.

Out of this uncertain numbness Gabriel Elk said, "Take the gag out of his mouth."

The coachman did so, stepping away as soon as the cloth was free. A film seemed to pass over our captive's eyes, he shuddered, his body feebly radiated its weariness.

Then the man began to curse us. He cursed vehemently, moving his head from side to side against the wall.

Gabriel Elk grabbed my arm and raised his voice over the belligerent cursing, "This is the other one, Ingram. No style, no subtlety. You killed the poet, the one with the flair. Did you know that?"

"Not until afterwards."

"Are you glad?"

"No," I said. I pulled my arm away. "Why should I be glad? Why should I be glad either way?"

The Pelagan stopped cursing, drawn to our disagreement. Gabriel Elk ignored him; the old man's eyes, amid leathery wrinkles, looked into mine with an intense and unsettling concentration. "You shouldn't," he said quietly. "You shouldn't be glad, Ingram. Forgive me."

"I don't know why I did what I did," I said. "I'd never killed a man before. Something happened to me."

"Never mind that now, Ingram," the old man said. He turned to his son. "He's run out of curses for the moment, Gareth; while he's quiet, put something on his wound. Clean it out first."

The boy moved to do his father's bidding. Arngrim Blaine said, "We needn't let our humanitarianism run past the cup's lip, Sayati Elk," but his voice carried no real rebuke and he didn't try to impede Gareth's bandaging of the captive.

The captive himself clenched his teeth while Gareth worked at his shoulder, but kept his eyes suspiciously on the boy, now and again letting them rove to our faces as well—where they seared their suspicion and disdain into our flesh. I tried to return the man's intermittent stares; in the attempt I noticed something utterly untoward and startling in his expression.

The barbarian's mouth reminded me of Bronwen Lief's. The dead girl shared with this archipelago dweller an almost imperceptible pout, a downtugging of one corner of the lower lip, that flawed an otherwise innocent and lovely face.

For the Pelagan was handsome. Despite the epicanthic fold, despite the darkness of his complexion, despite the hair on hands, arms, and face, he was imposingly handsome—in a ruggedly exotic way that no Ongladredan ever could be. But the set of his mouth! The set of his mouth sabotaged this alien handsomeness. That he should share such a flaw with Bronwen Lief, who had danced and declaimed as Gabriel Elk had programmed her to, amazed me. In the upland cold, the wind moaning through the rocks, I stared at him.

Then his eyes caught mine, and I had to look away.

Gareth was finished with him. "Are you going to take him back to Lunn in the coach?" the boy asked. He pulled the captive to his feet.

"No," Blaine said. "We have a dead man there already. The widow will ride with us, but I don't want Our Shathra Anna exposed to the Pelagan's presence any longer than is necessary; if possible, not at all. Ingram," turning to me, "I'd like you, young Elk here, and the ostler to walk the prisoner back to Lunn, if you would. We have no horses now but those on the carriage, and this man is too insolently disposed against us to bleed to death from his wounds on the trip back. I'm sorry to ask it, but I don't see any other immediate alternatives."

"Very well," I said. I didn't relish the walk, especially in the company of a man whose stare burned so piercingly.

Elk said, "You could leave the prisoner here tonight, Chancellor Blaine, and send someone back for him in the morning."

"No," Blaine said. "You may well have a secure place for him in Grotto House, but I want him back in Lunn as soon as possible. I intend to have him questioned quite thoroughly about the activities of Pelagan reivers and the likelihood of a concerted invasion by the entire Angromain. When? Where? How? I don't want there to be any chance at all that he might escape from your custody, Sayati Elk; the responsibility is too great."

"I'm not sure I want Gareth and Coigns on the Mershead Road tonight," the old man said. "They've been conscripted, yes, but their service doesn't begin until the day after tomorrow. Why should I let them go? A night is a long time, and it may be an even longer time after Gareth enters the Lunn garrison before Bethel and I see him again."

Blaine protested, "Ingram can't take this man back alone!"

"No," Gabriel Elk said. "The responsibility's too great. I don't propose that Master Marley go alone."

Arngrim Blaine pulled his cloak tight over his throat, crushing the lace there. His lips parted slightly; the carnelian tooth gleamed in the opening. He sensed some Elkian maneuver he would be powerless to avert. "Please, Sayati Elk, don't toy with me tonight. What is it you want?"

"Isn't it true you intend to cut short Master Marley's scrutiny of me and Stonelore? You're returning him to the palace?"

"That was my intention."

"I want him to stay."

"It was my impression you considered him a barely tolerable nuisance, Sayati Elk. He's been out here thirteen days eating your food, sleeping in your beds, an acknowledged agent of Our Shathra's Eyes and Ears—and tonight you decide you want him to stay? Why? Please enlighten me."

"The why is immaterial, Chancellor Blaine. My proposal is that I allow Gareth and Coigns to accompany Ingram and the prisoner *if* you send Ingram back to Stonelore on the day my son and the ostler report for duty—if not before."

"For how long?"

"Until Gareth and Coigns return."

Blaine looked at me with contempt. "You want to keep this indolent dirt-runner until the Halcyon Panic breaks, the Pelagans invade, the sloak crawls up, and Ongladred sinks into the Nathlin Trench? He's been on an extended sabbatical already, Sayati Elk, idling, idling every minute."

"I'll have work for him. Don't fear otherwise."

And so it was decided.

Our Shathra Anna and Rhia Lief climbed into the equipage with Arngrim Blaine, and the coachman galloped the tired horses through the Stonelore arena and down to the Mershead Road. Since there was no help for it, they went unguarded—although both the coachman and the Chancellor carried rifles on their laps.

As soon as they were gone, Gareth, Coigns, and I set off with our Pelagan captive, whose renewed curses required us to gag him again. Blood had welled up through the bandage on his shoulder, but the man seemed none the worse for it.

"See that he's treated humanely, Ingram," Bethel Elk said to me as we were leaving.

"Aye," her husband echoed her. "See to it."

Down from the upland arena we went on stiff legs. Wind rippled the tall grasses. The Shattered Moons passed their shadows through the wind and careened among themselves like drunken soldiers. We reached Lunn well before dawn. Robin Coigns and Gareth Elk returned at once to Stonelore, refusing beds and breakfast at the Atarite Palace. I refused only breakfast. I slept a long time, untroubled by any nightmares of the murder I had committed.

Later, I learned that representatives of the Magi had tortured the Pelagan captive for information. The man died on the second day after our trek back from Stonelore; he died without imparting a single nugget of intelligence—not his name, not his dead companion's name, not the Angromain island from which they had set out, not the purpose of their reiving. Not anything. Every torture he had endured, reviling his tormentors each time he could summon breath to do so. A remarkable performance, the representatives of the Magi said. I had slept through a good part of it, oblivious to his suffering. What would the Elks say to me when I returned?

Several days after the man's death, when I had firmly renewed my residence in Grotto House, three fishermen found a two-man boat nine kilometers north of Mershead. The boat had been concealed in a cave on the shoreline cliff faces; undoubtedly it had belonged to the men who had attacked us, killed our horses, and murdered Josu Lief and the chariot guards. A two-man reiving party. Together they had come at least thirty kilometers, mostly at night, in an open boat.

On the side of the boat, painted there in a thick indigo pigment, was a cryptic symbol. It looked like this:

X

Gabriel Elk indeed had work for me. The state had taken Gareth away from him, and the spring equinox drew inexorably nearer. With the equinox's approach came also the beginning of the old man's annual series of neuro-dramas. In preparation for these, he forced me to undertake a strenuous apprenticeship. I was to serve as Gareth's replacement in the comptroller room beneath the Stonelore amphitheatre. That I had little aptitude for such work Gabriel Elk refused to concede. He had need of me.

So long as no more than three reanimated maskers were taking part in the action in the neuro-pit, the old man required no help. But when more actors moved into the sunken "stage" from below, another comptroller had to assist him. I was to be the second comptroller. During the concentrated weeks of my training, the old man permitted me very little time to myself. I learned everything about neuro-drama that Elk could impart and that I was capable of absorbing.

I learned that none of Gabriel Elk's compositions called for more than six performers. When operating with a full cast, he controlled three corpses and I controlled three. Neural programming prior to each performance took care only of facial expressions and speech; the majority of the actors' movements Elk and I had to direct from beneath the neuro-pit by remote control. Stamina was required of us because each drama adhered to rigid Aristotelian standards of unity, and we sometimes held our swivel chairs—amid console banks, sweat-inducing light, and closed-circuit television screens—for more than two hours at a stretch. An additional burden devolved upon us because the plays also invariably made use of pantomimic elements from an Oriental form called the *Noh* drama; these posings and gestures demanded of us a kind of agonizing, empathic monitoring. Moreover, we had to take care of Stonelore's lighting, the operation of the pneumatic lift in the center of the working area, and the synchronization of musical scores with the action going on overhead.

One of my most vivid memories of that time is of my introduction to the dead actors; this occurred on the second day after my return to Grotto House, when I was beginning my apprenticeship.

"Come, Ingram," Gabriel Elk said. "It's time you lost your innocence. We can't really begin work until you've seen them."

Together we went by elevator from the main level of Grotto House down into the programming room. Into the rock, into the realm of cybernetic miracles. But we didn't stop here. Elk guided me through this first crowded vault to a massive door opening on the tunnel leading to the Stonelore comptroller room.

The tunnel, the entire underground complex, called up in me uncomfortable sensations of *déjà vu*—and not because I had once carried Bronwen Lief into the programming room; no, I felt as if in some indefinable past incarnation I had denied the light and entered a secret, subterranean mausoleum resembling this one, out of which I had emerged as pale as a dead man. The tunnel was lit by red lights; we stood for a moment in its mouth, looking toward the sealed comptroller room. Then we walked a few meters to a door on the corridor's righthand wall; here the old man admitted us to the dormitory of our dead colleagues, cohorts in Gabriel Elk's singular repertory company.

This room was cold, icily cold.

The corpses that Elk had purchased lay in hard white plastic coffins, or preservators, with crystalline lids. A rank of three preservators on each side of the room, a narrow aisle in between. Each unit had its own self-regulating cryostat; all shared linkage with a central system of storage tanks containing liquid oxygen, these ice-touched canisters ranged like bright, upended cannon barrels against the far wall. Or like organ pipes.

Yes, I thought, *like organ pipes.* As if each sleeping actor were listening to cathedral music in the numb privacy of his own death, forevermore plugged into the storage tanks' silent anthems, the seethe of unendurable cold.

I looked down through the unfrosted glass of a preservator at Bronwen Lief's face. Unchanged, she slept.

I moved down the aisle.

Through the crystalline lids I looked at the faces of four men and another woman. The masker woman appeared haggish and diseased. The men offered almost a cross-section of the male Mansuecerian population, two being relatively young, one stout and middle-aged, the fourth cruelly wizened by six or seven decades of Ongladredan winters. These were Gabriel's players.

I looked back at my host. He began telling me the names of the five performers new to me. About each he recited a litany of biographical information: birthplaces, families, occupations, accomplishments, failures, and, finally, manners of dying.

"Did you know any of them while they were alive?" I asked him.

"No." He looked at me, then exhaled another puff of breath. "But I found out as much as I could about them over the winter. I bought all of them this past winter—except for Bronwen. I had to wait for her."

"You buy every winter?"

"I have to. I burn them out, Ingram. One season at Stonelore burns them out, as life never really has the chance to do."

"Do you program every one of them before the season begins? Then re-program them before each new play?"

"The ones who have roles always require surgical adaptation, electrode implanting, cybernetic neural grafting—the last of which enables us to control our performers from beneath the amphitheatre, Ingram. I'll work extensively on the ones who carry the brunt of the dramatic situation, less thoroughly on the others. Sometimes a performer will be masked, easing the preparatory burden on me; sometimes an actor or two will not have a speaking part. But the work's there, it exists. Your own efforts at Stonelore, Ingram, will be confined to the mechanics of immediate control, as were Gareth's; I'm not even going to try to introduce you to the other. That's my specialty, my hands and mind are inured to its tediousness."

"And when the season's over, Sayati Elk? What have you gained? And our burnt-out company of players," sweeping my arm backward over the sleek, insidiously still coffins, "what becomes of them?"

"Cremation. The funeral of Atarites rather than Mansuecerians, since in their last days—their artificial, posthumous lives—they will have behaved like people touched with fire. A death they have—then a brief, violently intense second life here at Stonelore—then a second, incontrovertible death. After which we put their burnt-out bodies to the torch and let the smoke curl up to Maz from the autumn bonfires."

I thought of the sloak, of the fires burning on every beach, inlet, and strip of coast around Ongladred. What must those tiny pyres look like from the air? If the Parfects were indeed orbiting our planet amid the concealing Shattered Moons, wouldn't they realize the bonfires were cries for help?

Standing in Elk's cryogenic locker, I shivered and shook the thought away. "But you, Sayati Elk," I said, returning to an old question, "what do you gain?"

His pale green eyes, combining ice and fire, lifted to mine; then he turned and walked out of the chamber, forcing me to follow.

Materially he gained very little.

On the nights when Elk and I sat in our cramped control niches beneath Stonelore, the Mansuecerians who filed into the theatre and filled its concentric tiers always "paid" for their seats, not so much from economic obligation as out of a ritualistic impulse to honor the old man. No one was forced to give anything, but nearly every masker made a token donation of three or four mithras when he entered, dropping the small coins into an open-mouthed urn beside the theatre's inner doors. Elk fed this money back to the state, which taxed him mercilessly. Or else, in the autumn and winter, he used the small surpluses remaining to him to buy new performers and to acquire materials unavailable to most Ongladredans. Genius and madman, he was neither fish nor fowl, masker nor Atarite; he bridged the social order.

He bought materials and equipment from Atarites whose wealth, station, and access to the Old Knowledge had bestowed upon them the benefits of an incipient technology. In fact, throughout his life Gabriel Elk had striven to assemble as many pieces of the Old Knowledge as he could buy, extort, or cajole from those privileged enough to possess it. His library in Grotto House was a tribute to this effort: forty thousand microchips, meticulously catalogued, all of them facsimiles of those the Parfects had given to humankind when we were dropped off, like so many unwanted curs, onto the rocky, gong-tormented planet of Mansueceria. Twice the Old Knowledge had survived the dissolution of Ongladredan civilization; twice it had been at least partially restored by foresighted men who had found one another in the ruins. Now Gabriel Elk had his share of it, and the neuro-dramas, I discovered, both drew upon the Old Knowledge and radically augmented it, made it new. So perhaps this was one of the things Gabriel Elk gained from Stonelore, the satisfaction of an omnivorous mind communing across time and interstellar distance with its intellectual forebears. But that wasn't the whole of it. After all, the process had begun with Elk long before Stonelore, and it would have gone on until the old man's death, in different manifestations, even if the amphitheatre had never been built.

Why, then, this kind of agonizing labor, the reanimating of corpses, the sweat and the emotional stridency of control? I didn't really have an answer.

One night, during the first week of the dramas, while Elk—helmeted and wired—was directing the action in the neuropit, I leaned back in my swivel chair and stared with bleary eyes at my console's central television screen.

There the haggish old woman and the middle-aged man acted out their parts in Elk's drama *Agon*.[*] Life-sized figures projected as electrons through a cathode-ray tube and reassembled on the sensitized face of my receiver as tiny parodies of themselves. They hitched and spasmed on the screen, seemingly kilometers away, even of another universe; thin and metallic, almost garbled, their voices came through my headset. The spectacle grew violent as the woman brandished a temple knife and shrilly cursed her adversary.

How was our audience reacting?

I had no controlling to do for at least another fifty or sixty lines. I turned in my chair. I saw Elk across the room from me, his shoulders pushing forward, his arms stretched like knotted cables over the console top, his fingers curled beneath eight different switches at once and ceaselessly shifting among these. The cord-trailing helmet he wore gave him the look of a stocky, bellicose medusa.

Facing my own console again, I directed one of the cameras in the amphitheatre to scan our audience. I watched the lefthand monitor above my comptroller unit. In Stonelore's darkness the camera scanned by means of infrared floodlighting and a quartz-lens relay. Tier after tier of masker faces, all rigid beneath the movement of the camera, and because of the ongoing conscription program many of these faces belonged to women, the elderly, and the very young.

I halted the camera. I brought a section of the audience into startling close-up.

On my flickering monitor I studied the expressions on their faces. A revelation discouragingly grim, not because the maskers appeared either stern or disapproving but because their eyes and mouths betrayed no emotion at all; they sat, merely sat, gazing down upon our actors and partaking of Elk's surcharged dramaturgy as if it were no more real than an indifferent daydream.

Faces rigid with blandness; eyes too wide-awake and attentive to suggest apathy, but so noncommittal as to be damnnear inhuman.

As I watched the faces on the monitor, I began to feel that our audience wanted reanimating even more than had our dead actors, the ones who now vigorously shadowed forth Gabriel Elk's vision. The dead vicariously living through the dead, our audience seemed.

Then I had to go to work again. My visor came down. The pneumatic lift carried another actor into the arena, this one a young man under my direction. My eyes turned from the lefthand monitor to the screen in the center. Watching this, I let my hands direct the movements of my protégé's hands; I wandered into his mind, then activated Elk's neural programming of the speech centers, and withdrew. My presence was external then, a transferral of will conveyed by delicate mechanical means and the aching implementation of rote memory—mine. For twenty more minutes I sweated (eventually controlling Bronwen Lief as well as the young masker) while Elk deployed every one of his corpses and kept them all hitching and spasming about like the decrepit primitives they were supposed to be: a *tour de force* of comptrolling.

Then *Agon* was over.

Wearily I leaned back in my chair. I looked at my lefthand monitor and saw that the closed-circuit camera was still scanning our audience, relaying their images into the comptroller room as they sat unmoving and seemingly unmoved in the rising houselights. Again, that infuriating and universal expressionlessness!

Finally they stood and, talking desultorily with one another or saying nothing at all, filed out of Stonelore into the night, a regiment of automatons. When they were gone, the amphitheatre was no more quiet than it had been while they were there. I turned to Elk, who had unhelmeted himself and swiveled toward me.

"Three nights in a row, Sayati Elk. Are they always like that?"

"Yes. Usually." His sideburns were matted, the lower portions curled moistly over his cheeks; his eyes red-rimmed and narrow. He looked very old that night, every one of his sixty-three years.

"You mean we can expect a response no more lively than what we've had these last three nights?"

"Probably not a bit livelier than this, Ingram."

"A regiment of automatons," I said. "Blaine's conscripted almost all the men of fighting age, but there's still a regiment of automatons—several regiments—in Lunn, Brechtlin, and Mershead; they come out to Stonelore every night."

"Different ones come on different nights, Ingram. And they're not, as you would style them, *automatons.*"

"How judge a masker except on the basis of his behavior, Sayati Elk?"

"With the People Accustomed to the Hand one has to judge on the basis of *significant,* not just conspicuous, behavior."

I shook my head. "I don't understand you, Sayati Elk; I've sweated through this with you three times now and still don't understand why you do it. The money is nothing to you, and the maskers file out every evening as if they've simply wanted a warm place to sit for an hour or two. It demoralizes me, Sayati Elk, it guts me of purpose and initiative. Whereas you . . ." My unfinished sentence hung in the room between the two of us.

Then Elk said, "Whereas I notice that they come back, Ingram. No one forces them to come, but they come back—performance after performance in the spring and summer, year after year."

He stood up. "They always come back," he reiterated quietly.

Then we went about the task of securing the comptroller room and caring for our feverish performers. I worked without speaking, in a spirit of weary half-comprehension of what he had told me and of listless ignorance of what he had left out. We spent a good deal of time pushing the mobile preservators up and down the tunnel.

Afterwards I slept, slept dreamlessly. And woke on the next morning to anticipate another evening in the comptroller room—for, as usual, Stonelore would be full.

xi

Away from Stonelore things were happening. During the fifteen successive presentations of *Agon* events in the outside world threatened to break in upon us, to force us out of our isolation.

The far northern coasts of Ongladred, four hundred kilometers from Lunn, had begun to suffer the first of a number of Pelagan naval assaults. From what we heard, these were not merely the hit-and-run tactics of foolhardy reivers operating singly and apparently at whim, but the tentative strikes of a nation testing its full-scale capacities for war. Usually one or two large Pelagan vessels slipped through the veils of night and wind-whipped spray to fire their cannons at a coastal village and the small ships in harbor there. The bonfires crackling jewel-like at intervals along the coast to hold off the sloak did nothing but illuminate the barbarians' targets, betray the simple people who had set the fires.

Prows like dragons, sails like reptilian wings, banners like streaming serpents' tongues, witnesses said. Then, having wrought their sudden destruction, the ships were gone back into the night and the mocking sea wind.

But the little fishing village of Nogos, we heard, had not

escaped so easily; the Pelagans had come ashore, murdered most of the citizenry in their beds, abducted perhaps twenty more people, and then fled seaward. The following day several fishermen from south of Nogos found bodies floating in their fishing grounds; most of the corpses had been stricken at and mutilated by boarnoses (sharklike creatures infesting the iciest waters of the Angromain Run). On the second morning after the attack at Nogos, two or three more bodies were washed up by the tide near Thumbre.

Because of the latitude and their remove from the main islands of the Angromain Archipelago, the people in the north of Ongladred had felt themselves safe from this kind of brutal harassment. The Atarite Court in Lunn had agreed; most of the state's forces were positioned along our island's southern and eastern coasts, and not only because Arngrim Blaine wished to preserve Lunn over any other Ongladredan city. No. Lunn was vulnerable, that was all. The greatest portion of our navy, therefore, lay just off the coasts where our troops were encamped, a defensive barrier against the Pelagan fleet. Reivers had penetrated the barrier at night, yes, but Blaine reasoned that our enemies would have a difficult time sneaking a hundred large warships past us. Now it appeared that the Pelagans would not even try; instead they would sail their dragon vessels east from their own islands, away from Ongladred, circle then toward the polar cap, and descend on us from the White Sea and the multicolored Angromain Run.

Two days after the devastation of Nogos, four after the first hit-and-run raids on other villages, Our Shathra Anna ordered a reprisal.

She ordered seven of our galleons to strike swiftly and heavily at Orcland, the largest island of the Angromain group and the suspected seat of the newly centralized Pelagan government.

At Stonelore, Elk and I were preparing for the ninth performance of *Agon*. We were in complete ignorance of what was happening over seventy kilometers out to sea. Later we learned.

The reprisal strike had failed.

Several ships of the Pelagan fleet had intercepted our galleons more than an hour from the Orcland coast. Firing without warning, they had sunk three Ongladredan raiders, captured one ship, crippled two more, and sent the cripples limping home in the wake of our only unscathed galleon. Our enemies, it seemed, were strong, resourceful, and determined to establish themselves, eventually, as masters of Ongladred.

That much we learned; little more.

For the most part, Gabriel Elk ignored these developments, although on two or three occasions I managed to draw him into brief, unrevealing discussions. The only link he and Bethel recognized between themselves and the fortunes of the state was their son, Gareth. He and Coigns had been assigned away from the Lunn garrison to the infantry forces of Pavan Nils Barrow, now encamped outside the northern coastal city of Thumbre. Bethel Elk, from all external appearances, saw this link as much more significant than her husband did; she feared for her son, but she also feared for Field-Pavan Barrow and the people of Firthshir Province.

One day she asked me, "Do you think the Pelagans will land up there, Ingram?" She faced me stiffly, her back held erect by the brace.

"I don't know. Except for a few reivers, they've shown a general reluctance to put us to the trial down here—if that tells us anything. The raids on Nogos and the other villages must mean something, too, Mistress Elk. A clue to their plans."

"It's almost summer now," she said. "But it's still cold up there, isn't it, Ingram? Like winter?"

"Yes. Or very early spring."

"Gareth and Coigns have blankets and woolen coats. I hope the others are as lucky." Then she left me where I sat, in Grotto House's open courtyard, enjoying the warmth of pale Maz.

During the days, Gabriel Elk left me to myself.

He spent most of his time reworking the formal lyric passages of the dramas he had composed over the winter. A little time he spent in the programming room, forecasting the methods and the equipment he would use in preparing our actors for new roles. As soon as *Agon* was over, the mechanical work would begin. In the interval he concentrated on perfecting the odes and the rhymed variety of stichomythia in which he often had his characters speak, parrying epigram with epigram. All I could get from him was that the next two dramas completed a trilogy whose subject was "human suffering and achievement." After which pronouncement, he grinned.

First, *Agon*. Then plays entitled *Anabasis in Spring* and *Omega Thwarted*. The titles meant nothing to me, but Elk gave me to understand that the trilogy represented a new direction in his work. Again, I didn't know. I had neither seen nor read any of his previous neuro-dramas.

Now he was revising *Anabasis in Spring*. I had nothing to do but wander about Grotto House thinking on the frivolity of "enlightening" the masker population of Lunn, Brechtlin, and Mershead while the villages of Firthshir Province burned. An enlightened masker, as far as I could see, behaved no differently from one who dwelt in deadpan ignorance.

Then our fifteen performances of *Agon* were over. The island was growing into summer—real summer—with meadow flowers nodding yellow and blue heads among the dull upland grasses. Fifteen days we had; then Elk and I would be back in the rending, grey world of the comptroller room.

Our fifteen days out of the comptroller room were no vacation. Although we did get to see the anaita-roses fluttering—and the little blue flowers whose name I never learned (but remembered from Rhia Lief's embroidery)—and to feel the southerly sea wind, the *malooh*, blow like invisible velvet over our skins, these respites were rare. While Elk prepared corpses, I prepared myself. That preparation consisted of reading *Anabasis in Spring* and studying as well its diagram-laden companion, a Manual of Control. This last was a bleak little booklet in Elk's own minute longhand. Like some of the flowers around Stonelore, the ink (I remember) was violet.

As summer came on, so did the rumor and the fact of Pelagan hostility. On one of these days between dramas, during the period of preparation, I caught Elk in Grotto House's dining chamber and sat down beside him. "I'm afraid I'm beginning to be of Chancellor Blaine's persuasion, Sayati Elk. What we're doing, how do we justify it? I can appreciate the aesthetic experience of the neuro-dramas, or at least I can before the tedium of comptrolling blunts my responses—but too many things are happening beyond Stonelore, things of genuine moment, for me to rest easy here any longer. I'd like to go back to Lunn, to the Atarite Palace."

"Oh?" The old man leaned back in his chair, a heavy wooden chair with thick arms. "What will you do when you get back there, volunteer for a seaman's position?"

"As a member of the court, even as a relatively obscure dirt-runner, I'm—"

"You're exempt from any such demeaning service. I know, Ingram. So what will you do while 'things of genuine moment' confront your countrymen?"

"Whatever Our Shathra Anna and Chancellor Blaine require of me."

"Ah, duty; a noble sentiment, Master Marley." It had been a while since he had slapped me with "Master Marley." "For now, because Gareth's been taken from me, they require you to serve Ongladred by aiding me."

"The two are equivalent, I suppose?"

"No, no, Ingram. I don't suffer from that delusion. Besides, as you know, Arngrim Blaine doesn't equate the two. To keep you out here, I intimidated him."

"Then we're back to my original question, Sayati Elk. If my service to you isn't really service to Ongladred, why do we nearly kill ourselves for an audience whose only response is to come back as listless as they left? What are we accomplishing?" I had to pin the old man down.

But he said, "Service is of different types, Ingram, and some varieties of it lie outside the stagnant pale of nationalism and duty. This is one of those. What we're accomplishing, though, I won't try to tell you—won't even try to articulate yet for myself. I'm a selfish old man, Ingram. *Selfish* and *old*, those are the key words. And if I'm deluded at all, it may be in the assumption that my selfishness serves Ongladred better than would a dutiful renunciation of self. At least for now. This, like all things, may change. . . ."

And so we ignored the continuing depredations in the north; we forgot the fragrance of the anaita-roses, the freshness of the maloob blowing inland across a summer ocean.

Here is a summary of that time: The Ongladredan fleet overextended itself attempting to establish a defensive line across the coasts of Firthshir, Vestacs, and Eenlich provinces;

Elk and I, toward the end of our fifteen-day preparation period, began giving up great chunks of sleep time, courting exhaustion. Galleons burned; my morale sank. Rumors of impending invasion reached us via the itinerant tinkers and tradesboys who sometimes stopped at Grotto House; in my sleep I saw the amphitheatre filling with maskers who wore, under faces bitingly vacant, tunics emblazoned with this:

☯   Then, receiving only token resistance, the Pelagans landed an army of almost eight thousand men in Eenlich; on the evening of that day Gabriel Elk opened Stonelore for the first performance of *Anabasis in Spring*. Just as the Angromain barbarians had committed themselves in the north, we too had gone past the point of abjuration. Two darkly improbable enterprises had been set in motion, the Pelagans' and ours.

"How do you like the title of my play now?" Gabriel Elk asked me. "I'm a prophet in my own land, unhonored and indifferent to my neglect. The Pelagans, your erstwhile brothers, Atarites under the skin, march upon us. And my play predicts it."

"Pillars crumble. People die. And we—"

"—*fiddle*. Is that the word you're looking for? Remember one thing, Ingram: Gareth's up there in Firthshir, with Barrow's forces."

I turned away from him. So he was aware, coldly aware of the situation. Why, then, our singlemindedness in putting on a neuro-drama, in running corpses through an intricate, *unreal* series of events? Apparently Elk had his own satisfactions; I had only the sweat. My back to Gabriel Elk, I looked at the lefthand monitor.

Our audience was filing in.

"People die," the old man was saying, talking to the back of my head. "But not these. These still live, Ingram." I could feel his eyes fixed on my monitor. Together we watched the audience come in:

Women, children, old men, cripples of every conceivable sort:

The bent, the legless, the scarred, the humpbacked, even the blind. All of them People Accustomed to the Hand, maskers who had come to Stonelore for undivulged reasons of their own.

Then Elk swiveled away from me, faced his own control console, signaled to me that we were about to begin. I put on my helmet, shut out my thoughts, turned a dial, and plunged the amphitheatre into darkness. The sweat, the sweat of comptrolling.

And that night Elk and I, working together, working begrudgingly together, orchestrated a beautiful performance of *Anabasis in Spring*. The poetry came through my headset; the alternating grace and clumsiness of our actors poured into me like haoma. I was a part of Elk's poetry, I was a part of our actors' movement. The sweat of comptrolling turned into the sweat of participation.

In the neuro-pit above us two dead men are discussing the cycle of the sloak; I am both dead men, two young soldiers. Then enter the corpse of the haggish old woman, inhabited now by Gabriel Elk. She is masked like a demon, somehow enormous and dreadful in spite of her tiny bones and frail gestures. To the soldiers she is an apparition, a minion of hidden powers. In a long, image-crowded speech she tells them the sloak is real, that it does the bidding not of its own protoplasmic desires but of a watchful intelligence external to itself—an intelligence vastly more alive than Man's but different in kind. She dances while she speaks, and her huge, one-eyed mask seems to float between her upraised arms like a kite to which her thin, twisting body is the knotted tail. As the accompaniment of tabor and flute grows more insistent, her head—her leering mask—threatens to pull her aloft, lift her into soaring flight. But the music stops, her speech ends, and the hag disappears into the underworld. The two soldiers whom I inhabit stare after her in awe and consternation.

That scene, even in the observation of *Elk's* comptrolling, wrung me of energy. There were other such scenes.

Anabasis in Spring dealt not only with the threat of the sloak, but also with the problems of command in an army relentlessly on the march. It was not prophecy, as Elk had said it was, because one could not help feeling that the sloak and the army in this neuro-drama existed in an altogether different realm of experience, another world; everything was distanced, set at a remove—in spite of which the actions and feelings of the characters had an uncanny immediacy.

Still, though overwhelmed by the poetry and the detail Elk had lavished on this spectacle, I knew that it wasn't real. What relation did it have to reality? To the sloak and to the Pelagan forces? The real sloak, the real invaders? So absolutely powerful in Stonelore's comptroller room, Elk and I were ironically powerless in the face of these threatening certainties. Was Elk withdrawing into prophecy, abandoning the real for the sake of artificial order and contrived significance? He had said no. He had said that I ought to remember the dilemma of his son, which he had not forgotten either—which he could not forget.

Wrung out at play's end, I pushed my visor back and remembered nothing, thought nothing. The sweat of comptrolling, the sweat of participation, was dry on my neck. Elk stood behind me, a hand on my shoulder. Together we watched the maskers file out: the women, the children, the old men, the crippled and the deformed. Their faces were as dull as the underside of a leaf, their eyes were the wicks of guttered candles. Only a few of them talked.

"Nothing," I said. "Nothing."

We presented *Anabasis in Spring* on three more evenings. Then stopped—but not because of this lack of discernible response on our audience's part. No. Events intervened, events and Our Shathra Anna. Against history and royalty Gabriel Elk ultimately had no more resources than did the simplest masker. And on the following morning history and royalty came to Grotto House in the person of Chancellor Arngrim Blaine.

PART TWO

xii

His roan tooth glistening, slashing like a miniature tusk, Arngrim Blaine said, "The Halcyon Panic has broken, Sayati Elk. It's broken, and I believe your neuro-dramas have been instrumental in destroying our citizenry's calm." Anger lay under the planes of his thin, expressive face like a ripening bruise.

"Obviously you haven't attended a neuro-drama this season," I said. We were sitting in Gabriel Elk's quiet little study on the main level of Grotto House; the room contained leatherbound books—not microchips, but books. Both the Elks were present, in adjacent, meticulously carven chairs.

Bethel said, "The people have been kept abreast of the events in Firthshir, haven't they?"

"They have, Mistress Elk."

"Then how can you blame the people's distress—the breaking of the panic, as you call it, Chancellor—on my husband's dramas, not a one of which you have seen in its entirety? The Lief girl's performance doesn't count."

"I can do so, Mistress Elk, because things have culminated much too soon; the misdirected rage the young women of

Lunn have exhibited in the last two days comes well ahead of schedule, it defies the computations of the Magi."

Gabriel Elk said, "But then again, Chancellor Blaine, the Pelagan invasion has taken place sooner than the Magi expected."

"And the rage of the young Mansuecerian women, the wives of our soldiers and seamen," Bethel Elk said, "has been growing for a long time. That rage has been building since well before the Magi decreed the existence of a 'Halcyon Panic.' It's the product of a long-ingrained and periodically aggravated sense of helplessness, which I feel too, Chancellor Blaine."

"I don't doubt that you do. However, Our Shathra Anna—who is, as I shouldn't have to remind you, a woman too—says that the 'sense of helplessness' you speak of need not reveal itself in hysteria and acts of vandalism."

Bethel Elk said, "Our Shathra Anna's experience has hardly been typical."

A chill descended upon Gabriel Elk's study, like a dust of invisible snow sifting out of the very air. We were all as separate as corpses put up in our own sealed, sound-muffling preservators. Who would resurrect us?

I looked at Blaine, sitting cross-legged opposite me. He had come to Grotto House that morning dressed not as the Chancellor of Ongladred, nor even as a member of the Atarite Court, but instead like a reasonably successful masker tradesman. Two young guards had accompanied him, posing as his sons. All these precautions had grown out of the wish to prevent a visit as disastrous as Our Shathra Anna's last one. And yet the Chancellor had come himself, he had not sent a representative.

Coolly he said, "Listen to me. Two days ago—the day after your newest production had opened, Sayati Elk—a large group of young women left Lunn, marched out the Mershead Road, and began turning over vegetable booths and fish stalls. Not the ones run by old men or other women, but those tended by masker tradesmen whom we've exempted from military service—or else booths owned by minor Atarite officials. There was no stopping these women."

"In that case," Gabriel Elk laughed, "your choice of disguises could have been wiser."

Arngrim Blaine ignored this. "That night a pack of children—turned loose by their mothers, I've no doubt—ran into the thoroughfare beneath my offices and began chanting a litany to Maz, asking Him to blow Himself up and Ongladred, too, so that we might at least die in the light." The Chancellor permitted himself a wan smile. "We had no success either in catching the children or in driving them away; the ones whom the guards did catch were inevitably replaced by others, all crying together, 'Maz, Maz, destroy us in light. Preserve us from the slime of the sloak and the knives of barbarians. Let the lie die.' A litany drummed into them by women."

"Your sleep was spoiled," Bethel Elk commiserated.

"Oh, that episode has its amusing aspects; I'm not blind to them. But that same night some hysterical person, or group of persons, set fire to a row of dwellings on Lunn's southwestern outskirts. The houses all burned, and several people died, including children, Mistress Elk. A violet pall of smoke hung over the rooftops, quite lurid under the Shattered Moons, I assure you. And yesterday the wail of keening women filled the streets—issued from every house—from dawn until long after nightfall, a general lamentation the likes of which I've never heard in Lunn. I'm surprised you didn't hear it out here.

"Then yesterday—since the keening doesn't by any means end the matter—a procession of old women, as many as two hundred or so, walked all the way from Lunn to Brechtlin, on the point opposite Mershead, and disrobed on the beaches. After that, they waded into the sea and kept wading until their strength gave out and they drowned. These were widows, unmarried women, grandmothers. None of the Mansuecerian population tried to stop them; that they be left alone seemed to be the unspoken desire of even their relatives. We dispatched a few Atarite guardsmen to turn them back, but the women wouldn't be reasoned with—and simple coercion failed, from want of enough men to restrain them. Into the water they went, naked pathetic creatures obeying an hysteria beyond my comprehension, Mistress Elk. Even now they are being buried, all the washed-ashore corpses no one will come forward to identify.

"And these things—the arson, the keening, the senseless suicides—are *not* amusing, friends. They betoken the depth of our citizenry's fear."

A different kind of silence filled the study then. Arngrim Blaine had reasserted his dignity. The four of us sat there, self-conscious, in its palpable aura. At last Bethel said, "And you believe that *Agon* and *Anabasis in Spring* are responsible for these things, Chancellor?"

"In part, yes."

"I would like to think you are right," the old man said.

"May I ask why?" the Chancellor said curtly.

"Certainly. Everyone requires a degree of power, no matter how minute."

"Of this sort? Power to cause suicides and arson?"

"If one is weak, yes. However, I'm not a weak man, Chancellor, and that's not what I require in power. I see in these atypical patterns of behavior—this hysteria—the potential for something constructive. It's that germ of constructiveness I would like to think my neuro-dramas help nourish. In all the negative acts of the last three days there is a thin, affirmative thread."

"Very thin." The Chancellor's lips hardly parted. "Very thin."

I said, "The best explanation for this behavior is not the neuro-dramas, but the news from Firthshir."

"That figures prominently," Chancellor Blaine said. "Certainly I don't dismiss it. In fact, I ought to tell you that the Pelagan forces have pushed out of Firthshir into Eenlich Province, driving Field-Pavan Barrow's army before them." He paused. "There's no word of casualties. As far as I know, Gareth and Coigns are alive. On this point I can't say any more; I don't know any more.

"Messages have described the retreats as 'strategic,' but the fact remains that we're losing ground daily. Fields are being burned, early crops destroyed, animals slaughtered, and small hamlets overrun and subsequently abandoned. The enemy supplies himself at our expense. This is changing, however. A runner from Pavan Barrow reports that our people have begun to destroy any goods that may be useful to the Pelagans; the procedure now is burn and fall back, burn and fall back. We want to force the barbarians to be dependent on their own supply lines—in the hope that we can establish an unmoving front and then interdict at sea, destroy their own naval logistics system. But their troops have been reinforced almost three times a week, and we now estimate an invading army of almost twenty thousand men. If they continue to advance at twelve to fifteen kilometers a day, they will reach Lunn before the month is out. Ongladred will fall."

"Why have you made a special trip to Stonelore to tell us these things?" Bethel Elk asked. "Surely, Chancellor, you don't hold the neuro-dramas responsible for the Pelagan invasion?"

"No, not that, Mistress Elk." He turned to Gabriel. "Do you remember the conversation we had here at Grotto House after Bronwen Lief's recital, before the reivers murdered Josu Lief?"

"I remember it," the old man said. "You're not going to offer me the command of a Mansuecerian vessel again, are you?"

"No. That's not the portion of the conversation I'm referring to."

"Then which?"

"You and your son argued strongly that societies fail when their leaders fail. You cited inflexibility as the most dangerous sin of command. Do you remember?"

"I remember."

"And do you remember that Our Shathra Anna told you that one day you would have to include yourself among the number of Ongladred's leaders?"

"Yes, that too—more or less. Although I believe we made a distinction between intellectual and political leadership."

I almost laughed, but Chancellor Blaine was maneuvering craftily, as if born to the Socratic method; I watched him with genuine interest. Gabriel Elk, his large hands on his knees now, was also intrigued, a man ensnared in spite of himself.

"Distinctions such as that blur," the Chancellor was saying, "when the enemy plants his boots on our own soil, Sayati Elk. See me here before you," spreading his hands self-deprecatingly, "I am trying to bend. Our Shathra Anna bids me remind you that in these times we must all bend, particularly the leaders among us. If you feel that Ongladred is worth preserving, either for its own virtues or in preference to the barbaric code that would supplant our own, you too must bend, Sayati Elk. You must—"

"There will be no more performances at Stonelore this season, Chancellor. At least for a while."

Slowly Arngrim Blaine closed his mouth, cut off in mid-harangue. I, too, was surprised; the old man had said nothing to me about discontinuing the neuro-dramas. He had not even hinted at it. It was a course he had only just decided upon, it was his own preemptive strike—a means of regaining the initiative. And yet he struck out of belief, not out of wounded pride or insecurity; that his decision nonplussed the Chancellor merely increased his cold, grey delight in affirming a conviction. Elk leaned back; his hands came off his knees.

"Good," Blaine said. "That was easier than I expected."

"I don't do it to please you," Gabriel Elk told him, "but because Ongladred is threatened and I am not a fool. I had hoped that Field-Pavan Barrow and our ships in the channel would save me a decision like this one, but that's past recall now—a dead hope. The news you've brought tonight, Chancellor, wounds and frightens me, me a man almost inured to pain and too old to get very frightened anymore. Therefore, Stonelore closes."

"But what else does the Chancellor wish?" Mistress Elk asked. "Will you place Gabriel in command of a galleon?"

"No. That would be too little, Mistress Elk, a misapplication of talents. Our Shathra wants something more."

"A weapon," Gabriel Elk said.

Again Arngrim Blaine looked surprised, almost incredulous. He uncrossed his legs and extended them straight out before him. "Yes," he said. "An unconventional weapon, something that can be developed in twenty days or less, easily transported, and deployed in the field."

The old man looked at the ceiling and laughed, a sardonic yap. I started, so unexpected was this noise. Then Elk folded his hands in his lap and scrutinized them like a sculptor taking mental notes. "A weapon," he mused.

"That's principally why we want Stonelore closed," Blaine

said, "so that you can devote your time to this project—although my own feeling is that secondary benefits will accrue, the foremost among these being the return to calm of Lunn's populace. Our Shathra Anna wishes you to begin at once. Will you?"

"Why don't you put your Atarite scientists to work on this, Chancellor? They have the Old Knowledge, the materials, the technological capacity—or at least its potential." Elk clasped his huge hands together. "Why do you trek out here to ask of me this pretty little enormity?"

"Oh, we have the technological capacity to do everything you have done, Sayati Elk. We also have the materials, the physical resources. It's the psychic capacity that we lack. Were it not for this inhibition, an inhibition programmed into us by the Parfects several thousand years ago, the People touched by Fire would have created self-propelled carriages, atomic-driven ships, mechanized communication systems, even vehicles that fly—all of these things we would have developed long ago. The knowledge is there, but we don't permit ourselves to use it; we are inhibited, *psychically* inhibited, and even our recognition of this fact doesn't cure us, Sayati Elk. In this case, self-awareness is not power. We have heated and lighted the Atarite palace, and a number of Atarite lords have done the same with the houses on their estates—but beyond that we haven't ventured, we haven't *wanted* to venture. What you have done at Stonelore and Grotto House doesn't confound our intellects, it confounds our sense of propriety, it mocks something innate and immovable in our natures. That's what we've come to you for, Sayati Elk. Those are our reasons. Do you understand?"

"Yes. I'm an aberration."

"That's a pejorative term I would not have used. Please don't try to attribute it to me. What I mean is that you are not inhibited in the way of either those Accustomed to the Hand or those Touched by Fire. Your aggressiveness is intellectual as well as physical."

I said, "You're Ongladred's superman, Sayati Elk, Zoroaster's übermensch."

Ignoring this, Elk said, "The Parfects re-created Man in a strange, divided image, Chancellor Blaine. They did not want us to kill ourselves, but they didn't want us to die, either. Mansuecerians. Atarites. A strange, divided people struggling together to subdue Ongladred. Then, a thousand years ago, we divided again, and what the Parfects tried to provide against is happening once more. We're killing one another, but even as we do we excuse ourselves on the grounds that it isn't yet genocide, the extinction of the species. Neither the Pelagans or the ruling order in Ongladred has essayed a genocidal weapon; something in our shared unconscious will not allow the attempt. And yet today, Chancellor, you ask me to commit myself to the development of the first such horror on the road to just that end, the end of being able to destroy utterly, without mercy or discrimination."

"Because you have the skill," Blaine said. Then added killingly: "And the temperament."

"The temperament!" Bethel Elk said.

"Yes, Mistress Elk. The temperament that conceived and raised the miracle of Stonelore out of the dust of this upland arena."

"Oh come now, Chancellor. Your language apotheosizes my husband."

"Its intention, Mistress, is quite the opposite. It's because Sayati Elk is more 'human' than we," keeping his face composed, decorously humble, avoiding even the hint of smugness, "that we ask this of him."

"My difference from the members of the Atarite Court," Elk said, "is not so great that it frees me from the sanctions of our shared unconscious."

Arngrim Blaine sighed. Then he pulled his tradesman's clothes together, smoothed out the wrinkles in his breeches, and stood. "Very well. Then I'll tell Our Shathra Anna that although Stonelore is closing, you cannot bring myself to do something no Atarite will attempt." I was impressed, then, by Blaine's fairness; he might have said something as self-servingly crass as "cannot bring yourself to *save* Ongladred," but he had not: Conscience had prevailed.

"Sit down," Elk said. "Tell Our Shathra Anna that in twenty days—with the help of those Atarite lords who can supply me with information and materials—I will give her what she wishes."

Blaine eased himself back in his chair. "You have the complete cooperation of the court, Sayati Elk."

"Then I must also have your promise to return the weapons to me when we have defeated the Pelagans. The weapons will be small and deadly—but in themselves they'll fall mercifully short of any sort of doomsday weapon. Still, I want your word that afterwards, after our victory, the weapons will come back to me—without fail."

"You have it, Sayati Elk."

"Good. Then let's stop talking and have something to drink. Ingram, will you serve us."

I said that I would; got up; went down the hall to the kitchen. I could not believe that the evening would not find Gabriel Elk and me helmeted, wired, and perspiring in our swivel chairs in the comptroller room. Before I returned to the study, I had a solitary drink of haoma and let several scenes of *Anabasis in Spring* play through my mind. I would never see them again, except in my mind. Somehow that struck me—for reasons I then refused to consider deeply—as a poignant loss.

And that evening we turned away a crowd of masker women, children, and old men, telling them the amphitheatre had been closed. Unprotesting, they went back through the upland grasses, down to the Mershead Road, and returned from whence they had come—to tell their friends the news.

xiii

The following day Gabriel Elk began work. He used the facilities in the programming room under Grotto House. Bethel handled the correspondence that the project required, writing letters in her small, looping hand and sealing them with purple wax and the impress of Chancellor Blaine's ring. I carried the letters. To the homes of the landed Atarites, to the offices of our scientists, I rode. Always I returned to Grotto House; and soon wagons of materials—chemicals, metals, precious stones, boxed unknowables—began rattling up into the dusty arena and leaving behind their cargoes. On several occasions men whom I didn't know arrived with stern or expressionless faces, disappeared into the programming room, remained a day or two, then emerged and departed, not to be seen at Grotto House again.

Ten days passed. I found myself thinking that if not for the Pelagan invasion, we would have just concluded our second neuro-drama and begun preparations for the third.

Omega Thwarted. Appropriate title, it seemed. I had not even read the play, had no idea what sort of end it would mark to Elk's trilogy or which corpses he had hoped would carry the burden of its theme; for the moment, they all lay inviolately frozen in their preservators, darkness and ice weaving about them a smoky, blue shroud. In dreams, I saw the faces of the corpses growing a fine, weblike covering of hair, their eyes simultaneously narrowing—until they all resembled the reivers who had attacked us so many nights ago. Then I woke to the nightmare in the north.

Field-Pavan Barrow's forces had begun to slow the Pelagan advance—but the countryside through which they retreated, burning what our own people had built or planted, stretched away to the White Sea like a desert of ash. So our runners said. Firthshir, Eenlich, and Vestacs provinces had been transmogrified into the Fields of Astivihad; they were diseased deathscapes in which charred tree trunks and unfilled graves lay desolate under a thin sun and no birds broke the silence with their songs. At sea, several more of our galleons had been sunk, and even in Lunn we could feel the breaths of an animalish people hot and rank on our faces. The enemy was only a little more than a hundred kilometers away, momentarily stalled. Or so our runners told us and so we hoped. . . .

The fighting continued. Even young Atarite men were being sent to the front (those who could command were already there), and I expected at any hour to hear my own summons. At times I wished for it, so futile and anticipatory did my own privileged role seem. What was Elk doing? Though I slept in his house, I seldom got the chance to talk to him. At the front, I imagined, there would be continuous conversation of a lethal kind, the bass imperatives of cannon and the high-pitched yawping of rifles. Old, damn-near falling-to-pieces Yorkley rifles.

What kind of advantage was Elk going to give us?

On the sixteenth day after Arngrim Blaine's second visit to Stonelore, two empty, closed wagons arrived at the arena. Gabriel Elk directing, we spent the late morning and all the afternoon carrying equipment out of the programming room to the wagons. Up and down in the elevator, back and forth through the stone corridor. I worked with four masker laborers, handicapped men who had not been inducted; I struggled to preserve my dignity before them, sometimes attempting to lift more than I was able. Not long past, hadn't I come from these people?

Elk and I rode horseback (on creatures provided by the Atarite Court, animals which Elk eventually bought outright) beside the wagons on our way to Lunn. At sunset we reached the Atarite Palace and drove through the cobbled court to the great, white-stone recreation building. Here we unloaded our materials, setting them up in the vast athletic hall exactly as Elk told us.

Once, as I passed him, the old man said, "Your fire-touched friends will have to forego their genteel pellet-ball and fencing for a day or two, Ingram."

The hall was fiercely illuminated, the electric flambeaux rippled with the energy coursing into them, and the palace (as far as I could judge, outside, from the evidence of its muted windows) was almost dark by comparison—as if the recreation hall were draining some of its power away. Before we had finished unloading, Arngrim Blaine himself came out of the palace and approached the recreation hall; he came with two of the men who had been to Grotto House during the early stages of Elk's work. For the first time, their faces wore looks of ill-concealed excitement.

The wagons rattled away. In the shadow between two great buildings, we five men conferred. Chancellor Blaine said, "Master Gordon and Sayati Snow have told me nothing about this enterprise, Sayati Elk, except that it progresses. Does it?"

"No further, I hope, than it has already."

"What have you developed?"

"A device I call a photon-director. And I have merely developed it, not created it. The Old Knowledge preserved for us by the Parfects contains an incomplete and deliberately cryptic 'description' of the instrument and an abstract of its theory, including a list of applications. The applications are all benevolent—from precision measurement to the healing of retinal lesions."

"Then . . . ?"

"Don't fear, Chancellor. I haven't been working these last sixteen days to manufacture a machine of mercy. The Parfects explicitly told us nothing, nothing at all, about how to murder one another by such a device. But the information's there for minds profound enough to dig it out." The old man spoke as if each word scalded him. "Profound enough," he reiterated.

"And *flexible* enough. In times such as these flexibility is a cardinal virtue."

"And genius," the Chancellor said placatingly, sensitive to Elk's tone. And between Blaine's parted lips, the carnelian gleam of that tooth—a little tusk, a knife of discolored bone. And then the lips closed.

"Genius is a hag who flies in the heart," Elk said. "This was different, this was a toad squatting there."

"But it works?"

"It works. Master Gordon and Sayati Snow will demonstrate them for you in the morning, Chancellor. At first light."

"They know how to operate this . . . photon-director?"

"Yes. And they aided me immeasurably in their construction—there are three, you see. Three photon-directors. Apparently the Atarite inhibition against conceiving and developing an advanced weapon doesn't extend to mechanical matters like assembly and use, Chancellor Blaine."

"It's been rumored that I have Pelagan ancestors," Sayati Snow said. He was a man of my own age, a mathematician and abstruse theorist. His smile surprised me.

"And I," Master Gordon said, not smiling, "don't like being ruled by enzyme tags, plastic viruses, tampered-with chromosomes, any of that business. So I help with this." Gordon was an artisan, a stocky, dark-complexioned man with violet eyes.

"At first light, then," Chancellor Blaine said. He led the others to their rooms in the palace, and I found my own gloomy bachelor's quarters, deserted now since long before spring (with the exception of the nights I had spent there after bringing the Pelagan captive in from Stonelore), two rooms in the low building opposite the recreation hall. Amid the smells of musty quilts and stale air, I slept.

At first light Gordon and Snow demonstrated one of the photon-directors in the recreation hall. Gabriel Elk stood to one side, with Chancellor Blaine and me, and watched. While his terrible, sleek, streamlined machine burned holes of various shapes and sizes in several different target materials against one of the building's walls, the old man talked:

"The old name was laser," he said, "and oddly enough it was perfected on Earth *after* the weapon that twice—in Holocausts A and B—leveled the civilizations of mankind. That the Parfects chose even to hint at its existence suggests that they looked upon it as a device chiefly beneficial. Necessarily," he said, making the word sound evil, "we are going to pervert it to our own ends."

We watched as Sayati Snow triggered the device and a beam of intense, ghastly red light shot through the hall and burned a hole in a cuirassed dummy suspended from the ceiling. Gordon turned a small wheel on the side of the machine's casing and manually directed the beam to inscribe a valentine on the cuirass' left breastplate. When he had finished, a heart-shaped plug of bronze smouldered there. For a long time the plug did not fall; it was as if the metal didn't even know that it had been severed from its own contoured matrix, the torso of our hay-filled warrior. This inscription the photon-director made without even setting the strawman afire. At last, realizing its separateness from the cuirass around it, the plug fell and rang hollowly on the stone floor. Then Sayati Snow triggered the machine again and a brief stream of ruby light ignited the effigy. The dummy burned madly, and the breastplate, no longer having anything to support it, dropped to the floor with a hot clang of its own.

From where we stood we could still feel the heat the machine had generated and the scalding backwind of the destroyed dummy.

Then, after a time, Blaine: "And these will save us?"

"Unless the Pelagans are more cunning monsters than we," Elk said. "I suggest that you send Master Gordon and Sayati Snow, each with a photon-director, to the front. Then, position each man on a flank of Field-Pavan Barrow's line of defense. Ingram and I, with the third machine, will go aboard a warship to the northern run—to halt the barbarians' supply fleet."

"Why not a direct assault on Orcland and the Pelagan capital?" Chancellor Blaine asked. "That would be surer. Much surer than trying to intercept the supply fleet in the White Sea fogs—with one vessel and a dubious weapon."

"The weapons are far from dubious, Chancellor, and I'm requesting two escort vessels in addition to the warship carrying the machine itself. As for the *lasers*, they're to be used only defensively."

"And returned to you?"

"And returned to me."

"Very well, Sayati Elk."

That afternoon, accompanied by a guard of Atarite retainers, Gordon and Snow left Lunn for the northern provinces. Elk and I rode in an unguarded wagon to the little port of Brechtlin and there, as two old masker stevedores carried our boxed weapon aboard the warship *Paradise*, watched the landward gulls flashing their wings in the day's last light.

A seaman pointed out to Elk and me the stretch of beach where the widows, grandmothers, and spinsters from Lunn had waded into the indifferent water and drowned themselves.

xiv

We sailed in the morning. Around the southeastern cape of Ongladred we went, passing the village of Mershead and picking up an escort of two heavily armed galleons. The weather was good, the wind blew from the south, a late maloob, and our sails bellied out like so many linen-shirted paunches. For nearly fifty kilometers we followed Ongladred's coast, staying within the line of defensive warships positioned ten kilometers off the land at intervals just permitting each captain to see the vessels on his flanks; then we were swept out in the Angromain Channel and journeyed northward as a trinity of solitary freelancers, glorified reivers, our task the crippling of our enemy's supply efforts, a task we would have to accomplish amid an archipelago not of rocky, knife-edged islands but of glittering, tabular icebergs, all of them perilously in movement. Through the Angromain Run we sailed, into the cliff-littered White Sea.

On this trip Gabriel Elk taught me how to aim, activate, and control the beam of the photon-director, which we had mounted on the raised forward deck of the *Paradise*. I spent two hours one afternoon burning holes in the improvised sails of a dinghy being dragged at a safe distance behind one of our companion vessels; then I sank the dinghy, setting both its sails and hull ablaze. The sailors on the *Sea Drake* cut the little boat's tow line and waved cheerily at me. I think I grinned. The maskers at Stonelore had never reacted with even half the effusiveness of the seamen; not once. Those on the *Mandragora*, our other companion, even fired a cannon. How much more powerful than this could one feel, I wondered.

"Good, Ingram," Gabriel Elk said. "Soon you'll use your new-found skills against the Pelagans."

"Me? Why not you, Sayati Elk?"

"I've done enough, Ingram. This is for you."

We did not talk about how Snow and Gordon were faring, nor about how the forces of Field-Pavan Barrow were acquitting themselves. These were things out of our control. We could only hope that the Pelagans had not altered their manner of supplying their own forces and that we could intercept them in the White Sea. But although we didn't talk about the land war, it wasn't hard to see that Elk frequently thought of it. In more than one sense, his own blood struggled in that conflict, strove both to honor itself and to pulse for its nation—even though the old man and his son were driven more by abstract ideals than by any fanatic nationalism.

The wind continued brisk, and on our third evening at sea we entered the southernmost reach of the Angromain Run, that corridor of indigo- and vermilion-shot water between Ongladred's northern coast and the overarching scorpion's tail of the barbarian archipelago. Most of these islands are little more than rocks, and uninhabited. Of our voyage into this region I remember principally the bitterness of the night air and, off to port, the small, pearl-like fires burning on the coast. These were now and again visible when a jut of land, like the nub of a gigantic finger, poked out accusingly from our island-nation's usually unobtrusive shore. Parallel to Firthshir Province's eastern coast, we saw no more of these fires; the enemy had let them go out—apparently they did not fear the sloak, or had forgotten about it, or (the most likely alternative) had insufficient men to keep the fires going.

But even without the coastal bonfires the *Paradise* sailed on a mirror surface of rich, darkly rich light; the Shattered Moons illuminated the Angromain Run as if it were a floor of marble and swirled the icy water with deeper indigos, more elusive vermilions. Was it really true that in the wake of the Pelagan advance our country was becoming a gutted ashpit? At sea, it did not seem possible, for the moonlight had an aurora-like brilliance and the very air sparkled. At night I spent as much time as I could on the *Paradise*'s decks, just to see these things—the immemorial wheeling of stars, and of water, and of curdled satellites.

"The moons are brighter out here," I told Elk on our third night.

"One or several of them are artificial," he said.

"How do you know that, Sayati Elk?"

"The Parfects carried us out here six thousand years ago, carried us out here eight hundred light-years from Earth. At least one of the Shattered Moons, perhaps the minutest shard, is an instrument of observation, data-accumulation, and relay—the Eyes and Ears of the neo-people who attempted to re-engineer their own progenitors. Mankind was given genes for morality. You and I, then, are integers in a modestly cosmic experiment, Ingram, and the Parfects therefore have a small vested interest in us—they would have wanted to see how their experiment turned out, they would have made provision for monitoring this hemisphere of Mansueceria, at least."

"But how do you—?"

"It doesn't stop there. They would have wanted a means of interfering in our affairs, of altering the balance of historical forces in Ongladred—if the need arose. Their satellite or satellites among the Shattered Moons fulfill this purpose, too."

"Robin Coigns told me once that he believed the Parfects would return and repair our botched world at the third coming of the sloak. Surely you don't believe that, Sayati Elk?"

"No, Ingram. One property that we can't lease out is the equivocal terrain of our fates."

"An epigram," I said with a cruel inflection that surprised even me.

"If you like, Ingram. But true for all that. In spite of the Parfects, we're alone, and we are also accountable."

"But this instrument in the sky, the Eyes and Ears of the

Parfects, how can you be so certain it exists? What proof have you?"

Sayati Elk looked up at the curling, night-darkened sails; then, grinning like a sly adolescent, he said, "Faith. Simple faith, Ingram." And he went down from the forward deck to his own private cabin.

On our fourth morning we were in the White Sea, traveling northwest out of the Angromain Run. Since we had no idea into which of the many sinuous fjords at the top of Ongladred the Pelagans were running their supplies, our little fleet stood well out to sea and waited. Eventually the barbarians' hideous ships would have to sweep down the arc of the Angromain's scorpion's tail and reveal themselves—or else, for want of provisions, our invaders would soon have to plump out their bellies on ash and gunpowder. Several kilometers out from the coast we tacked about and faced to the east, our three vessels now strategically placed and separated in order to cover the wide, white mouth of water out of which our enemy must sail, dragon-prowed and sinister. *Evil* was the word I thought, knowing that Sayati Elk would have merely laughed at the literalness of my imagination.

We had nothing to do but wait. Nothing but wait and watch the icebergs drift down from Mansueceria's polar cap, sedate and reflective—like hermetically sealed, buoyant cities of crystal. Or like imperturbable monsters of glass.

We saw five icebergs on our first day of waiting, none so close that it posed a danger to the *Paradise* but all near enough to incite our wonder. The closest to us had inlets and firths like an island, although its sides rose up from the White Sea so steeply that none of these afforded a landing place; an eerie sucking roar emanated from the iceberg's caves as the sea rushed in, and a reverberant echo followed each guttural shout. The ice itself was a thousand different colors, mostly shades of blue that purpled the water beneath the iceberg and, as the evening drew on, turned the sky behind it a brittle cobalt. Maz went down early; but not before we saw this nearest leviathan calve and heard the thunderous groanings of her birth pangs as the ice tore apart. Another night to wait, but our first night to worry about ramming the progeny of a multicolored and fecund ice-creature.

Captain Chant, apparently, had seen service in the White Sea before, and we survived the night intact.

The fifth morning greeted us with cottony banks of fog, all of it rolling down from the archipelago's last few islands. The *Sea Drake* and *Mandragora* disappeared, faded away into the gathering gauze as we watched—like apparitions becoming once more invisible. We were enshrouded, we were made a bobbing universe to ourselves. Now our fears were that the icebergs would demolish us or, even worse, that the Pelagans would glide by us in the murk.

Again, we could do nothing but wait, muffled in this hanging fog. Maz was a wan dream somewhere on the other side of our anxiety, and fog dropped down on us from the masts and spars like a ghostly moss. Then night fell, a night that sealed us into ourselves.

All that reminded us of the worlds beyond our own was the intermittent ringing of the *Sea Drake*'s and the *Mandragora*'s ships' bells. The bells' notes, blurred by the fog, drifted through the darkness to us like parachutes of iron sound. Where did they come from? How did they reach us? And then I realized that the *Paradise* had a bellman of its own, that he was on the forward deck (by Gabriel Elk's canvas-covered machine), and that our bell, too, occasionally sent out peals of hollow warning.

"Aren't we just giving ourselves away to the Pelagans?" I asked a masker seaman on the *Paradise*'s main deck. I nodded forward.

"Oh, the bell. Perhaps, Master. But it's better than banging up against our sister ships, and the Pelagans—if they're out in this—have most likely ceased to run, so as to let the soup blow off. They've got fellows with passable heads, too, you know."

I said: "Our bells won't keep the icebergs off. They don't listen."

"If we bump we bump, Master. It may mean giving up a sail or two, but we'll pull her by. So, too, the *Drake* and the *Mandragora*."

His confidence was pleasant but not contagious. I went below decks and tried to sleep.

XV

On the sixth morning the fog was shredding. Shredding into a series of staggered curtains, some of them standing open, some of them closed but for a hairline of blue where sea and sky parted them. Our sister ships became visible once more. Ahead of us, still partially veiled, the mouth of White Sea water from which our enemy would have to come. Feebly Maz was parting the veils, revealing the icy glitter, the stretch of predatory sea, that had been curtained from us.

A voice cried out: "Dragons floating! Six in flight!"

Gabriel Elk came by me, wrapped in furs. Sailors began moving on the *Paradise*'s decks.

Paralyzed, I watched, watched everything.

In a crush of moving bodies the old man halted, twisted his wide face toward me, said, "Up here, Ingram, up here," and strode purposefully through the swarming men, a distinct and preeminent figure. I watched him climb to the forward deck. His stocky form teetered above me, disappeared. Then it was at the head of the ladder again, gazing down on me— though I couldn't see the old man's eyes, only the light pouring down over his shoulders and through his akimbo arms. "Ingram, get up here, damn you! Is all the fog in your head now?" These words overmastered the confusion; somehow, though spoken in an almost conversational tone, they were audible.

In only a moment I was beside Gabriel Elk.

Looking forward over the prow of the *Paradise* I saw nothing—nothing but twinkling water and, slightly to our left, a single iceberg. No other icebergs were visible, only this one rectangular block whose length was several times that of our ship's. It loomed, loomed just out of our intended course. Again, the cry from aloft: "Dragons floating! Six in flight!" And I wondered if the man up there weren't simply reading his own apprehensions into the facets of this solitary iceberg. Maybe the dragons floated in his mind, nowhere else.

"There," Elk said, pointing, and I saw the sail: the first sail.

It seemed to rise up out of the White Sea like the wings of a pelagic, half-frozen pterodactyl, crisp and crimson-brown. Fog scattered as these wings beat through. The prow rising up beneath the Pelagan vessel's sail was carven into the shape of a horned, reptilian head—like that of a dragon, or a fire-lizard, or even an ancient Earth saurian. Exact identification hardly mattered. The impression was that of the entire ship's having emerged hungry from a long sleep in the cold sea. Now the monster was hunting, and the only prey in its path was the galleon on whose forward deck I stood.

One by one the other five sails breasted the horizon, popped into view as if propelled upward from the White Sea's bottom. We saw them, they saw us. And the other five Pelagan ships were as hideously accoutred as the first, bright banners streaming above their dried-blood-colored sails.

On the *Paradise* orders were called out. Gabriel Elk tenderly and quickly drew the piece of padded canvas off the photon-director. It hit me that I was going to operate the machine, I was going to trigger it, I was going to control the intensity and the direction of its scorching needle-flare. More orders were called out; I didn't know where or from whom. The old man said something to me, bumped me into place. My gloved hands were on the photon-director's obscenely neutral-looking controls, a curved trigger and a simple metal wheel. And out in front of me: water like frozen milk, a single bluey-green berg drifting toward us several hundred meters away, and the distance-dwindled but still terrifying Pelagan warships. The only fog I saw now was peripheral, every wispy curtain drawn into the wings of our theatre of battle. Inside my heavy gloves my hands were sweating.

"Are we in range?" I somehow asked, the words atremble with two different kinds of cold, my voice hoarse as if from shouting.

Elk said, "Only a target beneath the horizon is safe, Ingram."

"Do I fire?"

"Did you hear Captain Chant?"

I looked at the old man—at his face under the fur cap, at the iceberg-green eyes, at the snowy sideburns standing away from his cheeks. How long had I known him? Why was he talking to me?

Quietly, guardedly, he was saying, "Captain Chant wants you to wait—to see if they'll turn now that they've seen us, turn and go home." *Was this true?*

Absently I said, "I didn't hear that order."

Then, from aft, I heard a megaphoned command. "Commence firing, Master Marley. COMMENCE FIRING!" The order echoed aloft, the air reverberated with it, the immense northern sea swallowed the echo.

Gabriel Elk pushed me away from the mounted machine, pinioned my arms. "Captain Chant, Captain Chant, I've decided that this man will fire at my word! At no other word but my own!" Then he released me and shoved me back into place.

My hands gravitated to the laser's controls—and I was very conscious of the sharp rippling of the highest foresails. My gums burned with the otherworldly chill, my ears throbbed acutely, and the *Paradise* seemed frozen by Sayati Elk's legitimate, but irregular, usurpation of the galleon-captain's command role. No one moved. Captain Chant's megaphone was stilled.

The Pelagans' little supply fleet had indeed begun to turn—but not out of either fear or surprise. Two of the dragon-prowed ships were maneuvering away from the other four, off to the west. The remainder continued to run toward us, but with their starboard hulls slightly open to us and cutting across the wind. Like ours, the ships were all three-masted, but the sails differed from ours in being serrated and ornamented. Each topgallant bore the yin-yang symbol which Elk had once told me the barbarians had appropriated from legendary Cathay. I stared as ships and sails alike came on.

"Do you know what to do, Ingram?"

I nodded. I could tear cloth with the photon-director, I could burn clean holes, I could set lacerating fires, I could incinerate men on deck, I could sear off mastheads, I could open ragged vents beneath the ships' water lines. What could I not do?

—Turn the barbarians back with a shouted word, with a wave of the hand. No hope of that; none.

Therefore, I would wield Elk's re-created machine as if it were a funnel for all my frustration and rage.

"For Maz' sake, Sayati Elk," Captain Chant called out from the pilot's deck, "let the young master fire!"

"Stay your hand yet," the old man whispered fiercely in my ear.

Numb, I obeyed. I saw a puff of smoke appear as if by magic on the starboard side of the foremost Pelagan vessel. Momentarily I feared that I had triggered my weapon by mistake. The puff of smoke tattered into greasy threads and blew away on the wind; a roar followed, pinched-sounding at this distance. Then, about fifty meters out to sea, a spout of water suddenly kicked up in front of the *Paradise*; air and water vibrated with the shock. It was as if someone had poured liquid mercury into my ears, that painfully deafening.

Another puff of smoke, followed rapidly by another; two muted barks in succession; then the shock of impact as the milky sea broke under the weight of Pelagan cannon shot and water spiraled up in two separate fountains off our bow. I could see individual drops glistening in the midmorning air, miniature prisms tracing their own kaleidoscopic parabolas of descent. Altogether numb, I watched.

"Sayati Elk!" Captain Chant was shouting. "Let him fire!"

"Fire, then," the old man said in my ear.

I pulled the trigger with my gloved finger, then released it. The machine's needle-flare blazed out over the White Sea like a radiant, resilient thread snapping from one point to another—as if its light had originated at the target point and then simply reeled the instantaneous beam out of the photon-director's tubular throat: *Fffffthup!* An obscene, rapid sucking. Afterwards the air seemed changed—but the beam itself shot past the enemy warship; was bewilderingly absorbed by the charged, electrically cold air.

Had my finger touched off this raylike lightning, this gone-astray miracle of fire?

Bursts of smoke formed and dissolved on the sides of two of the Pelagan warships; spray kicked up all across the bow of the *Paradise*, the noise was almost insupportable, water leapt up to us on the high forward deck so that we were drenched with its lashing fallout.

"Again, Ingram!" Elk shouted at me. "Again!"

I swiveled the laser on its mount, I pressed the trigger and held it back with all my will. Rage, frustration, bewilderment, longing for power, impotence, hatred, pride—these and more spun out of me in the swift embodiment of the photon-director's luminous, ruby ray. Almost blinded, I swiveled the machine, turned the wheel controlling the beam, and, teeth achingly clamped, willed the disintegration of everything that was not Ingram Marley.

I stitched the sails of the first Pelagan ship with fire, I sheared off all three masts above their topgallants, I scorched a line of black piping along the middle of its starboard hull. There were drops of water on my eyelashes, tears of half-frozen spray, and the red lambency of the emotions streaming out through the tube of the photon-director was reflected a thousand excruciating times in these tiny beads of ice.

The cannon aboard the first Pelagan ship ceased firing; no more innocent-looking puffballs of smoke. Aboard the *Paradise* we could hear men screaming, men shrieking like the winter ghost-wind. Their full-voiced terror was ludicrously out of phase with the placidity of the northern sea.

We could hear the splintering crack of wood; we could see the severed mastheads toppling, catching, and ultimately tearing through the adjacent sails to crash against the warship's decks, indiscriminately crushing men and equipment alike. The hull of the Pelagan ship was filling with water and ineluctably beginning to capsize—sails hanging and aflame, banners altogether scorched away, the dragon-prow glaring balefully out of one burnt-out eye and nodding ever seaward.

Finally I released the trigger, stopped swiveling the photon-director.

The booming of cannon growled over the water again, but this time from the *Mandragora*, which lay a little behind us and over a hundred meters to our right. A hollow booming, full of antiquated fury. Spray began geysering up in front of the enemy vessel that I had already effectively demolished, a line of violent punctuation marks. They added nothing at all to the unequivocal statement of the photon-director.

"They're jumping," Gabriel Elk said. "The Pelagan seamen who are still able to, Ingram, are jumping. They won't last ten minutes in the White Sea. If that long." The old man was not looking at me, but at the sinking warship. "If that long," he reiterated.

I remembered something. "Where's the *Sea Drake*?"

"There." He gestured off to port. "Those two warships that split away from the main contingent are bearing down on her, trying to use that iceberg as a screen between her and us."

They were moving west, but because of our position I had to look north to see them. Already they had got behind the iceberg's striated, azure-and-rose cliffs and, in a moment, were cannonading the *Sea Drake*—a cacophonous, echoing barrage. At the same time, the three remaining vessels assaulting us and our other companion continued to come on, undeterred by the demolition of their leader or the ungodly shrieking of half their crew. Apparently no effort was being made to pick up the overboarded sailors; the Pelagans knew what Gabriel Elk knew, that they were dead men. Three warships, then, bore down on us; their two fellows attacked the *Sea Drake*.

Captain Chant was shouting orders again; masker seamen scrambled about frantically on the *Paradise*'s main deck.

I was drained, trembling.

"What should I do now, Sayati Elk?"

"Take the ones closing in on us, Ingram. I see nothing else for it."

Swiveling the photon-director, I aimed at the Pelagan vessel negotiating its way toward us from behind the wreckage of the first. In ten minutes I had reduced it to a smouldering shell, masts down, hull precisely ignited. More men were in the water, and smoke trailed away to the north like a tattered banner. Even through my gloves I could feel the heat coming off the casing of Elk's machine. Inside my fur clothes I was sweating, profusely sweating. My face felt hot—but in my eyelashes, those frozen beads in which I could see the distorted reflections of the scene before me! No longer was I firing out of rage, or frustration, or hate; cold resolve sustained me, that and Sayati Elk's droning, almost perfunctory encouragement. For these things I had created wreckage.

"Now the third, Ingram; now the third."

I destroyed the third ship, even though it had finally begun to turn away from the conflict; its captain had witnessed enough. No doubt he died with a terror in his heart more dreadful than that his ship's painted sails and grotesque dragon-prow had ever provoked in his enemies.

The fourth Pelagan warship fled. Successfully.

"Let it go, Ingram. Let it go. Someone must carry word of this back to the archipelago, back to Orcland."

Off to port, off to the northwest, the *Sea Drake* was suffering the methodical onslaught of the barbarian ships shielded by the now seemingly immobile iceberg. Their cannonade continued. The booming was deceptively melodic, deep and sweet. We could already see, however, that the *Sea Drake* would not survive the encounter; its foremast and several of its staysails were down, and she was returning fire only rarely, a tacit acknowledgment of her doom. Neither the *Paradise* nor the *Mandragora* had taken a direct hit.

"Can you help her?" Captain Chant shouted.

"Can we?" I asked.

"If you can burn through that berg, Ingram, if you can split it up and give yourself an aisleway to your targets."

"Can I do that?"

"Probably not. I don't know. Its volume may be too great."

Again, I swiveled the laser on its mount. Again, I adjusted the intensity and width of its beam, allowing for maximums in both. Again, I pulled the trigger back and held it in place.

At once the iceberg erupted in an almost volcanic billowing of steam, white clouds pouring over its table-top and sweeping off like thin gas. Hissing and creaking accompanied this eruption. When I finally released the trigger, the photon-director had done little more than bore an uneven tunnel whose depth I couldn't gauge.

Ships fell to this weapon more readily than did the calves of Mansueceria's polar cap. Still—with time—I might have won through. It was just that we didn't have the time. . . .

The *Sea Drake*, gently capsizing into a foam scarcely whiter than the surrounding sea, slid out of our sight; gently she went, incredibly gently. If her crewmen were screaming, we did not hear them. Maskers often die without even a sigh of protest, and the officers of Ongladred, the Atarite elite, must emulate their stoicism, even in death. We watched our sister ship go down, we watched her slide with broken but commanding dignity into the indigo-riven deeps. And all on the *Paradise* were silent, stilled by our comrades' last end.

"Wait for the bastards," the old man told me. "Wait for them, Ingram, until they have to pull out."

Fetched up with the *Mandragora*, we waited, we waited for the Pelagan renegades to sail out from behind the iceberg. I am certain that they knew we were waiting, that they had seen what we had done to the rest of their fleet.

A half-hour went by, then forty-five minutes. And when the barbarian ships came out they came out on opposite sides of the azure-and-rose ice plateau, cannons booming, their captains apparently determined that one crew would sacrifice itself for the other.

The water was pockmarked with shot, deliquescent with spray.

"Incinerate them," Gabriel Elk said. His voice was flat.

Working first on one ship, then on the other, I did just that. I alternated until they both went down, blackened husks crumbling into ash on the waters. We were not hit. When it was over, Gabriel Elk stalked away from me, descended to the main deck, strode the length of the ship, and without a word to anyone ducked into the passageway leading to his cabin.

I looked on my work: the sinking ruins; the flotsam of boards, boxes, and men bent double like shrimp-things, all bobbing hopelessly in the White Sea; and the smoke curling and dissolving above it all.

Then, the photon-director. On its swivel it sat: a slender, single-eyed beast no more remorseful than the snake that strikes and soon afterwards sleeps. I covered it with a piece of canvas. That way I could continue to look at it.

I looked at it for a long time.

xvi

That evening as we sailed southward, the sky still smoking behind us and the *Mandragora*'s masts and sails silhouetted against that sky's brownish flame, I went below decks. I knocked on the door of Gabriel Elk's cabin. He had not been seen after our victory over the Pelagans; he had not joined Captain Chant and the other Atarite officers in the mess. So I went to Sayati Elk's cabin, and knocked.

"It's open," he called, his voice still disconcertingly flat.

He was sitting on a stool in the middle of the small room, and over him leaned a middle-aged masker seaman with a razor. A basin of sudsy water rested on the writing surface next to Elk's bunk. The masker, a thin little fellow with no eyebrows, was shaving Elk; he grinned at me when I opened the door, then went back to work.

"This is Gnot," the old man said. "Yukio Gnot. He's a barber as well as a yard-trimmer and buntline-tender."

I squeezed past the two men and sat down on the narrow cabin's bunk, a sort of wall cot. The little masker bowed. The hand holding the razor was extended gallantly out behind him. He recited,

> *"I am Gnot, the man
> You think I am,"*

and resumed work for a second time; all this he did completely humorlessly, with dead-pan seriousness in fact.

Elk was wrapped to the throat in a khaki-colored apron, his face partially lathered, unnaturally pink where Gnot had already shaved him. Then I noticed that on the desk next to me, as well as the barber's soap-filled basin, there was a pair of heavy shears. What did all this mean?

For a time we listened to the groanings of the *Paradise*: Elk in his khaki tent, Gnot concentratingly ignoring the sway of the ship, and I somehow excluded from the intimacy of shaver and shaved. Between groanings I thought I could hear the almost frictionless scraping of Gnot's razor; it was as if the razor were scraping at the wet inside of my skull.

Would no one speak?

"I'm sorry I deserted you, Ingram," Gabriel Elk said. "I'm sorry I made you do what I made you do."

"You did desert me, didn't you?"

"Yes. But no more certainly than I deserted myself after we closed Stonelore—and created again that thing out there."

"That was for a cause, Sayati Elk. What about this morning's desertion? What about leaving me?"

"For the cause of my own sanity, Ingram. As the goldhearted beauty of the Stews once said, 'It's nothing personal, Master, nothing personal a' tall.' But I regret the desertion mightily for what it seemed to imply."

"Why are you being shaved at this hour?"

"An ablution of sorts," puckering his mouth as Yukio Gnot scraped at the grizzled whiskers near his Adam's apple. "Perhaps I should be bled clean. Gentleman Gnot, an extra mithra if you go into the jugular neatly."

The masker stepped back. "There's nothing neat about that operation, Sayati Elk. As for the mithra, I'm Gnot for nothing and all's for Gnot in this barbering. You owe me nothing, for all the pleasure's mine." It was patter, amusing but sadly hollow. The little man leaned over Gabriel Elk again, his browless eyes naked and vulnerable—like ripe, peeled grapes.

His hands flashed expertly. Then I saw that he was shaving away Elk's sideburns.

I said, "Gentleman Gnot, was that requested?"

Elk threw me a sidelong look, the whites of his eyeballs like little quarter moons. "All of it's requested, Ingram. Jaw, cheeks, and skull. All of it."

"The masker mourning cap," I said. "What for?"

"For today."

"You aren't one of the People Accustomed to the Hand," I said, "and you haven't lost a relative. Did you do this when your two eldest sons died?"

"I didn't, Ingram—because I wasn't a Mansuecerian, though born of them, and their customs weren't mine. Today I revive the custom of the mourning cap. Why? Because I mourn and don't know how to express it, the expression of it's gone out of me, all of it out. Today was a day I relearned everything but its expression, Ingram, and so I turned to Gentleman Gnot for help. I'm no longer young, I'm nearing death, in fact—but I've never understood the element of affirmation that may exist in mourning, though I know that it *does* exist.

"The Atarite practice of mourning has always struck me as defeatist; the Mansuecerian, as cold and ritualized. But today—a day of my own making—requires this atonement at least. Already a kind of feeling flows in, behind Good Barber Gnot's fashioning of my cap. The outside will teach the inside. What say you to that, Ingram?"

"Nothing. Nonsense from Our Genius."

"Exhibitionist nonsense?"

"Your words, your doubts."

The old man shifted under the khaki barber's cloth. The wall candles flickered together; the cabin filled with interlocking shadows, most of them pooling and ebbing around the two men in the center of the room. Delicately Yukio Gnot wiped the lather from Gabriel Elk's face; the old man's face was then naked, as if newborn. I wondered if I would have been able to recognize Elk if I had not seen the transformation. "I'm a dramatist and poet," he said confidently. "Introspection and exhibitionism have been my trades. No doubts whatever in that, Ingram. This that I do now has nothing to do with my trades, however. It has to do with my humanity and mortality. How the world interprets it, I little care."

He gestured at the spry, shadow-tattered barber and said, "Proceed."

Gnot took the heavy shears off the cabin's writing desk (I had to move my feet for him) and began sclip-sclipping at Elk's massive head, the ring-curled, silver-white hair tumbling over the shears' blades like wool. Satyr's wool, I thought: Elk was smiling cryptically. Like the parings of old dreams the hair fell. In the shadow-filled cabin it almost floated, each curl a fleck of time, of coil-wound chronology, cut and discarded. Individual hairs clung to the drab bib or laced the floor with their dead, frightening beauty. I could not help thinking that this was something more than a simple barbering: I thought of the Parfects, I thought of the Pelagan reiver I had murdered, I thought of denatured animals and the resurrected performers of Stonelore. A sense of elation; a sense of loss. And the hair kept curling away from the blade, emphatically white.

When Gnot had finished with the shears, he lathered Gabriel Elk's shorn head, stropped his razor, and began scraping away the stubble. "Harvest time," Elk said. He sat perfectly still under the little masker's hands. Then, the operation complete, Gnot laid the shears aside and washed his patient's liver-spotted skull. Strangely, Elk did not look ludicrous—maybe because his bald head didn't shine like a tunic button, but more probably because his face, in its runneled candor, green eyes hemmed in like a tortoise's, was already humorous at its own expense.

"Done, Sayati Elk. You needn't pay me. I'm Gnot for nothing."

"I'd rather, Gnot," Gabriel Elk said, shaking the apron out on the floor and giving the barber a few coins.

The barber bowed; he grinned. "Oh, that's amusing, Sayati Elk, that's amusing how you put that. I'm appreciative, I am."

I said, "I'm doubled with laughter myself, tied up in a Gnot."

"Oh, Master Marley," he said, looking at me, "you, too. You, too. All's for Gnot, it is. All's for Gnot."

In disgust, I looked at the floor.

"I'll clean up, Gnot," Elk said. "You needn't feel obligated for that, too. You're a seaman and a barber, not a mercenary in the broom brigade." This time the *not* wasn't a pun; the old man's voice had changed.

"Oh, no. I must do it, you know." He took a small horsehair brush from the inside of his jacket, knelt, and swept the fallen hair into the barber's apron, which he had spread out on the floor as a receptacle for hair, dust, and any other oddments he could rake together. Speedily done, he pulled the four corners of the apron together and tied them up as best he could, careful not to spill either dirt or severed curls. He slung the resulting bag over his shoulder. He bowed to Gabriel Elk; he bowed to me. He looked like an archetypal giftbringer, but one whose generosity has dissipated him into a posturing—and anemic—clown.

"Take a few of those shavings," I suggested, "and paste on some eyebrows."

The masker, alerted to something *unkind* in my tone, stared at me in utter incomprehension; his nonexistent eyebrows were quizzically raised. Elk opened the cabin door for him, let him into the hall.

"Thank you, Yukio," I could hear him saying. "You're a skillful man, and a good one. Let's hope we find our country and families safe when we put in at Brechtlin."

"Yes, Sayati Elk. Let's so hope."

Elk returned to the cabin. He sat down opposite me, pulling his stool around as he sat. His naked, gravely humorous face was as unfamiliar as a map of Austernmere, the Brobdingnagian continent sprawling over a quarter of Mansuecceria's southern hemisphere. The naked, unfamiliar face looked at me, simply looked at me.

At last I said, "Oh, that wasn't so bad, Sayati Elk. I've sunk five ships today, drowned nearly eight hundred men in an icy sea. Insulting Gentleman Gnot was one of my less murderous sallies of the day." I wanted to cry. Instead, I pulled in my bottom lip and tried—tried very hard—to stare the old bastard down.

"A Mansuecerian, Ingram. A simple masker—"

"Why are you trying to shame me?"

"Oh no, Ingram, I don't mean to shame you, just to explain

that his shaving my head was my idea, not his. To explain that he speaks as he does because he's a simple, untouched creature."

"But the banality of it, Sayati Elk, the endless banality of it." And my eyes filled with wet candlelight, diamonds of melting, detonating color that washed the old man's unfamiliar face away. I couldn't control my shoulders. *"The terrible, utter banality . . ."*

Then I could smell the old man's lather-sour warmth, feel his heavy arm and strong hand pulling me like a child into his side; he was sitting on the bunk next to me, a reality that had swum through my blurred vision to assert its realness. The voice was warm against my face. "It's a banality which touches us all, Ingram—and we all attempt to transcend it, in whatever ways we're able. Even Yukio Gnot. Even the maskers who come to Stonelore." His huge hand squeezed my biceps. "But for pushing you to this, I'm sorry. My mourning is for you, too."

"Will what we've done make a damn bit of difference?"

"That's hard to gauge."

"Won't the Pelagans send more ships, and more, and more?"

"One escaped today. That one will return to Orcland, and the news its captain gives of his compatriots' end will soon be broadcast throughout the archipelago, both as rumor and warning. Or so I hope."

I pulled away from the old man. In the melting-diamond light I found my feet and crossed to the door. "Goodnight, Sayati Elk." I went out without waiting for his reply. Inside my fur-lined parka my shoulders became a part of my body again, settled almost comfortably into me.

In the cold I found my way to the forward deck. There I directed two masker seamen to take the photon-director off its mount and carry it to my cabin. Under close-hauled sails, tarnished-tin stars, and the shadow-pocked moons, they did so.

They put the machine on the floor in the center of my cabin, and I sat on the edge of my bunk for a long time looking at it. Then I extinguished my lamps, undressed in the dark, and lay down under several ragged quilts.

(Pulling them up, I remembered a quilt with blue flowers embroidered over its silken squares.)

The *Paradise* groaned, gently rocking. The shadow of the photon-director, the sinister bulking of its silhouette, drew my attention, and I stared at it as if compelled to wrestle with the implications of its shape. I was past crying. I lay in the dark and relived the morning and early afternoon, oh, eight or a thousand times. Then was rocked into dreamless nightmare, a series of floating images without correlatives. . . .

xvii

On the morning that we rounded the southeastern cape of Ongladred, a strange thing happened. Captain Chant was wringing the very air for wind, so motionlessly still was the day; our sails were expertly trimmed, the yards finically dressed, and we were moving homeward—but only just. The *Paradise* rode the shallow, almost nonexistent waves sluggishly, and the *Mandragora* had fallen back half a kilometer in our languid wake. Aloft, our banners scarcely fluttered.

Because the sailing was so poor along our island's coast, we rounded the Mershead Cape well out to sea—far enough out so that land was no longer visible. Although we were now in waters lapping quiescently against uninvaded territory (the civilized heartland of our nation), we saw only five or six ships of all of Ongladred's fleet, and all of these out of hailing distance.

It was an odd morning, a subdued and lonely sort of homecoming.

Gabriel Elk and I stood with Captain Chant and his helmsman on the pilot's deck. Maz shone with a thin but elemental vigor; he did not seem a likely one to nova, to explode us all back into primordial plasma. Therefore none of us wore parkas or overtunics; we basked in the uncommon autumn mildness. And wondered at the absence of wind and the tranquility of the sea.

"Where are all our ships, Sayati Elk?" I asked.

"On a day like this," Captain Chant answered, "their captains would hope to be in harbor. Perhaps that's where they are today."

"But we ought to see a few. A precaution against the Pelagans."

"The Pelagans, Ingram," the old man said, "are defeated. I know it. Last night—and the night before—we saw the bonfires on the coast. Having beat back one enemy, our people are turning their energies again to the threat of the sloak. Like Captain Chant, I believe most of our ships to be in harbor."

"But the sloak," I said, "is no threat at all; a superstition."

"Perhaps not a superstition," Gabriel Elk said. His uncovered head struck me again as shamefully naked, a violation of character. Captain Chant's eyes caught mine once and their irises seemed to surround a question.

But our desultory talk continued. Meanwhile, on the *Paradise*'s decks our sailors worked with quiet, insectlike efficiency keeping the sails open to whatever breath of wind they could smell or intuit in the listless air. We were bound for home, we were bound for home, and only that mattered. The strange thing that happened that morning came too late to be an ironic comment on my refusal to see the sloak as a threat; too much time had passed to underscore my words with irony. Or so I tried to convince myself.

This is what happened:

Suddenly, with no warning, the sea beneath the *Paradise*—and everywhere else around us, insofar as we could judge—began to heave and surge, surge and heave, lifting and dropping in great, vaguely peristaltic swells. Our masker seamen turned their faces to the skies in disbelief, shouting to one another, checking braces and halyards. Captain Chant roared unintelligible orders over their shouts and scufflings, his megaphone jutting out before him like a supernatural trumpet. Officers on the other decks trumpeted these misheard orders back and forth over the sailors' heads, and the whole ship was atremble and ajostle with split-struck confusion.

Great slappings of water pounded our hull. It was as if a team of ocean-breathing giants—seaweed for beards and driftwood for bucklers—were playing at toss-the-blanket on the bottom of the Angromain Channel, oblivious to depth and pressure as impediments to their play. The flap-and-fall of their monumentally water-logged blanket translated itself into the lift-and-plunge that we aboard the *Paradise* were experiencing, into the running swells everywhere around us. It had to be giants. Since there was no wind, since our banners were still hardly billowing, this quaking of the sea, this ferocious faulting, had to originate from *beneath* the surface. I think that even I realized that, even I was aware of the odd nature of the channel's intransigence—and could do nothing but pray that the giants grow weary and desist. But, with Sayati Elk, I remained on deck, watching.

"The sloak!" I heard a voice cry out.

"Aye, the sloak!" in answer.

"The sloak it is!"

"The sloak!"

I grabbed Gabriel Elk's arm and shouted, "I don't believe that! This is some kind of tidal anomaly, isn't it?" I had to repeat my words, but I got the old man to face me.

"I've never seen a tide like this, Ingram!"

"What about sea-bottom volcanic activity?"

"Who can say, Master? Who can say?" He was reveling in the surge of the waters, the cry and scuffle of our sailors. Me, he had no immediate concern for; I couldn't question him while this untoward pounding made our bilge echo and our masts passionately thrust and fall back. Men were mocked in this, their tenderness and pride both mercilessly battered, and the old man laughed and drank it all in. Every haughty wave.

I shouted, "Do you—do you believe it's the sloak?"

But he didn't answer me, refused to hear me. Beside him on the pilot's deck I waited for an immense mythical creature to capsize and drown us on a transcendently fair day. The masker seamen, hauling line and climbing, kept us afloat, and then, in a split-struck instant, the seas calmed and the *Paradise* settled into a gently bobbing element scarcely even foam-flecked. The giants had wearied of blanket toss and gone on to more delicate amusements.

—Like subduing boarnoses to their clammy hands, I thought. I could imagine the sleek, sharklike creatures undergoing training.

After we had ridden for a time on the freshly stilled waters, I began to force my questions on the old man. We stayed abovedecks in the midmorning sun, a little away from Chant and his helmsman. "Was that really the sloak, Sayati Elk? Not freak vulcanism nor a quirk of the tides, but this creature you and the maskers call the sloak?"

"I believe so, Ingram."

"Why?"

"Because that answer, to my mind, is the only one that truly works, the simplest and most legitimate."

"Then do you expect this gelatinous monster to smother the coastal bonfires—haul itself irresistibly over our island— and destroy Ongladred for a third time? That seems to be all we can hope for?"

"Ingram, I am past expectation. Past prophecy and vision. But I don't think Ongladred will be destroyed again. At least not by an entity as remorselessly out-of-nature as the sloak."

"If you believe in the thing, why not?"

"Because what we've just experienced, Ingram, was meant as caveat and warning, it was directed specifically at us aboard this ship and the men on shore who witnessed the turbulence's batterings, the men of our nation."

"Caveat and warning," I said incredulously. "From whom? The sloak?"

"No, but from those who control it. It's a thing out-of-nature, Ingram, an anomaly in its own right, a product of smug and juridic intelligence. It has no will of its own; it executes the judgments of this 'higher,' all-ruling intelligence and does so in the guise of an apocalyptic but wholly natural phenomenon. The sloak exists, Ingram, but it's a lie."

"I don't understand you." —Although this argument was somehow familiar. I had heard it before. In Stonelore. From a haggish old woman in one of Elk's neuro-dramas.

"I'm speaking of the Parfects. The sloak is a quasi-organic creature, a biological construct which the Parfects have twice before activated in order to pull us back from forbidden knowledge. For them, the Old Knowledge is the limit of what we may know; the sloak, the unweaponlike weapon by which they fix the parameters of our knowledge. Once again, Ingram, we begin to encroach on the boundaries of the permitted: We have employed technology—proscribed technology—to kill. Hence this warning, a warning especially vivid to us on the *Paradise*, wielders of stolen fire."

"Your interpretation, Sayati Elk, hardly seems the simplest and most legitimate; it's infinitely complicated."

"It's the simplest explanation that accounts for the arrogantly directed history of our island, Ingram, and by 'arrogantly directed' I don't mean to imply that we—Atarite and Mansuecerian alike—don't share in the shame of our failures and the simple pride of our glories, only that we have been measured against an alien standard and made to suffer unduly for the squalid aspects of our nature—even though They have altered that!" He delivered this little oration heatedly, as if it had been rehearsed a thousand times but never before spoken.

I said, "Aren't you seeking a scapegoat, Sayati Elk, a scapegoat external to ourselves?"

"I absolve humanity of nothing! At the same time I refuse to designate humanity itself as a scapegoat, as the Parfects decided six or seven thousand years ago it must be so designated. That view is abhorrent to me, as abhorrent as the utter denial of our guilt. —I resent the suppression of humanity, I resent the Parfects' self-undertaken Sitting in Judgment."

"And if humankind destroys himself?"

"He must be free to do so, even if he does it over and over again until the last sterile coupling of the species. Or until he learns."

"And if he doesn't learn?"

"Then his viability as a creature worthy of the cornucopian gifts of chaos has proved altogether too weak and he must die—cursing himself, mind you, not that cruel but munificent chaos. His passing will have, must have, the grandeur of tragedy. That much is evident, Ingram, that much is clear."

I looked away from his intent, naked face. Ahead of us, off to the right, the hazy blue line of Ongladred's southern coast was becoming visible; we had successfully rounded the cape. The ships in harbor at Mershead and Brechtlin must have had to endure the shock waves of the pounding we ourselves had ridden out at sea. Now, however, the clear sky and the windless air mocked our memories; the planet basked.

"Could your sloak—whether native or quasi-organic—have caused an upheaval like the one we just survived, Sayati Elk? Legends have it that the thing's so thin its body has almost no width at all."

"The legends are legends, and even if true, the activation of the monster's biocybernetic consciousness from the Parfects' orbiter would generate enough energy both to thicken the sloak's immensely attenuated membrane and to stir up the sea in the process. Once drawn together for its assault on Ongladred, the sloak becomes as formidable a sea beast as any that has ever lived—either in Mansueceria's oceans or in Earth's."

"For everything, you have an answer." *Didn't Sayati Elk's resurrection of the dead for the purposes of his dramaturgy have a kind of parallel, a kind of affinity, with the Parfects' "activation" of the sloak (assuming of course, that the old man's hypothesis was correct)?* That was a question which I didn't ask, but which I decided to think about. There were a great many questions that I would have to think about in the days, the years, ahead.

"No, not answers, Ingram, *theories*—all of which I intensely believe in, since they are better than all others and since they are mine."

Gabriel Elk said this without a hint of haughtiness, but I wanted to deflate him somehow, wanted to disabuse him of his own intricate but annoyingly logical theory. I asked, "What about the two-thousand-year cycle of the sloak? Isn't that too regular for an expedient that you claim is punitive? Does humankind reach the brink of forbidden knowledge with so inhuman a precision each two thousand years?"

"The sloak has come only twice before, even according to legend. How can we compute its cycle with any accuracy? Besides, Ingram, this—the Year of the Halcyon Panic—is not the only year that men have predicted the return of the sloak, the destruction of the species. Men are superstitious beings; they read numbers into everything. Eventually their mystical numbers become the basis of a numinous science. Oh, it's beautiful and frightening, this becoming, Ingram, one which always unworks itself only to evolve again. The cycle of the sloak? It is science and superstition compromising their separate integrities through the mediation of numbers."

"Dear Maz," I said. "Spare me more of this. Spare me."

Gabriel Elk threw his head back and laughed, laughed with hearty abandon, as if his breath would puff our sails in the breathless day and billow us jauntily into Brechtlin's harbor—a galleon of heroes ready for their gallons of haoma, a crew of gallant murderers hoping to inundate their crime in the masker panacea.

Amazingly enough, in two hours Captain Chant and our seamen, having wrung the air for its faintest stirring, took us into the recently wave-lashed but now silent harbor, and after fifteen days at sea we disembarked upon our native soil. Behind us, a sky full of masts and sails. Before us, the port, a road, and all of Ongladred.

In the flush of this excitement I forgot that it was I who had incinerated the enemy, nearly eight hundred human beings—until, as I left the *Paradise*, I saw Gentleman Gnot staring after me.

xviii

Gabriel Elk and I rented a wagon in Brechtlin, had the photon-director loaded into it, and drove not to Lunn but along the coastal road toward Mershead. "The weapon is mine," the old man told me. "I don't have to take it back to Chancellor Blaine; he'll discover soon enough, without our telling him, that the *Paradise* is in harbor." It was dark when we reached Stonelore. Oddly, I felt that I had come home too; that this arena of rock and sand and artificial light belonged more certainly to me than did any of the tract on which the Atarite Palace sits.

Bethel and Robin Coigns met us in front of Grotto House. That there were only the two of them was in itself an ominous thing.

Bethel kissed her husband. Then she stepped back from him, her hands still on his shoulders, and said, "Gareth is dead, Gabriel." Then she ran her hand slowly over her husband's head, backward from the brow. "Someone has told you already?"

"No. You are the first." He pulled his wife to him, and they embraced—a silent, undemonstrative, somehow expressive embrace. Coigns and I stood apart, not so much excluded from this sharing as simply incapable of comprehending its intensity. Then Gabriel Elk drew his wife with him toward the house, the woman almost an extension of himself, he almost an extension of her, the two of them incomprehensibly and reproachfully whole. "Ingram," he said, "Robin, come with us." We followed. Silently.

Later, in the arras-hung dining chamber, we talked—while the beardless Gareth's almost tangible presence hovered in our words and breaths. The stone table was between us like a funeral slab; the Atarite Palace and the provinces of Ongladred were reduced in our minds to ghostly greys on a battle chart. Before a single dead loved one, the concepts of civilization defended and honor reaffirmed dissolve into fume and blow away, like cannon smoke. Even with no one of my own to mourn, I knew that much; the knowledge had grown in me.

"He was killed four days ago," Robin Coigns was telling us. "Those machines that Sayati Snow and Master Gordon brought up to below Firthshir had turned it all around, the fighting, you know, and the Pelagans had started back up north, all the way through Vestacs and Eenlich, too, it looked like. The boy he was killed in the per-suit Field-Pavan Barrow ordered right after the machines turned 'em around. Then, when he sees they can still kill us, you know, while we're per-suing 'em, ole Barrow calls it all off and we just let 'em go, just let 'em run—but Gareth he was already dead, Sayati Elk, he was already lost, along with a mess of others, all of 'em on-the-line fellows, too."

There was silence.

Bethel Elk sat with her hands folded in her lap, as regal in her silken green gown as I had ever seen Our Shathra Anna. Gabriel kept his gaze down, apparently directing it at his heavy, rope-veined hands.

Then he said: "An irony, Robin. An almost maudlinly predictable one. Irony, a part of my trade; a philosophical joke to work on my creations. Now it comes home to haunt me."

Bethel said, "Forget that, Gabriel. We will mourn awhile."

The old man looked up; he looked at Robin Coigns. "Where is Gareth? Was he buried in the north?"

"He's under," Robin said simply. "He's in the tunnel 'twixt Grotto House and Stonelore."

"Here?"

"Aye, Sayati Elk."

"How?"

"He took a rifle ball in the throat, sir, through the Adam's apple so his wind was cut; the ball lodged there, you see. It wasn't meant for me to be beside him then, I guess. Others came running for me and took me back, but by then our officers knew him for your son and called for haomycin to go into his blood so as to get him back here 'fore he stiffened. I was shunted off to one hand, Sayati Elk, and most near cried, and watched 'em do what they had to. Gareth he lay in the midst of all this scrambling, you know, and bled the life all out and couldn't see me no more than if he was blind, his eyes gone back and his face just as still as old milk. He got home 'fore I did, Sayati Elk—*preserved*, sort of. They took him off that way, with nothing for me to do but watch. I near cried, sir."

"We put Gareth in a preservator, Gabriel," Bethel said.

"Which one? They were all full."

"They're empty now, Gabriel. Except for Gareth's, and Bronwen Lief's. After you left, I had some men come out from Lunn and give the other dead ones their second funerals. They were burned, our actors, all of them together—in the place we always burn them—at the end of the summer. I couldn't leave them sleeping in that heartless ice, Gabriel."

"Why did you spare the girl?"

"I don't know. Because she was new—newer than the others. Because I had seen her dance."

"I want to see Gareth," the old man said.

I asked, "May I go with you?"

After an almost imperceptible pause the old man said, "Please, Ingram."

We excused ourselves. Bethel and Coigns permitted us to go without them. They had seen the boy, and they knew Gabriel's wish for what it was, a plea for one last, unhampered moment of communion. Perhaps I was less sensitive than they, for I knew this, too, and should not have gone with him— but I felt that he would have refused to let me go if my presence had threatened to throw up a wall between him and his dead son. I had to go with him. Down into the programming room, into the dark tunnel, into the dormitory room for corpses. Sensing my need to accompany him, Elk had said yes.

And so we left the dining chamber, walked down the hallway of luminous panels, and rode the elevator into the very womb and bowels of Grotto House. My sensation of going home grew more pronounced, more and more uncanny.

Then we were in the icy preservator room, among the ranked coffins and the upended storage tanks of lox. A faint musical seething played in my ears. Our breaths took shape in the air like dreamlike sails; we had voyaged into a numinous place, a world whose deities were enshrined in ice and plastic. Four of the shrines were empty, but in the two closest to the door we found the daughter of Josu and Rhia Lief and the newly slain son of Gabriel and Bethel Elk. These young people were the numens of the preservator room, guardian spirits whose frozen youth mocked their guardianship. Were they not too primevally vernal for such a custodial godhood? I stared through crystal at first the woman, then the young man—whose throat was swaddled in a wide bandage.

Bronwen Lief looked different to me. Her face was not a whit altered from the first time I had seen her, long ages ago, back before the spring had come. But the smirk I had then read in the twist of her mouth seemed not at all sinister now; it was not even a smirk, it was instead a wholly natural flaw, human and therefore reassuring.

As for Gareth, he looked no different, no different at all— except that his sparse, adolescent beard had matured into stubble. If Bethel had had him shaved before committing him to the preservator, then even in death his facial hair had continued to grow. So: His corpse's features were fresh and youthful, but touched with the beginnings of a revivifying weariness.

Wearing frost-gloves, Gabriel adjusted the cryostat on Bronwen Lief's preservator. With the cryostat he could take the temperature within each coffin up and down a limited scale of cold in a very brief time, although the preservator room itself remained at a constant 0° C. in case of separate cryostat malfunctions. As the temperature in Bronwen's unit rose toward that of the room itself, the old man leaned over his dead son and studied the boy's face. "He was growing into himself, Ingram. He was just on the verge of growing into the wholeness of himself."

My hands, for warmth, were in my armpits. I was behind the old man, and as he leaned over the preservator I noticed for the first time an angry red gleam on the back of his head, his mottled, naked skull. It was a nevus, a birthmark, a magenta discoloration just to the right of and a little above the brain stem. Before I could stop myself I had reached out and touched the tiny mark.

Gabriel Elk turned slowly and looked at me. I withdrew my hand, the image of the nevus clearly before me even though the old man had turned. "You have a mark back there," I said.

Briefly his face was inscrutable. Then he smiled and his eyes crinkled into almost Mongoloid slits: a pleasant, joy-etched smile. "Ingram, I'd almost forgotten the mark. When I was little my father used to brush my hair aside there and tell me that I'd been branded by the Evil One, by Ahriman himself."

"Yes," I said. "It's like a scorpion, a little scorpion with its stinger raised."

"My father always told me of the blemish with a smile, as if joking, but he upset me more than he knew, and for a time I dreaded his touch—his reminder to me of something I knew was back there but couldn't actually see for myself. My father was a Mansuecerian, Ingram, a masker, and I knew that I was somehow different from him. For a long time I believed the difference lay in the scorpion mark, that it and only it was what set me apart from my family and everyone else."

"That mark probably made your father uneasy, Sayati Elk. It's frighteningly perfect, it might almost be a tattoo."

"He told me that, too, Ingram—though not in those words. And when I reached adolescence I ceased resenting his uneasy banter about the birthmark; I understood his uneasiness, his ill-expressed love. I understood what I was and how the differences in what we were didn't finally matter. But I kept waiting for him to express—in some uncharacteristically flamboyant way—the love he didn't know how to articulate." Gabriel Elk rubbed the spot I had touched. "Oh, those are mostly good memories, Ingram, almost from another life, they're so far away." He rubbed the spot and smiled.

Then he abruptly turned and began disconnecting some of the apparatus affixed to Bronwen Lief's preservator. Apparently he was not going to let those memories overwhelm him. As we had done several times during the summer, he pulled the coffin on its coasterlike wheels out of its moorings and pushed it toward the door. He gave me a pair of frost-gloves.

"What are you doing?" I asked.

"Going back to work. Will you help me?" He returned to the young woman's preservator after giving me the gloves and began to roll it toward me. I opened the door for him, and together we pushed the gleaming white fuselage through the tunnel and into the programming room. I couldn't believe that it was beginning again, I didn't know how to react.

Once inside the programming room, however, the old man said, "Go upstairs and go to bed. Take Gareth's room. I want you to have it."

I hesitated. "Sayati Elk, I can't tell Mistress Elk I'm taking her son's room. Not now."

"Tell her. She'll understand."

"Are you going to stay here?"

"For a while. Go on. Go upstairs. Go to bed."

Reluctantly I rode the elevator up. Alone in the main hallway, I felt like a figure in a photographic negative, like the light-blackened obverse of myself. Then, in her silken green gown, Bethel Elk came toward me out of the glare of the corridor's wall panels and restored color to the microcosmic world of Grotto House.

I told her what her husband had told me to tell her. She put her hand on my arm. She led me to Gareth's room. The door opened for me. She said, "Go in, Ingram, and sleep well." The door closed behind me. And momentarily I felt again like a black figure on a white ground—until I brushed against a wall panel and a flood of yellow light reversed things once more.

The room was exactly like the one I had slept in before Gareth's death—except that at various places about the room Gareth had put on display pieces of his idiosyncratic statuary. Sinuous trees carved out of stone, every piece a gnarled and leafless tree. I picked up the sculpture next to my bed. It was unfinished, almost as if the boy had realized that no matter how expert his hands became or how exemplary his vision, in execution his trees would inevitably be dead and petrified before he could complete them; as if he had realized this and given up the attempt as foolish.

The tree I was holding may have been the last one he ever worked on. I set it down and stretched out on the dead boy's bed.

xix

The next day Arngrim Blaine appeared at Stonelore. His arrival coincided with Robin Coigns' departure for Brechtlin in the wagon we had rented the previous afternoon; the ostler was going to return the wagon and ride back to us on the horse following the wagon on a short tether.

As Coigns left the upland arena and joggled on the wagon seat down the dusty hillside, we saw the Chancellor's equipage approaching from Lunn. In a red billow, wagon and carriage passed each other. Only two Atarite guardsmen rode beside the Chancellor, and they did not venture into the arena with his sleek, ebony coach; instead, they halted and took up positions outside the rock wall, as had the charioteers on that night when Bronwen Lief danced and the reivers drew down on us from their blind. Had we learned nothing? But the war was over, I reminded myself, we had successfully beat back the bringers of ruin. I had murdered a few myself.

"Welcome," Sayati Elk said when Chancellor Blaine stepped down from his coach. "Once again, we're honored."

The man with the roan tooth tilted his head and clasped the old man's hands in his own. "It's I who should extend the welcome, Sayati Elk. Welcome home to Ongladred. Your countrymen and your countrymen's rulers have proved to be more flexible than many"—the Chancellor gave me a significant look—"felt to be possible. Our Shathra Anna has fathomless reservoirs of flexibility; she ordered me to pay you a visit when it became apparent that you weren't going to come into Lunn of your own volition."

"An inconvenience to you," Gabriel Elk said, "for which I apologize."

The three of us were crossing the arena, walking slowly. I said, "Why exactly did she send you out here, Chancellor Blaine?"

He didn't answer at once. But finally he did say, "To offer both congratulations and condolences, Sayati Elk. And these tasks I undertake willingly. Don't speak of inconvenience. There is none, none whatever. I'm only sorry that your son's death diminishes the joy you must feel in your homecoming."

Elk said nothing. He opened the wrought-iron gate across the foyer to Grotto House and led us inside. Bethel joined us, and since the day was fair and unseasonably warm, we went through the foyer to the house's open, central courtyard. All of us but the old man took up seats on the stone benches there. Elk, his bald head absorbing rather than reflecting the sunlight, stood with his back to us. I could not help looking at the scorpion mark above his runneled nape. It focused my attention.

I heard him saying, "Robin tells me that Sayati Snow and Master Gordon swept the enemy before them with the ease of minor deities. And that we pursued our retreating enemy."

Blaine responded, "And Captain Chant tells me that Master Marley destroyed six Pelagan warships as if they were soap bubbles waiting for the lance."

"Five," I said.

"Was that pursuit necessary?" Bethel asked, picking up a dropped thread.

"That's a determination only Field-Pavan Barrow could make, Mistress Elk. I am no tactician."

"Where are the photon-directors that Snow and Gordon used?" Gabriel Elk asked. "They must be returned to me, Chancellor, that was a principal stipulation of our agreement."

"In safekeeping at the Atarite Palace, Sayati Elk. Where is the one you and Master Marley used aboard the *Paradise*?"

"Beneath Grotto House. Coigns carried it down for me last night, and I removed its chemical power source." Elk turned and faced us. The leaves of the blood lily behind him caught the sunlight and showed us their velvet, crimson underbellies. "It's a disemboweled machine, Chancellor. Dead."

"Well, while it lived, it reveled. So be it."

This remark seemed to be inordinately tactless. I stood up. I walked off a few paces down one of the stone paths in the courtyard. Then I halted, still within speaking distance of the others. Around me: blood lilies, autumn azaleas, the hard yellow berries of the ahura-wood, the inner walls of Grotto House. Gabriel, Bethel, and the Chancellor formed the points of a triangle which excluded me—until I realized that I had simply extended the geometry of our disenchantment. I was a fourth point, I meant too.

"You've offered congratulations and condolences," Sayati Elk said. "Surely that doesn't comprise the whole purpose of your journey?"

"Actually it does. The only other thing Our Shathra asked me to do was to bring Ingram back to Lunn with me. He's handled his responsibilities capably, and we desire to reward him."

"Then let me stay here," I said.

Arngrim Blaine looked at me as one looks at a presumptuous child; but for the carnelian flash of his tooth, his smile would have been fatherly. "A decision such as that is out of my hands, Ingram. Nor could Our Shathra Anna make it without knowing Sayati and Mistress Elk's feelings."

"Does Our Shathra Anna seek to reward me, too?" Gabriel asked.

"Certainly." The Chancellor's eyes blinked rapidly.

"Then I ask as my reward that which Ongladred owes me. A son. If Ingram Marley wishes to stay here at Grotto House, we wish him to stay as our son."

Bethel said, "Grant Ingram his request, Chancellor Blaine, and you have granted ours as well."

"Ingram is rather old to be acquiring parents, Mistress Elk."

"Oh, indeed yes," she said.

"Besides, it's not only for his personal qualities that I wish him to stay here," the old man added. "A fortnight from now I intend to present a neuro-masque in the Stonelore amphitheatre, and Master Marley will be of invaluable assistance to me in the comptroller room. Tell Our Shathra Anna that she is invited, that the masque will commemorate her reign in dance and song."

And so it happened, in that exchange of words, that I gave up my place in the Atarite Court, my status as a dirt-runner, my incompetently executed duties as a member of the Eyes and Ears of Our Shathra Anna. As the Chancellor and Sayati Elk and Mistress Elk talked, my past fell away.

I looked up at Maz. I was conscious of the fluttering colors of the courtyard, leaves peripherally afire with burnt red and smoky emerald, and of the wan circle of the sun shedding its summer scales down the sky. My past had fallen away, even that part of it including my sojourn with the Elks. It had not disappeared; it lay at my feet like dead leaves or shed scales, and I had the power either to collapse into it or to stride out of its alluring, brittle debris. I was still held, but the coils were off, the colors were golden.

The conversation of the others went on around me as I tried to read the future in Maz' outlines, to adjust to the new skin that I still had no right to. The morning passed, the afternoon passed, and somewhere in this evanescent progression Arngrim Blaine found a moment in which to bid us goodbye and depart.

Before I could think what had happened to me, to all of us, I was in Gareth's bed once more, hypnotized by the tangled shadow cast upon the wall by one of the young Elk's meticulously carven stone trees. I could not sleep. My mind was in the branches of the shadow. I lay tangled in the flown, leafless day. Too many things had happened, but the only one who seemed aware of their significance was I. Then, faint footfalls began to resonate in the shadow's branches. It was an illusion. The footfalls were coming from the hallway, from the corridor outside my door. I lay listening to them even after they had gone. A long time later I got up and left Gareth's room. Down the illuminated corridor I walked, placing my feet in the shadows of the footfalls that had preceded me.

I was in front of the elevator. I rode the elevator down.

In the programming room I found Gabriel Elk bent over the corpse of his son, working with liver-spotted and untrembling hands to turn the boy into an actor. As he worked, he talked. He talked in a low, almost emotionless monotone whose very lack of coherence was poignant.

Beside the table on which Gareth lay was the preservator I had seen him in the night before. It stood open and empty, like the casing of one of those fabled bombs that had so long ago virtually destroyed our spawning place, making our planet the home of a preemptive neo-human species that had exiled us, masker and Atarite, to the darkling islands of a northern sea on a world eight hundred light-years from Earth. The whirring of a small computer and the tiny hands sweeping across each tube in an array of cathode-ray tubes (these last on the face of a toposcopic unit opposite the table itself) made the room an eerie place. Gabriel Elk's voice droned on above the sound of the computer; his hands continued to wire, and probe, and snip, and hover, lingering now clinically, now out of something profoundly unscientific.

Before the old man could see me, I turned and left the programming room. Upstairs, the boy's inert trees were waiting for me, frozen in time, tangled in my own nascent memory.

XX

I have been at Stonelore almost two years. The sloak has not returned to Ongladred, and the bonfires on the beaches have long since been allowed to go out. Perhaps there is not any such creature; perhaps the Parfects—in their infinite, condescending wisdom—have granted us their penultimate reprieve. I don't care anymore, I live as if my fate were in no one's hands but my own. When I look at the night sky, I see only the Shattered Moons, nothing sinister, nothing quietly malign—and I hold my breath and genuflect before their random, concerted beauty.

The photon-directors that Sayati Snow and Master Gordon used against the Pelagans have still not been returned to us. Our Shathra Anna and Chancellor Blaine have each been to Stonelore twice since the morning I was granted my freedom from the Atarite Court, and they now assure us that the weapons were dismantled in Lunn.

I don't know how we should accept this news. Gabriel Elk doesn't believe it, he thinks Blaine is lying.

As for our enemies, they have ceased to attack our goods and people even in the small reiving parties for which they